LONG LIVE THE QUEEN

KATE LOCKE

ORBIT

First published in Great Britain in 2013 by Orbit

A CIP catalogue record for this book
is available from the British Library.

ISBN 978-0-356-50145-1

Typeset in Times by M Rules
Printed and bound in Great Britain by
Clays Ltd, St Ives plc

Papers used by Orbit are from well-managed forests
and other responsible sources.

LONG
LIVE
THE
QUEEN

It was time. Eighty years had passed since the Great Insurrection, and aristos had garnered just enough negative attention lately to spark a new level of distrust and hate.

Honestly, I couldn't blame the humans. Though it would be easier if they would just sod off. I wasn't one of the aristos who had hurt anyone, so I didn't deserve the animosity. I'd been a prisoner in one of those awful laboratories, and yet I was hated perhaps even more than a typical vampire or were, or even a goblin. The reason was simple: I was different. After years of being told the bogeyman could only come out at night, or could only get you underground, suddenly there was me – who could walk in the sun and looked relatively harmless.

I'd be afraid of me too.

*This book is for Steve, for putting up
with the madness and doubts, for helping with
plot, for reading every bloody word, for being my biggest
fan, and my toughest critic, and for sticking around.
Oh, and for backrubs. Yeah.*

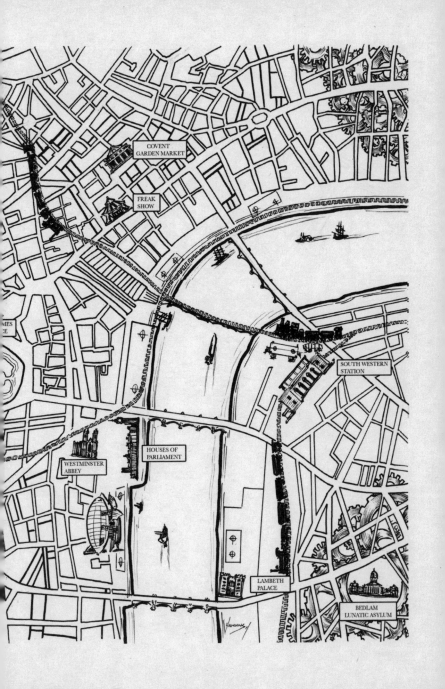

CHAPTER 1

AND HAIL THEIR QUEEN, FAIR REGENT OF THE NIGHT

I had a corpse over my shoulder when I walked into the goblin den. It had been dropped off outside my house by a cheerful young man who seemed to have smoked a full stone of marijuana before getting behind the wheel. My nose still tickled from the scent.

Far beneath the streets of Mayfair, below the wreckage of Down Street station and beyond, was where my goblins made their home. They lived in catacombs and grottos amongst forgotten treasure, astonishing technology and inexplicably thriving horticulture. Pieces of pottery had been worked into the patching of a wall, and a tattered medieval leather shoe had been repurposed into a child's doll.

I almost stepped on the doll as I entered the great hall. I skipped over it just in time, the corpse on my shoulder almost sliding down my back. I hitched it into a better position before laying it down on a stone altar/sideboard against the far wall.

The goblins knew I had arrived, and word spread throughout the den. By the time I unzipped the mortuary bag, tens of furry bodies were crowding behind me as the smell of flesh mixed with the smells of the den – earthy smells, with a touch of metal and fuel from the Met trains.

The girl inside was human, a little on the plump side and totally naked. A Y-shaped scar divided her torso. She looked younger than I'd been told she was, but it didn't matter now. Her blood was of no interest to the hospital, nor was her DNA. She was an organ donor who had signed her body over for medical research and who had no trace of aristocracy in her blood at all.

I suppose feeding my gobs could be loosely filed under "medical". Her heart and eyes had gone on to help others who needed them, and the rest of her would keep the plague from hunting. It was a winning situation for all. One body didn't supply a lot of meat when divided between every gob in the den, but they ate animal flesh as well, and were omnivorous. Human was what they hungered for most, and what made them strong, but they didn't have to eat it all the time.

I pushed the bag off the girl's shoulders and manoeuvred it beneath her until it slid free altogether. I wasn't even squeamish over handling her – or what was to become of her. She'd feed my flock, and then her bones would be incorporated into furniture, her hair braided into rope. Nothing went to waste in the plague den.

I stood back and gestured to the feast I'd provided. "Eat."

They did not need to be told twice. The goblins descended

upon the corpse with delighted yips and growls. I'd already eaten, so I left them to it and went in search of William, my second in command and friend. Usually he greeted me when I came to the den. I was a bit peevish that he chose tonight to deviate from that habit.

I'd discovered I was a goblin a few months ago now, back in the spring/summer. I looked like most other half-bloods out there, with my candy-red hair and lack of fur and snout, but inside ... well, I was a wee bit of a monster.

Imagine my surprise to discover that I liked it.

In the social hierarchy of my world, Queen Victoria was at the top. She was the first vampire queen and had ruled the British Empire for 175 years. At the top of the food chain, however, were goblins.

As a furless goblin who could walk in the sunlight, I was considered dangerous. Extremely dangerous. I think I'd disappointed quite a few people by not living up to the hype. I'd a hunch that there were those who were just waiting for me to steal a baby or something. Maybe eat a nun while defecating on the grave of William the Conqueror.

If only they knew. *Ha*. If they knew, I'd be dead. There'd be a bounty on my head bigger than Victoria's ego.

As I wandered through the halls and catacombs of what was essentially my kingdom, I let my nose lead me to my prince. Goblins had an earthy scent, like smoke and damp earth, and each was unique. I reached a room at the end of a darkened corridor. Something sweet hung thick and heavy in the air, irritating the inside of my nose and making me want to sneeze, only this time it wasn't pot.

Opium. I ought to be accustomed to it by now.

The door was shut, but I knocked once and opened it. I

didn't care that we had an opium den. If humans were hatters enough to get fucked up at the mercy of shameless flesh-eaters, that was their problem. Free will and all that.

And no, I didn't tell myself that to make me feel better about the situation. I honestly didn't care about the human users who frequented this dark place. It wasn't as though they were lured down here like rats mesmerised by a magic piper. They came here because they'd already screwed over and stolen from everyone who ever loved them, and a few who hated them. They came to the goblins because they were so in debt no one cobbleside would sell to them.

A billowing cloud rolled over the threshold to meet me. I didn't bother holding my breath; any effect from the drug would wear off soon enough.

The room was dark save for a few candles. I was surprised to find only two people in it. Well, neither of them was technically "people", as that was a word generally applied to humans. One was William, and the other was Rye Winter.

Rye was a surprise. He lay on one of the narrow cots with a pipe, and a small smile on his lips. He looked more like the boy I'd once loved rather than the scarred and broken man I'd rescued from a laboratory that used halfies – half-bloods – as mice. They'd experimented on him for years.

William looked up from where he stood at Rye's bedside. He made a motion with his hand/paw for me to leave, and then started towards me on slightly haunched legs.

I ducked out and he immediately followed, closing the door behind him. My head began to clear almost instantly.

"Xandra, lady. A pleasure." His voice was low and growly. At one time it inspired so much loathing and fear that it made me want to vomit. Now, I found it comforting.

"William, what the ruddy hell is Rye doing getting dazed in the den?" I frowned. "And why didn't I know about it?"

He took my arm and drew me further away from the door – presumably so that Rye wouldn't hear us through his poppy-glazed haze. "One month has the wolfling sought our help."

"I don't think getting him wasted is entirely helpful."

William smiled without baring his teeth, the silky sides of his muzzle pulling up. He was wearing a new eyepatch – this one was burgundy leather, tooled with an intricate design.

"The wolfling had become dependent on laudanum in the Tower. The plague will wean him like a pup."

That analogy conjured the not so pleasant image of William holding Rye to his breast. "You're trying to get him off the dragon?" It was a tricky process. Halfies metabolised alcohol and drugs very quickly. Rye had been almost constantly sedated for years. Trying to come off that would be dangerous indeed.

"Aye, my Xandra lady is correct."

It would be remiss of me not to notice that since I'd become queen, the goblins in this den had improved their speech somewhat. Normally William sounded like a dyslexic Shakespearean actor on mushrooms, so any improvement was just that – an improvement.

"That doesn't explain why I wasn't told."

William regarded me with his one good eye. The warm amber had more than a century of wisdom in its depths. "The wolfling asked that the lady not be told."

"And you agreed?" A frown pinched my brow. "What the hell for?"

"Upon our honour the wolfling requested our silence."

I made a face – a very attractive one, I wager. "You and

your bloody honour." A thought suddenly occurred to me. "Does Vex know?"

Vexation MacLaughlin was alpha of the UK wolf pack, and my mate – for lack of a better term. As a wolf half-blood, Rye was under his care. Vex wasn't obliged to care for the king-dom's wolves, but he extended the blanket of pack and protection to all who wanted it. It was one of the things I respected most about him.

William's muzzle twitched. Look at that, I'd made the big bad goblin uncomfortable. This killing machine was intim-idated by my little self. Brilliant. My temper wasn't *that* terrible.

"It was your wolf that brought your halfling to your prince."

My wolf. *My* halfling. *My* prince. It wasn't lost on me that when William used "your" in this context, it was meant as a ... suck up, a ploy to puff me up with my own importance. Most times it worked.

This wasn't one of them.

I wasn't pissed off – right, that's a lie. I was pissed off, but I wasn't certain on whose head to lay my anger. To be fair, I could also see why the three of them would leave me out – empathise, even. I simply didn't like it.

"William, I know your word is your honour, but please don't keep things from me."

He bowed his shaggy, furry head. "Aye, lady."

Scowling, I gave one of his ragged ears a tug. "Stop that. I hate it when you play at that subservient rubbish."

He bowed his head further, but not before I saw a flash of fang. He was grinning. "Your word is rule, lady."

I gave him a shove. "You arse."

Goblin laughter can be a terrifying sound. Depending on the

goblin, it can sound like growls, whines, yips, or like a Dobermann being eaten alive. I was becoming used to it as well. Turns out gobs have more of a sense of humour than I would have previously given them credit for.

A few months ago I wouldn't have thought it possible to feel anything but hatred and fear for goblins, let alone the protective love I now had for the furry little bastards. Yes, they were monsters, but they were *my* monsters.

There were still a few who weren't overjoyed at the prospect of having me as their matriarch, but I was determined to be a good queen. The goblins had never once let me down, and I was beginning to think of William as more of a father figure than the man responsible for my vampire half – the half that was mixed with the genes passed through my mother when she was attacked while pregnant with me. The combination of all that aristocrat, plague-bearing blood was what made me a goblin.

The waves of plague that had struck Europe over the centuries had caused the mutations within certain people – mostly those of noble blood – that resulted in vampire and werewolf births. Both groups could be found in all European countries, and in very small numbers in other parts of the world. Genes were genes, and the peerage of Europe liked to spread theirs around. There were even full-bloods in America. The ones publicly "out" were mostly actors, models and socialites.

I'll say this for the Yanks, the majority of them might have sprung from common stock, but they didn't treat their full-bloods like monsters. They made them into celebrities. I supposed if it all went to pot in the UK, I could always move to New York and make a sex video cylinder – get myself some notoriety.

Right.

"I brought meat," I said. Using that slang term in regard to humans still felt wrong, even though I had little love for a lot of them, but it was better than saying "a corpse".

From my pocket I took a package neatly wrapped in butcher's paper and tucked inside a plastic bag. Blood clung to the inside of the bag where it had soaked through the paper. It wasn't the first time I'd come into this den with a treat for him. "This is for you and baby Alexandra."

William accepted it like a child receiving a present on Christmas morning. He sniffed, and I knew he could smell it through the plastic. If I could, he could. His one eye widened. "Lady?"

I put my hand on his wide shoulder. The fine burgundy wool of his coat was dusty and shabby, but he still managed to look regal in it. "It was already dead when I got it, don't worry. I didn't kill for it." I wouldn't – not for what was in that package.

That took some of the shock out of his expression. "Your prince would share ..."

"No." I said it with a smile, despite the silent screaming of my conscience. There were some lines I refused to cross, and tender young meat was one of them. Not because I was morally opposed to it – which I was – but because I was horribly certain I'd like it.

It was one thing to think of yourself as a monster; quite another to prove it so.

"I will take this to the pup now. She grows stronger every day."

Little Alexandra was the first goblin born in ... well, I don't remember how long William had said it had been. That made her special enough, but she'd been named after me, and that made her even more special.

"What about Rye?" I asked.

He glanced at the door, then consulted his pocket watch. The shiny metal looked out of place in his leathery, fur-trimmed hands. "The lady's other wolfling will shortly arrive to take him home."

My other wolfling? Aw, bloody hell. "Ophelia?" Was I the only one *not* included? I should have known that Fee would be involved. My half-sister was one of Vex's half-bloods. She was also part of our mother's group of Insurrectionists who wanted to overthrow the aristocratic rule. Still, Vex treated her as his, despite her duplicitous nature.

When William had left, I stood in front of the heavy door and peered through the small window in it at the man lying peacefully on the bed. He wasn't the boy I'd once loved any more. Those feelings had drifted away as I mourned him. I cared about him, but I didn't love him like I used to.

There were lines on his face, but he was still beautiful. He'd put some weight on, which was good, and his skin had a healthier colour to it. If anyone could help him kick the dragon it was the prince, my trusted right hand. But it would be Fee who got the credit for saving his life. I'd pulled him out of that laboratory, but she was the one bringing him back to the world.

"Xandra?"

Speak of the devil. I turned my head and met my sister's wide blue gaze. Her eyes were almost the same salt-water blue as her hair. I had the Vardan green eyes that all my paternal siblings possessed while Ophelia looked more like our mother, though there was no denying that we were sisters.

"Hello, Fee. Come to fetch Rye, have you?" And being sisters meant I could take the piss out of her for a moment or six, so I adopted a very chipper demeanour – one she would be certain to interpret as restrained aggression.

She regarded me warily. I reckon she hadn't quite got over the time when I tried to rip her throat out with my teeth. "Yes."

"He's still asleep. Do you need help with him?"

She squirmed – literally squirmed. "Uh, no."

That was when I smelled him. Maybe it was the fact that his scent clung to me anyway, but I knew Vex was there before he came around the corner.

Over six feet of Scottish alpha, Vex was muscular without being bulky. His reddish-brown hair was naturally wavy and his eyes were a faded blue-grey that reflected the knowledge of over a century of living. He wore the MacLaughlin tartan, rugged black boots, a cream-coloured sweater and a black leather frock coat. He looked good enough to eat, while I had my hair up in a messy bun and was wearing old bloomers, a plain corset and a nondescript knitted top. At least my boots had a bit of flash – pink and burgundy with an hourglass heel.

While I was comparing our combined fashion sense, Vex stood quietly watching me. It wasn't until I returned my gaze to his that he spoke, "I will take him."

Carrying a full-grown halfie would be nothing to him. I opened the door and stepped back as the last of the smoke drifted out. Vex walked in, scooped up Rye and came back out in the length of time it took me to glance at Ophelia. She looked sheepish, but not afraid. Good. Family shouldn't be afraid of each other. I believed that even though I knew it was naïve.

Vex looked down at me. I looked up at him. There wasn't a

flicker of guilt in his gaze. Right then, I knew no one meant to slight me. Rye had trusted them in a way he couldn't trust me.

No, that was self-pitying bollocks. Rye hadn't wanted me – his first love – to see him as weak, and that was it. I didn't like it, but I had to respect his wishes. I would have done the same were the situation reversed.

"Don't tell him I know," I said.

Vex inclined his head. "See you later?"

I nodded. "I'll be home by midnight or so."

"Coming?" he asked Ophelia.

"In a mo," my sister replied. "I just need to speak to Xandra."

We both watched him walk away, though I noticed Ophelia's gaze wasn't as appreciative as I imagined mine to be, which was all the better for her.

"What?" I asked.

"There's a raid planned on an aristo facility tonight," my sister replied. "Want to come? Vex is leading us in."

I did, actually, but I'd forgotten it was happening that night. "I can't. I have an audience with Her Majesty in half an hour."

Fee looked horrified at the prospect – a fact that did nothing to make me feel better. When the most reckless, daring woman you know looks as though she'd rather step in front of a train than trade places with you . . . well, that's when you know you're doing something *really* stupid.

"You're not going alone, are you?"

I chuckled. And just *what* was so comical? "Yes, I am actually."

She grabbed my arm. "Xandra, she'll kill you if she gets the chance."

It was no secret that I didn't care much for the Queen, and

that she cared even less for me. Historically, queens of England have reacted poorly to new queens popping up – like blade-of-an-axe poorly.

"If she kills me, she'll have the goblins after her, and she doesn't want that. If the humans rise up and war comes, she wants to know the goblins will fight for the right side."

"Hers?"

"I'll give her more credit than that. We'll tear apart anyone who challenges our safety, and Queen V knows it."

"That whole enemy-of-my-enemy thing?"

"Something like that." She still looked a little twitchy. "Something else, Fee?"

My sister glanced about as though making certain we were alone. It was a little ridiculous, because goblins had incredible hearing – as did wolves.

"Have you talked to Mum lately?"

Not what I expected. "No." To be honest, it was still a bit of a sore spot. I hadn't even known the woman was alive – and relatively sane – until she popped up as leader of the Insurrectionists and my youngest sister Dede's new role model.

"She's been acting off lately. All secretive and smiley. Sneaking about. The other night I heard her talking to someone on her rotary. She said something about giving them a tour of 'the facility' and then got all giggly at something they said in response. It's not like her."

Ah. "She's having it off." When Ophelia blinked at me, I explained. "You know, having sex." I could tell this hadn't occurred to my sister – in true daughter fashion. Who wanted to think of their parents bonking?

"But she's sneaking out." Fee frowned. "She's seeing someone from outside Bedlam."

I almost asked what the big deal was, but then my brain caught up to my mouth. For years our mother hadn't left Bedlam for any reason other than to check up on me and lead a few rescue missions. She was seeing someone Ophelia didn't know, and more importantly, someone she didn't know if she could trust.

"Follow her," I suggested. "She hasn't said anything to me, but if you're worried, go and find out what she's doing. And who." I laughed at the face she made.

I checked my pocket watch. "I'd best be off. Her Nibs hates to be kept waiting."

"Hey, Xandra?" Fee fell into step beside me.

"Yeah?"

"Don't be too angry with him, okay?"

"Who? Vex? Nah, we're good."

"No, I mean with Rye. Don't be angry with him."

I stopped walking and turned to face her so she could see my expression. "I'm not."

"Good, because he doesn't want you to see him as less."

"He survived for years in one of their labs. He's one of the strongest people I know."

Her gaze locked with mine. We were about the same height, so it was easily done. "He still fancies you. He says that thoughts of you were what got him through."

Was that jealousy I heard in her tone? "That's lovely, but he'll soon figure out I'm no one's fantasy, won't he?" When she didn't immediately respond with a smile, I frowned. There were times when being ... unpredictable was a pain in the arse. "He's in no danger from me, Fee. The last thing I want to do is hurt him, but I let him go a long time ago. My hopes for him have nothing to do with romance."

She nodded. "Fair enough."

Of course, I wanted to ask if *she* had hopes of romance where Rye was concerned, but I held my tongue. It was none of my business, and she and I weren't quite at the share-everything level of sisterhood just yet.

"Be careful tonight," she told me as we parted company cobbleside. Wise girl that she was, she hadn't asked any questions about the feast my goblins were having. And she'd kept her gaze focused straight ahead when we walked past the great hall. I knew that she could smell it, however.

"You too," I replied. "People have killed to protect those labs and what goes on there. I don't want you to be another casualty." The facility I'd rescued Rye from had been under the control of my stepmother – the Duchess Vardan. She'd ended up dead before I could get any information out of her. Pity, that. I'd been so looking forward to slapping her about a bit.

My sister smiled. "Aww, look at you being all caring and what not."

I grimaced. "Don't get used to it. Off with you, wench."

She drove away in a little bright red Daimler sporty thing. For someone constantly in trouble with the law, she certainly liked to draw attention to herself. How many strings did Vex have to pull as her alpha to keep her out of Newgate? As I took the lift up to my flat, I decided I didn't care.

A few months ago, I'd moved into the building above the old Down Street station, which marked the entrance to the goblin den. It was a good location for me as their queen; it meant I didn't have to live underground, which I simply refused to do. I would miss daylight, and I didn't want my comings and goings watched.

And if I was completely honest, I would have to admit that giving myself over that completely to being a goblin was terrifying. Being part of the pack was fabulous – leader of it even better – but I needed to hang on to what was left of the old me for a little while longer.

I unlocked my front door and stepped inside. There were boxes stacked in almost every room – bits and bobs that had yet to be unpacked and put in their place. Some of the contents had belonged to my sister Dede. She'd been dead almost six months and I still couldn't bring myself to look at her things. I couldn't bear to part with them either, so here they sat, boxed up and waiting.

The place was nice – a little old-fashioned, with its Georgian façade and Robert Adam plasterwork, but I liked it: it was just a touch shy of pretentious, with a side order of obnoxious tossed in. All the pale blues and greens on the walls had been painted over with reds and violets – strong colours – and I'd taken down the crystal chandeliers and wall sconces and had them replaced with ones that were a tad more art nouveau.

I ran up to my en suite to brush my teeth – I'd fed before the goblin den – and check my appearance. There was blood on my shoulder from the corpse ... er, meat, and I smelled of opium. Brilliant. I had enough time to change my shirt but that was it. Her Majesty would just have to put up with my scent.

Now, what did one queen wear to meet another? I wondered as I opened my wardrobe. The first thing that came to mind was easy.

Armour. Especially around the neck.

CHAPTER 2

PATIENCE IS BITTER

During the Great Insurrection of 1934, Buckingham Palace had been attacked and set ablaze, requiring extensive renovation to repair the damage done by weapon- and torch-wielding humans. If not for halfies, there would be a lot fewer aristos alive, including our sovereign. That was when considerable effort began to produce larger numbers of these half-human births. Because the first British half-blood on record had been born to the Duke of Marlborough's mistress, the title of courtesan was given to those women whose genetics made these births possible, and they became instant celebrities.

Some people forced their daughters to be tested for the gene. Of course, back then, the only test was to have sex with an aristocrat. People didn't exactly shove each other out of the way for a spot at the head of the queue.

After the smoke had cleared, and her husband was buried, Queen Victoria retreated to her home, and hadn't made an official public appearance since. I used to think it was because she expected everyone to come to her, but lately I'd begun to understand her fear of humanity. The Insurrection happened long before my birth, but I'd witnessed what the Human League was capable of when they firebombed Vex's car. They were completely hatters zealots who wouldn't stop until we were all dead.

Security at the palace was a bitch, but I'd be paranoid too if I were Victoria. I was already paranoid enough, and I wasn't queen of an empire where the majority race was gearing up for another insurrection. Although I reckoned more people had tried to kill me than her. Human League violence had been on a steady rise over the past few months. Aristo-friendly businesses had been bombed or sacked. Rallies and demonstrations against Victoria's rule took place on a weekly basis. Guards had been doubled at the gates to Mayfair and those around the palace as human protests happened on an almost daily basis. The tension was so thick you could smell it. Literally.

My goblins kept an eye on much of the city – little voyeurs that they were. I was fairly safe in my new home, close as it was to the walls that surrounded Mayfair, but I knew of many aristocrats and halfies who avoided venturing outside of the safety of the West End.

I wasn't one of them. It wasn't that I was stupid – well, perhaps I was a touch foolhardy or too proud – but I wasn't going to live my life in fear. For one thing, I had no idea just how long my life expectancy might be, as goblins lived a bloody long time. And for another, I couldn't abide bullies. Never mind that I'd been known to be one on occasion.

And then there was the fact that I had a hard time sitting still for very long, let alone living out almost an entire century without leaving my immediate neighbourhood. Hell, I had yet to make it to the quarter-century mark and I'd already lived in five different homes in various parts of the city.

No, I wasn't afraid, but I was wary. The only weapon I had on me was my lonsdaelite dagger – it was harder than diamond and so sharp you'd never see the wound if blood didn't pour out. It had been a gift from my mother a long time ago, and it didn't set off the hounds at the palace. It was just rock.

But if by some chance Victoria did go for my head, I could at least try to take hers as well.

I walked through the hounds – they were like metal detectors, but were designed to "smell" a body and pick up any traces of gunpowder, harmful chemicals, metals and what have you.

The bloody thing started screaming as I stepped through. "What the fu—" I froze. Eight palace guards surrounded me, weapons drawn. Most of their ammo would be designed for human physiology, but I didn't kid myself that they weren't equipped to take me on. You didn't invite a goblin into your house unless you could hurt it if things went wrong. These guards – some of whom had been my classmates at the Academy – had to have silver-tipped tetracycline-filled bullets.

I held up my hands. "I don't have any weapons."

Two came forward to pat me down while another checked the hound's printout. The dagger was in a sheath concealed in the bust of my corset, so they didn't find it, thank God. Unless you were part of the Royal Guard, or Peerage Protectorate, carrying a weapon into the palace was tantamount to treason.

Notice that the possibility of being sentenced to death didn't stop me from bringing the dagger altogether. I rarely had cause to use it, but I felt much more at ease having it with me.

The guard at the hound – he couldn't have been more than

nineteen – looked up. "It detected traces of goblin, human and opium."

I flashed a grin – and a little fang. "It was a positively brilliant party. You ought to have been there."

He stared at me, face totally blank. Then, as he consulted the appointment book, his left eye twitched and the colour drained from his cheeks. "Are you . . . ?" He cleared his throat as he raised his wide eyes. "You're Alexandra Vardan."

I nodded. No point in denying it, especially when his bladder-clenching anxiety was so entertaining. "Yeah. I was in the plague den before coming here." That didn't make him look any less tense. Probably wouldn't help if I mentioned that I'd been delivering a corpse for luncheon.

"Look, Her Majesty is waiting on me, so if we're done here, perhaps one of you brave lot might escort me to her?" Really, they should have asked my name when I came in. If Church was still alive, there'd be hell to pay for knobbing up their duties.

But Church wasn't alive.

"I'll take you, ma'am," offered one of Mr Pee Pants' partners. She was perhaps all of five feet tall, with shiny turquoise hair and almond-shaped eyes. All halfies had funky-coloured hair as a result of the plague's effect on that particular pigmentation. To be honest, I hadn't understood it when they explained it at the Academy, and I didn't care to now. It only mattered because my own candy colour was fabulous camouflage, making me look only half aristo when I was actually fully plagued. My particular red wasn't common, but it normally allowed me to move about in relative anonymity. Or it had before the city started to heat up with racial tension.

I appraised my escort. She looked familiar, though she had

to be fresh from the Academy. She must have ranked very high to be put into the Royal Guard so young.

"Are you one of Sayuri's?" Sayuri was one of the courtesans my father "visited" while doing his duty to the Crown. My brother Val was the result of that transaction.

"Yes." She began walking, so I followed. "And before you say anything, I know who you are and that you and I share a brother. Believe me when I say that is *all* you and I have in common."

I arched a brow – it was my go-to expression. "That and a penchant for bitchiness, apparently." I had to admire her ... pluck. It took balls to provoke someone like me, and I'd be lying if I said I didn't wonder how the marrow of her bones might taste as I sucked them dry.

That whole thing about being a monster? Yeah, sometimes I liked it, I'll admit. There were times when it frightened me, but I *liked* being scary. It was a better high than opium, and it lasted longer. So long as I didn't get too cocky and forget that I could die, I'd be fine.

She stopped walking and turned to me. "Are we going to have a problem, ma'am?" Maybe I was just overly sensitive, but her tone sounded hopeful.

Or maybe I was the hopeful one. "How do you reckon it would play out if we did?"

"I graduated top of my class." How very modest of her. Another commonality between us. "I am proficient in hand-to-hand combat as well as sharps and ranged weapons. I am incredibly fast and agile, and strong too."

I moved without giving it too much thought. Fast as a blink as we rounded a corner, I grabbed her, spun her and slammed her into the wall. I held her hands behind her back, between our bodies, as I yanked her head to the side and exposed her jugular. I held her like that for a few seconds and let her contemplate her own mortality. To her credit, she stayed very still, but I felt the fight in her muscles.

"I'm somewhat proficient myself," I informed her before I released her and continued down the corridor. I half expected guards to come running, but no one came. I wasn't certain if that made me feel better about the situation.

To the girl's credit, she didn't try to attack me from behind or retaliate in any way. She simply fell into step beside me, her face flushed. "An excellent lesson, ma'am. One I won't soon forget."

Ah, there was the family resemblance with my brother. She had that same attitude as Val that everything was a challenge or an opportunity to improve herself.

"There's always someone badder than you," I shared – rather sagely, I thought. "Always someone faster or stronger, smarter or prettier."

"Lord Churchill taught us the same lesson – without the prettier part."

I smiled, despite the conflicting emotions conjured up by thinking about Church. "I reckon he did." Of course he had – he'd been the one to teach it to me when I got so puffed up I wasn't fit for company.

My companion was quiet for a moment. A maid in a crisp uniform passed us, eyes averted. Only a glimpse of bright orange peeking out from beneath the ruffle of her cap outed her as a halfie. Of course Victoria would be too paranoid to have human servants, but halfies were meant to be fighters and protectors. They were not born to empty chamber pots or do laundry.

Then again, Church always stated that our – no, *their* – purpose was to serve the aristocracy. At the time, I hadn't taken that quite so literally. I suppose I should consider myself fortunate that I had been as good as I was at violence, because there was no bloody way I'd empty someone's piss-pot.

Still, the hierarchical thing bothered me more now than it ever had when I thought I was a halfie. I didn't know then what I know now about the aristocracy, humans and goblins. My world had gone from stark black and white to muddy grey, and my naïve assumption that "aristo" was synonymous with "good" had been trodden into the ground like horse shit in Hyde Park.

"May I ask a personal question?"

I slid a sideways glance at her. "Can't guarantee I'll answer, but go ahead."

"Do you miss being RG?"

That was a loaded question, was it not? "Sometimes," I replied. It was the most honest answer I could give – and the most non-committal.

The girl seemed satisfied, or perhaps it wasn't worth further digging. Regardless, she was silent for the next few moments before stopping in front of a set of large double doors.

"Someone else will probably meet you here to escort you back out."

"I'm sure I can find my own way."

"You know no one's going to let you wander around unattended, right? There are closed-circuit cameras all over this place."

That she was so serious made me smile. She sounded – and looked – so much like Val. "Yeah, I know. I have every intention of behaving myself, no worries."

She didn't look convinced, and I can't say that I blamed her. I wouldn't trust me either.

I raised my fist to the door and knocked.

"Good luck." That was the last thing she said to me before leaving me alone to face the woman I'd come to think of as my nemesis. There were those who would think Victoria mad to have a private meeting with me. There were more who would think me mad for agreeing to meet her one on one. Mostly because we were on her territory, and there was no such thing as one on one.

The door was opened by another halfie – this one a girl still in her teens. She must be here as part of a work assignment from the Academy. When it looked as though a halfie might not be inclined towards protection services, they were put into various other stations for trial periods so that their talents and skills might be evaluated. That was how the orange-haired maid had ended up here. The plague was a fickle thing, and sometimes even the best genes couldn't guarantee the perfect halfie. I was a good example of that.

I hoped for this one's sake she was better suited to anything but picking up V's dirty knickers.

She didn't meet my gaze, but gave me a curtsy so deep her knee must have touched the ground. "Come in, Your Grace."

Grace? I wasn't a duchess, I was a queen. It was a deliberate snub – and not on the part of this girl, of that I was certain.

I smirked – not that she saw it – and crossed the threshold. "Thanks."

"Her Majesty will be with you shortly. Would you like tea while you wait?"

I was going to refuse, paranoid that it might be poisoned,

but I had to think Victoria would be smarter than that. "I would, thank you."

She bowed her head and left the room, leaving me entirely alone. Now what?

I sat down on a chair that had to be at least a hundred years old, and about as comfortable as a church pew, despite a little padding. Would it kill her to update the decor in this place?

The maid returned a few moments later with tea and some sandwiches, which I dug into. Then, with a cup of tea and a reasonably full belly, I sat back in my chair.

And waited.

I was done waiting. Queen of Britain or not, Victoria could go bugger herself. Thirty-five minutes went way beyond my capacity for bullshit and patience. Not to mention how there was only so much snooping about a girl could do before she grew weary.

I would not be treated like a lowly serf, and I would not give her the bloody satisfaction of waiting on her any longer, the cow.

My hand had just turned the door knob to let myself out of the ostentatious parlour when I heard a slight creak behind me. I turned, and caught sight of my hostess closing a not-so-secret door in the far wall. Her gaze went to the chair where I had been sitting. She seemed surprised to not find me in it.

I dropped my hand, the latch clicking back into place.

Slowly, the Queen of England turned to me. "Alexandra, there you are."

"How fortunate you came along when you did," I replied

with the same false sincerity. "I was just about to take my leave."

"Without giving me an audience?" Her voice was sweet, but had a core of razor-sharp steel so often possessed by tiny women. "How very rude that would have been."

I was more than half a foot taller than she was, and out-weighed her by at least two stone, if not three, and yet she looked at me as though I was an ant in her path. That blatant disregard dug at me like a finger in a wound. Vex told me it was my primal side – the predator – that rose up when some-one tried to assert dominance over me.

I reckoned it was also plain, old-fashioned defiance.

Goblins were known for their arrogance, and I knew myself well enough to admit I was no exception to that rule. No midget-leech was going to treat me like a recalcitrant child.

"No more rude then being made to wait half an hour, *Victoria*." If she was going to use my first name, I was sure as bloody hell going to use hers. "Your time might not be so pre-cious, but mine is."

Cool blue eyes narrowed. "Yes, I suppose it would be, given that most of it is spent in the company of illiterate dogs. Tell me, how often do you have to put down fresh newsprint?"

Oh, how I longed to snap at her bait. Instead, I looked around at my opulent surroundings. "You must find the palace so lonely after Albert's murder." A murder she was rumoured to have committed during the Great Insurrection. I nodded at her mourning gown. "Black widow ... oh, I mean *widow's black* suits you."

She stiffened, and the room crackled with energy – the kind that made the hairs on the back of my neck stand on end. I'd felt this before once when Vex had been angry. It was as though the powerful old ones were capable of generating an electrical charge with their emotions. If only I had such useful parlour tricks.

I met her gaze. "Are we going to whip 'em out and see whose is bigger, or are you going to apologise for intentionally making me wait to have a discussion that was *your* idea?" We might be on her territory, but I wasn't above pissing on it.

She drew herself up to her full height, which wasn't terribly impressive. At one time I would have been intimidated regardless, but not any more. She couldn't touch me because the goblins would retaliate, and I couldn't slap her around because she could make life miserable for a lot of people I cared about.

So we stared at each other for a moment, and then she sighed. Her chin lifted. "Forgive me for keeping you waiting."

I seriously doubted she was sorry at all. In fact, I'd wager the only thing she was sorry for where I was concerned was not commanding I be killed immediately after my birth. I knew that my mother would have been made to have an abortion had my father, the Duke of Vardan, not intervened.

What had my father told his queen that had convinced her to let me live? What promises had he made, and were they worth it? Somehow, I doubted that as well.

"Sure." I wasn't about to waste any more of her time or mine being a prat. I returned to the chair, which had started to mould itself to my arse, and sat down once more. Victoria seated herself on the sofa across from me.

"Since we've dispensed with small talk, I'll get right to the point." She called *that* small talk? I might have to respect her a little after all. "We have a common enemy, you and I."

"I assume you refer to the humans?"

She gave a regal nod. "Specifically the Human League."

Ah, they were a proper toothache to be sure – relentless, unexpected and impossible to ignore. They'd bombed a halfie/aristo bar a while back and injured Ophelia. They'd also blown up Vex's car – luckily he wasn't in it. And then they'd torched my house in Leicester Square. I hadn't lost much, but it had pissed me off, and made the smug little bastards feel like they had the upper hand.

Since then, they'd become more and more public. My mother had come out of hiding to speak against them, but she had her own agenda and her own reasons for wanting to abolish the monarchy.

What no one seemed to understand was that this façade of hierarchy was the only thing preventing an all-out war. Violence was unseemly, but humans gave those of plagued blood a reason to drop the pretence. If Victoria was cut down, aristos and halfies would band together to defend themselves, and then it would get messy.

Very messy.

I cut right to the bone – no chewing around it. "What do you want from me? Other than for me to go away, that is?"

She shot me a rather cross look. What? Did she expect me to forget that she wanted me out of the way? It was only my usefulness that prevented her from calling for my head on a pike. "I would like to negotiate a treaty between the vampires and the goblins."

I frowned. "What about the weres?" I was sleeping with the alpha after all.

She arched an imperious brow – it was a favourite expression of my own. "It is common knowledge that the MacLaughlin will align his wolves to your goblins."

Blimey, she didn't even try to sugar-coat it.

I made a show of looking around. "Odd, I don't see Vex here. Did his invitation get lost in the post?"

"You are a most infuriating girl. I've no idea what Churchill ever saw in you. Then again, he's proved his poor judgement."

Right, most of the world thought Church was still alive; just that he'd fled England and Victoria's wrath. I had to make sure I remembered that and didn't talk about him in the past tense. That wasn't the reason for my hesitation, though. There was something in the Queen's expression. Something strange.

Something vulnerable.

"Fang me. You were sleeping with him." Now some of her hostility made sense. No wonder she had a hate-on for me when Church had had plans to marry me – not that I ever would have said yes.

She could never, ever find out that I'd killed him – no matter that she never would have married him herself. Good enough to screw, but Church's mother had been American, and that kept him from being suitable for anything else as far as the aristocracy was concerned.

And I would never tell her that he was behind the attempt on her life.

"Fifty years," she admitted. "He was my consort and trusted friend, and he betrayed me."

I met her gaze. "He betrayed us both." I refused to think of Dede, but I let a little of that rage simmer in my gut.

Some of the coldness returned to her expression, as though she'd cracked a shell to let me peek inside and now snapped it shut again. "I will *not* watch everything I am, everything I've built crumble under human feet."

I felt for her. Call me a sucker or naïve, but I did. I wasn't about to hug her or plait her hair, but we seemed to have found common ground, she and I. Who would have thought that resenting Churchill would be that blood-soaked, unhallowed, corpse-concealing ground?

I didn't want to think too hard on that, either.

"Schedule another meeting," I told her, leaning forward so my forearms rested on my bloomer-covered thighs. "This time you invite Vex and William as well, and we'll figure out what to do about the League. Together."

I thought I saw a hint of a smile on her lips, but it might have been a twitch. "You are very democratic, Xandra. I don't have to tell you how unattractive that is. The secret to handling men is to make them *think* they have a choice, not to actually give them one."

Was that a hint of admiration in her tone? I shrugged it off. "Let me put it to you this way – it's the only solution that has any chance of getting you what you want."

That seemed to be the deciding factor. "Fine. I will call a meeting of the faction heads." She rose to her feet and I followed. She offered me her hand. I stared at it.

"Shake my hand, girl. That is how honourable bargains are sealed."

I took her much smaller hand in my own. She might be dainty, but her fingers closed around mine like tiny steel vices.

"Does this mean I get to keep my head?" I asked.

This time there was no denying her smile. Sharp fangs bit into her lower lip. "For now," she said.

Bitch.

CHAPTER 3

FEAR IS PAIN ARISING FROM THE ANTICIPATION OF EVIL

I returned home from the palace the same way I got there – through the labyrinth of tunnels and catacombs beneath London. Seriously, it was a wonder the city hadn't caved in on itself yet.

The last few months had given me plenty of time to learn various routes and short cuts, and also to become comfortable with the underground. It used to make me feel vaguely claustrophobic, but now it was more like my own little adventure land. A private treasure hunt. Sounds ridiculous, but it was true. In the last fortnight alone, I'd found three Roman coins, part of a fresco and a hand-hammered gold ring that I now wore on the middle finger of my right hand. Granted, sometimes I found things like discarded condoms and old chamber pots, but still, it was more fun than not.

Although who would be horny enough to risk goblin attack

by having underground sex? I knew the thought of danger got a lot of people off, but there was fun danger and then there was *danger*. That made me think of humans who had sex with goblins, and my mind didn't want to go there. I was learning to love my furry kin, but their sexual behaviour wasn't something I wanted to explore. They were all kinds of freaky, and didn't seem to care if anyone watched or not. Not that the humans seemed to mind either. No one that I knew of was ever hurt, but it worried me, letting humans into the den. Everyone was searched first, but what if someone came into my territory under false pretences? What if they managed to kill a few goblins before they were ripped apart?

What if they brought a bomb, or tetracycline?

I viewed gobs as the organised crime of the aristocratic world. Some of the things they did were all right, and others were more of a morally grey area, while a few were just outright wrong. However, they'd been doing them long before I came along, and there wasn't a person in the UK – human or otherwise – who didn't know the possible consequences of doing business – or pleasure – with goblins.

I'd eaten my mentor's heart, so I wasn't exactly in a position to judge, was I?

When I reached the forgotten ruin of Down Street station, I climbed on to the platform rather than continuing down the track to the entrance to the goblin den. Feeling lazy, I chose to take the lift.

I was distracted by my visit with Her Nibs. What the hell had I got myself into by shaking her bloody hand? I didn't trust her, but she was right that we had to prepare for the human problem to escalate. It was time. Eighty years had passed since the Great Insurrection, and aristos had garnered just enough negative attention lately to spark a new level of distrust and hate.

Honestly, I couldn't blame the humans. Though it would be easier if they would just sod off. I wasn't one of the aristos who had hurt anyone, so I didn't deserve the animosity. I'd been a prisoner in one of those awful laboratories, and yet I was hated perhaps even more than a typical vampire or were, or even a goblin. The reason was simple: I was different. After years of being told the bogeyman could only come out at night, or could only get you underground, suddenly there was me – who could walk in the sun and looked relatively harmless.

I'd be afraid of me too. Still, it would be lovely if they'd just leave me alone.

The lift jerked to a stop. I walked out of the cage into the kitchen and immediately headed to the ice box. I put the cherries I'd snagged before leaving the den in a bowl to nibble on later, took out a bag of blood, then put a pot of water on the hob and popped the bag into it when the water began to boil. I preferred drinking blood heated this way than by a radiarange. I didn't trust those things, and used them as little as possible.

Did Victoria even know what a radiarange was?

Fang me, but she was mad. Full-on hatters. Still, not having to worry about her cutting my head off – at least for the present moment – was a welcome respite.

I was lounging on the chaise with a book and a glass of Scotch when my rotary rang. I grabbed it off the coffee table and checked the incoming number. It was Ophelia.

I hesitated. This was a bit of alone time before getting together with Vex. I was really enjoying this book and didn't feel like chatting. Still, she rarely called, and she had been off to raid a lab. I pressed the connect button as the infernal device rang once more. "'Lo?"

"Get your arse over to Vex's now."

I sat up at her overly dramatic, sharp tone. "What is it?"

"Just hurry the fuck up." The line went dead as she severed our connection.

I could dismiss it as typical drama-queen behaviour if it was my other sister, Avery, but Ophelia's life was even more dangerous than mine, and if she told me to get my arse over to Vex's, she meant I should do it and do it *now*.

And then it hit me. There was only one reason she would make such a call.

Vex.

My mind went blank. No thought except getting to him as fast as possible.

His house was on South Street – close enough that it was faster for me to run and trespass on other properties than it was to drive the sometimes tiny and twisty roads of Mayfair.

A group of aristos having an outdoor gathering hissed and shouted at me as I ran through the middle of their party. I growled and kept running. A couple of gasps followed on my heels, and I knew from the sound that I had "gobbed out". If it made me run faster, then I didn't care how I looked.

Goblins had the ability to shape-shift like weres, but not to the same extent. William could have hands or paws, or something in between if he wanted, but it would be next to impossible for him to look human. I could look partially goblin but not change completely. It was a little brilliant, to be honest. And more than a little terrifying. I literally looked like a monster, with my huge eyes and elongated fangs. I even had something of a muzzle.

I launched myself over a stone wall and twisted in mid-air to land on my feet still running. When the weres guarding the door to Vex's house – a sure sign something was wrong – saw me coming, their eyes widened. They threw the door open and got the hell out of my way. It wasn't until I slipped in my own blood on the foyer floor that I realised I hadn't even stopped to put my boots on. The soles of my feet were gouged and dirty. Shredded.

It didn't matter. My feet would heal. The floor could be cleaned.

Ophelia met me at the top of the stairs, looking like a wild, feral thing. Her hair was a mess, and she had blood on her face. Her nose looked broken, and she was missing a tooth. She would be good as new in a couple of days, but for now she had to be hurting.

"Where is he?" I demanded.

She jerked her head towards Vex's bedroom. "Xandra, there's something you need—"

I ran before she could finish. Whatever she had to say could wait until after I'd seen Vex. I raced down the dimly lit corridor to his room and shoved open the door.

At least a dozen weres and halfies stood gathered round his bed. Two of them snarled when I barged in, ready to attack. I stopped in my tracks, forcing my face back to its normal state. I didn't even wince at the discomfort any more.

The wolves watched me warily. I knew some of them continued to be displeased with the fact that Vex and I were together, but most were pretty relaxed about it. This was not relaxed.

Ethan MacGreggor, Viscount Sinclair and second to the alpha, stepped forward. "Lady Xandra." I'd finally got him to

stop calling me "Majesty", but he was a peer, and all this lording and ladying was part of that society.

"What happened, Ethan?" I tried to peer through the weres
at the bed, but they blocked my view. My lips pulled back
from my teeth. I'd rip their throats out if they tried to keep me
from Vex.

"The alpha accompanied a raiding party on an aristo exper-
imental facility, similar to the one you discovered in the Tower."

Discovered, my arse. I'd been imprisoned in it. I dragged
my attention from the bed. "He was attacked?"

Ethan's expression grew guarded. "He was, yes."

"How bad is it?" I frowned when he just stared at me.
"What?" Did he not realise how close I was to losing it?

Apparently he did, because he didn't touch me, he simply
gestured for me to go to Vex. "Let her pass."

They did. Some of them continued to stare at me with open
hostility until I reached the side of the bed.

I was not prepared for what I saw there.

Next to William, Vexation MacLaughlin was the strongest
man I knew. The figure on this bed looked as though he'd been
used as a chew toy. Only when his eye – the one that wasn't
swollen shut – opened and looked directly at me did I know
that it was Vex.

"Xandra." His voice was a hoarse rasp. "You're okay."

The hand that reached for me was smeared with dried blood
and bandaged all the way to the elbow. Tears scalded my
cheeks as I wrapped my own fingers around his. I didn't care
if his wolves saw me bawl and snot like a child.

I raised his hand to my lips and kissed his battered knuckles. I smelled something strange on his skin – a scent that was
both foreign and familiar. I couldn't place it.

"Don't cry, love. I'll be fine in a few hours. It's not as bad as it looks."

I choked a little then, as a sob caught in my throat. "What happened? Who did this to you?"

Vex's gaze went to Ethan, so I turned my head and caught the gathered weres watching me warily. There were more at the door, staring as though as I was on trial and they were the jury.

"For fuck's sake," I snarled. "Tell me!"

"It was you!" Ethan snapped, voice turning into a growl. He shook his head, pulling himself together. "Whoever – whatever – it was, it looked just like you."

Obviously such a dramatic statement required a rational follow-up. "Are you fucking wasted?" I demanded.

On the bed, my injured wolf protested. I turned my attention to him, shutting out the others. I stroked the blood-crusted waves of his hair, and watched as one of the more shallow wounds on his forehead slowly began to close. He wasn't healing as quickly as he ought. I gave him what I hoped was a reassuring smile.

A nearby halfie growled at me. Without thinking, I reached out – without taking my gaze off Vex – and backhanded him hard enough to knock him on his arse. Vex had declared me his mate, and I'd shown my devotion to him in front of many of these people. No little runt was going to bare his teeth and snarl at me like I was beneath him. Like I was a threat.

I bent down and kissed Vex on the forehead – where the wound was healing. If I could, I'd give him my blood to speed the process along, but my blood was toxic to anything but another goblin. I could very well kill him.

"Who hasn't given blood yet?" I demanded to know, my gaze searching the room. A few raised their hands – both were and halfie. "Do it. Now. Your alpha requires it. He needs meat as well."

One of the weres looked to Ethan, who nodded. I bristled, but held back. I was still new to some of the pack, and they held Vex's second in a higher regard than his girlfriend. If we were married, there'd be no question of hierarchy, but as it was, I had little or no authority.

I turned to Ethan. "Let's go and talk." I told Vex I'd be back soon, and left him to be cared for by his pack.

"You know it wasn't me, right?" I asked, once we were out in the corridor. I wasn't about to put any more distance between me and the man I loved.

Ethan nodded. I hadn't noticed before, but his hands and arms were bandaged, and he walked with a limp. Something had seriously kicked his arse, and Ophelia's – and almost killed Vex. "The scent wasn't yours, though it was similar. But, my lady, it wore your face. Even your hair."

"That's not possible." Of course, six months ago I would have said a furless goblin wasn't possible either. You'd think I'd learn.

He ran a rust-stained hand through his thick dark hair. "Yeah, right, I know. That's why everyone's in such a knot. It looked like you, smelled something like you, but it had claws like railroad spikes and fangs like something prehistoric. *It* did that to Vex. One creature, the size of you, almost killed our alpha."

A new sensation twisted my insides at that moment – a

feeling of nauseous rage. I've never had the urge to kill and puke at the same time – shortly after one another, yes, but not all at once. "Tell me you killed it."

His expression added to the sick feeling. "All we were left with was a human corpse. The creature got away."

"What?" Oh, fang me. This wasn't good. Something that dangerous running loose in London. Bloody hell. "But you destroyed the lab?"

He nodded. "Bastards did it for us – had a self-destruct installed."

Just like the Tower had. That was all the thought I gave to the prison where I'd been kept and made a victim of.

"One of the guards hit the release switch on the cage the thing was in just before pulling the alarm. We thought it was you – that someone had grabbed you again. Vex and Ophelia were the only ones who could tell it wasn't, and by the time they realised what had happened it was too late. She was on us and the place was about to burn."

I swallowed. That was an awful lot of killing and maiming for one creature. Maybe it was shock that made me numb, but I wasn't as shocked as I should have been. We'd known there was a covert group of halfies and aristos – mostly aristos – doing experiments on halfies and plague-carrying humans. It had started as a bid to improve aristo live-birth rates, and quickly turned into something more nefarious.

When I was put into one of the labs, I was only there for maybe two or three hours, but in that time they took eggs from my ovaries. They could have taken other stuff too, for all I knew. If this creature looked enough like me to fool Vex's people, then it had to have been some sort of clone. Right?

Albert's fangs.

What else could it be? A baby killing-machine with enough strength to take down several wolves and halfies, and their alpha. Vex was the best fighter I knew – better even than Church. I doubted I could best him. William probably could, but that was it.

And the creature that had almost killed him was loose. In London. With my face, huge fangs and more strength than anything I'd ever seen. And a taste for blood.

Fucktabulous.

"We need to have a meeting," I told Ethan. "Now. Send word to the palace that you and I and the prince are on our way." I'd no sooner finished saying the words than my rotary rang. It was William.

"I'm at Vex's," I said by way of greeting. "Gather everything you've got and meet me at Buck House."

"Aye, lady." A slight pause. "The wolf lord?"

"He's healing, but he won't be joining us." I would not think about what might have happened. I could not.

"Your people are here for our lady and her wolf."

My eyes prickled. Crying was so not helpful at the moment. "Thank you, William. I'll see you at the palace."

As I disconnected, a servant passed us carrying a large covered tray. I could smell the blood and flesh from where I stood. It was cow, but it was fresh and dripping with iron-rich blood. It would help speed Vex's recovery.

"I want a moment with him before we go," I told Ethan. "Alone."

He looked apologetic. "My lady, the pack . . . "

I took a step towards him. He was bigger than me, but that had never stopped me before. "It wasn't a request. I understand your position, but I don't care if this thing freaked you and the pack out. All I care about is Vex, so clear that room or I will."

And my way would not be polite or neat. My way would only complicate things even further, and while I didn't care, Ethan did. And Vex would as well. Ethan nodded. "You are one bossy woman. No wonder he likes you."

I managed a small smile. "Flatterer."

Ethan smiled back. "Give me a moment." He went into Vex's room. I wasn't alone for long, though, as Ophelia walked along the corridor towards me.

"You all right?" I asked. She looked better than she had when I first arrived – she'd washed the blood off.

She nodded. "Few bites and cuts. Vex wouldn't let most of us at her." At my glance she added, "He knew it wasn't you immediately. As soon as I caught her scent I knew too."

"You've been in these labs before. Have you ever seen anything like this?"

Her face paled. "Once. There was a halfie who they repeatedly allowed to be raped by a goblin. There's no other word for it. It resulted in a birth, but it didn't survive long, bloodthirsty little monster that it was. It was a quick pregnancy, though," she added, as though that somehow made it all better. Most likely it only meant that the poor girl was raped again all that much sooner.

I thought of the girl Dede had shown me in the lower levels of Bedlam – where there lived halfies who had been badly damaged by these experiments. She said that the girl had been impregnated by goblins. Was this the same halfie Ophelia was talking about?

"He's going to be all right, you know."

I looked up.

"Vex. He's going to be okay." She said this so earnestly I had to smile. I didn't tell her where my thoughts had gone. She'd lived at Bedlam, and if she hadn't thought of that girl, she would soon enough. And Vex ... well, I knew he was going to recover simply because he was still alive. He wasn't the sort to give up.

"Thanks. It's very ... scary to see him like that."

"It was horrifying to see it happen."

I didn't even want to imagine it. "Did he tell you not to call me?"

She nodded. "I figured after what happened in the den earlier you wouldn't appreciate being kept out of the loop again."

"Indeed." I wouldn't have either, and I would have made that clear in a spectacular display, no doubt. "Well, thanks for the consideration."

Fee looked at me – really looked at me. "Xandra, you're my sister. You're also his mate, and friend to this pack. You've saved my life; of course I'd tell you."

I arched a brow in the hope she wouldn't notice my eyes were a little wet. "I also tried to rip your throat out."

She shrugged. "No one's perfect."

It was such an absurd remark that both of us chuckled. I was still smiling when Ethan came out of Vex's room, followed by every pack member. My mirth soon faded.

Some of them showed deference towards me, but others retained an air of defiance. Were they daft? By now, all of them knew it wasn't me at that lab, so what the bloody hell were they snarling at? How was I the least bit responsible?

"They'll come round," Ophelia whispered as they paraded by. "It's easier to blame you than them. Have to blame someone, right? Otherwise they're powerless."

I supposed I understood, but it was still rubbish. "Do me a favour? Tell Ethan to let me know when he's ready to leave."

She said she would, and left me outside Vex's door. I was nervous as I turned the handle. I knew he wouldn't blame me for this, but there was a part of me that thought the pack was right. Maybe I was responsible on some level. More rubbish, but there it was.

He was sitting up when I walked in. A mountain of pillows supported him. He watched me with his good eye as I approached, and what I saw there warmed me. He wasn't angry. There was nothing but love in his gaze. Love and concern.

"We have to stop this thing, sweetheart," he said. No declaration of affection, no jokes, no telling me not to worry. I suppose I should appreciate that he respected me enough not to attempt placation.

"We will stop it," I promised, as I sat on the side of the bed. He didn't flinch, so that was a good sign. "But right now I'd just like to sit with you for a minute, if that's all right."

He smiled. God, he was a mess. A beautiful, battered mess. "Of course." He reached out and touched my cheek. "I didn't need to catch her scent to know it wasn't you. Even if I was blind and had a human's sense of smell, I would still know you."

One of the tears I'd tried so hard to hold back trickled down my cheek. Vex brushed it away with his thumb as I leaned in to kiss him. Whoever, or whatever, this creature was, she had almost taken Vex from me.

I was going to kill her for it.

CHAPTER 4

HAPPINESS WAS BORN A TWIN

Queen V was no more pleased to see me again that night than I was to see her. Still, this was bigger than both of us, and required immediate attention. If the thing with my face was running around London, no one was safe. And if it could take down Vex, it would have no problem eating a tiny little morsel like her.

Her son, Bertie, Prince of Wales, was with her. He was the official vampire liaison and heir to the throne, and he'd been getting a fair bit of attention lately as he lobbied for peace between humans and those of plagued blood. He was very well-spoken, and presented a much kinder face to the public on behalf of the aristos than that of his mother, who was perceived as a cold bitch.

If they wanted to persuade humans to like us, they should hire a couple of actors from the US to put a pretty face and spin on things.

I understood that Bertie was considered handsome amongst

the aristocracy, but I'd always suspected that applied more to his money and power than to his face. He lacked a certain ruggedness, or robustness, that humans seemed to find attractive. It wasn't that he was ugly, just that his face was ... soft – except for a sharp nose. He was fairly lean and wore his brown hair in a very current style, but his clothing – at least while at court – favoured the more late-1800s sensibilities preferred by his mother.

In fact, my snug velvet trousers and blood-red frock coat made me more of a peacock than him.

I wondered if he knew his mother had offered him to me as a potential husband some time ago. *That* was how much she wanted to keep an eye on me. Offered up her firstborn like a fluffy little lamb. Enemies closer than friends and all that.

"Lady Xandra," Bertie greeted me, "it is a pleasure to see you again, despite the tragic circumstances of our meeting." His voice was pleasant, and when he smiled I could see why he was rumoured to have bedded every woman with even a hint of plagued blood in her. He was charming, and had a way of making a girl feel as though she was the only one in the room.

I bowed my head to him. I was a bloody queen, so I wasn't about to curtsy. Still, etiquette and proper address had been part of my training. "Thank you, Your Royal Highness. It is good to see you as well."

Niceties were exchanged as quickly and with as little formality as possible. Still, I was a little twitchy; aristos did everything so bloody slowly.

William brought digital footage of the creature. This was no surprise to any of us. Goblins were like the old women that used to run the switchboards – they knew everything that went on in the city because they were unapologetically nosy. They were tapped into security cameras all over London, and had even installed some of their own. They didn't have footage from the actual raid, but only because the lab had done something to render nearby cams useless. Regardless, they'd picked up the escaped subject on several feeds afterward.

"Thought it was our lady at first," William said as he popped another video cylinder into the playback machine. "So wrong was your prince." That was directed at me rather than Victoria. William considered her nothing more than a bloodsucker – beneath him. And she treated him like he ought to be in a zoo, or better still, laid out as a rug in her den.

A somewhat grainy image appeared on the screen of the fifty-odd-inch box in the family room of Buckingham Palace. Victoria never struck me as the type to sit down and watch VBC 1 with her children, but this room definitely had more of a lived-in feel than the others I'd seen. There was a box of Cadbury's chocolates on the tea table, next to a battered Wilkie Collins paperback novel. This decor was a far cry from the black-draped gothic nightmare I would have conjured for her.

We all looked at the screen. The lab had been located in Notting Hill, which was part of the Greater London area known collectively as the North End. The district name was Windsor, but few people called it that. The area surrounding the laboratory was nicknamed "Mostly", as it was mostly made up of human relatives of noble families, those born aristo who didn't carry the plague – rare, but it happened – and retired courtesans. Everyone there was "mostly" human, but important enough to the Crown to warrant their own neighbourhood and close proximity to Mayfair.

I spotted the creature as soon as she appeared on screen.

She didn't look anything like me at all! Her hair was a fright and her clothing abysmal. And when she turned her head, the light lit up her eyes like a cat's. But her face . . .

Albert's fangs – she *did* look like me. Eerily so. I had to sit down on the arm of the sofa. If I didn't know better, I'd wonder if maybe it was me too. Granted, she was dirty and wild-looking, but there was no denying her features.

Was she my twin, or a coincidence? My mother would surely remember giving birth to another child, but whether or not she'd tell me the truth was the question. After all, I'd thought she was insane, or dead, for years before I found out the truth about what had happened to her.

As far as parents went, mine sucked – literally and figuratively.

Instinct told me this creature was too new to be my twin. Too young. She had been created, I was certain of it. Animal cloning had been going on for decades, and scientists already knew how to fabricate new organs. Hell, they'd cloned a human in the US six years ago. The whole thing was still tied up in a legal battle, and was illegal in Britain, but neither of those things would stop someone who truly wanted to give it a go. Parts of Europe had such facilities set up. Just last month doctors in Germany had announced that they had successfully grown new organs for a woman who'd had a complete hysterectomy due to cancer. She was pregnant now, I believed.

It made sense that this would be the point of the labs – to genetically engineer future generations.

Victoria stepped forward. "The resemblance is uncanny, but this footage is time-stamped during our earlier meeting, which proves that it is indeed someone else."

The scene on the box switched to another camera. I watched

my blood-soaked doppelgänger as she moved southwards, pausing occasionally to sniff the air. What was she looking for?

Thankfully, there was very little pedestrian traffic, and most of what there was was on the opposite side of the street. To be honest, I was surprised she didn't attack. And then, I saw her head turn. She stared as a motor carriage stopped at a traffic beacon.

This was not going to be good.

I think we all jumped when she leaped through the air on to the bonnet of the vehicle, crushing it like foil wrap. She tore through the windscreen and roof like a child ripping open a bar of chocolate.

She ate the driver in much the same manner.

"Dear God," Victoria whispered, pressing a hand to her mouth.

I stared at her, frankly astonished. I knew she couldn't feel sorry for the human. Could she? After all they'd done to us. To her. Had she never seen such violence before? Surely she had. After all, she'd been alive for almost two centuries. She'd survived the Great Insurrection. Had fought in it.

"She just ate that man's liver." Victoria's eyes widened as she stared at the gory scene. "While he was still alive."

I exchanged a glance with Ethan, who had accompanied me in Vex's stead. The Scot looked as alarmed as I felt. This side of Victoria went against everything I'd ever heard or thought about her.

"Yeah," I said, rather lamely. "She did. He's dead now, though." The tearing-off of his head made sure of that.

I watched as her face settled once more into the resolute countenance to which I was accustomed. Not one trace of emotion remained. What did it say about me that I was more comfortable with this side of her than one capable of feeling?

"Word of this is going to spread. Human deaths at the hands of an aristocratic abomination is just what the Human League requires to start a full-fledged uprising." She looked at me. "Something has to be done about it."

"That's why we're here." If I'd added "eejit" to the end of that, I couldn't have sounded any more condescending.

Victoria's blue eyes narrowed. "I mean that someone has to get to the scene of that accident and clean it up before humans find it."

"So dig out your wellies, Vicky, and get to it. I'm more concerned with finding her than cleaning up her mess."

It didn't help that William decided to snigger at my tone. Victoria's cheeks flushed. "I am the Queen of the British Empire. I do not dispose of human remains."

"Oh, I think we both know you've disposed of your share of remains. You'll just have to find someone else, then. I'm going looking for my feral twin so that I don't end up with an angry mob outside my door calling for my head."

"If I thought your head would appease them, they'd already have it."

I smirked at her. "Good luck with the clean-up. Maybe the humans won't blame you, the Blood Queen, for an attack on an innocent human. Maybe when they attack this time they won't bring tetracycline or silver with them along with weapons and fire." It was a prickish thing to say, especially knowing she'd sequestered herself to this posh prison years ago because she was so afraid of humans.

"Your Majesties," Ethan interrupted, "I'm sorry to break up your pissing contest, but she's moving."

Both Victoria and I turned our attention to the insubordinate wolf, who pointed at the screen. On it, the doppelgänger was considerably south-east of where she'd started. The time-stamp showed twenty minutes ago.

"Where do you reckon she's heading?" Ethan asked. As a were, he spent most of his time in Scotland with the rest of the pack and took care of business there while Vex was here in the city. He didn't know the layout of London like the rest of us did.

I watched as my double stopped again. From what I could see of her surroundings, I reckoned she was near the Serpentine, either in Kensington Gardens or Hyde Park. She lifted her head and sniffed once more.

"Tracking," William said. "The not-lady is hunting."

"Hunting?" There was a tremor in Victoria's voice. "What is it hunting?"

"Something it smelled at the laboratory where it was found?" Ethan suggested.

"Or someone," Bertie added.

"Oh my God." Nausea slammed hard into my gut. How could I have been so utterly, totally, stupid-arse, straight-up hatters not to realise it before this? "We have to go. Now!"

I grabbed William by the hand and pulled. He came along willingly. I couldn't see the question in his eyes, hidden by the dark glasses he had to wear above ground, even at night.

"What is it?" Ethan demanded, following us. Victoria stayed where she was, brooding. Too bad. She could take clean-up duty – or charge Bertie with it. I didn't care. I was on the verge of hysterical panic.

"I know where she's going!" I yanked open the door.

"Where?"

Fang me, couldn't he just come with me? "Mayfair," I shot back. "She's tracking Vex."

William dug a rotary out of the pocket of his shabby frock coat and dialled a number as we ran out of the palace. He barked – literally – into it before telling whoever was on the other end to haul arse to Vex's house. I felt marginally better that the goblins would protect my wolf. If my doppelgänger could hurt Vex so badly, the only hope I had of protecting him was with the gobs.

Sirens wailed in the night – not unusual these days. At least a few of them had to be headed to that twisted wreck of a car – and man – the creature had destroyed.

At the gates of the palace I could hear protesters, even at this late hour. These humans were either incredibly brave or incredibly stupid to be causing a fuss during aristo hours. Safety in numbers was a fallacy – for both sides.

There were vehicles with flashing lights – red and blue and amber. Both coppers and paparazzi. Reporters were set up with their microphones and camera crews. Others took photos for their scandal rags. The authorities tried to keep it from getting out of hand.

Shouts rose as we were spotted exiting the palace. Voices shouted questions – almost incoherent as they tried to talk over one another. We ignored them, even as the odd word got through: "Freak!" "Monster!" "Murderers!"

Then someone yelled something about tonight's incident. They already knew about it. Fuck. There wouldn't be any covering it up. This was going to be so very, very bad. The Human

League was going to love it – not that someone had died, but that the aristocracy could be blamed for it.

Right now, I didn't care. Vex was more important than any of this. If humans wanted my head, let them try to take it. They'd either succeed or they wouldn't.

We opened a partially concealed door on the north wall of the palace and leaped down the stairs to the dusty floor below. All I could think about was Vex. If she hurt him again, I wouldn't rest until I'd ripped her apart myself or died trying, which was the likely outcome.

What had they been thinking, creating a creature so strong? How had they planned to control it? She had to be an accident – a deadly one.

Ethan's normally ruddy cheeks were pale. "If that thing is headed for the keep, I have to get back there."

I opened my mouth to say something sharp, but words failed me as I watched him shift effortlessly into wolf form, his clothes dropping to the dirt around his paws. He howled once and took off.

Weres might look like fairly normal wolves, but there was nothing normal about them. My two legs, regardless of how incredibly fast they could move, could not keep up with four preternaturally fast limbs.

"Lady!" William called, his voice sharp with bark.

I stopped and turned to see him remove his coat. "William, there's no time."

What he did then I knew I would never forget. I watched as he went from bipedal to all fours, his body changing, morphing, until he stood before me as a huge dog-like creature with a thick chest and long limbs. Bigger than any werewolf I'd ever seen.

"On my back," he growled.

I somehow managed enough thought to pick up his coat – let Ethan come back for his own kit – and climbed on to his broad back. He didn't have to tell me to lean low, gripping the fur at his neck. I bent my legs and lifted my feet so the tops of my boots rested on his haunches. Once I was secure, he bolted.

Albert's fangs, but he was fast! The tunnels were nothing but a blur of grey and graffiti as we raced through them. We passed Down Street and the den, onward to the exit nearest Vex's house. When we reached it, I jumped off William's back. The goblin was back in his normal form and shrugging into his coat before my foot hit the second rung of the rusty ladder.

We came out cobbleside a block away from Vex's. I ran as fast as I could with William right beside me, boots pounding hard on the street, breath rushing in and out of my lungs. When we reached the house, our goblins were already there.

Stephen Argyle, Vex's secretary, met us. "Ethan told us what's going on."

I glanced behind him at the other pack members gathered in front of the house. Vex's second stood with them, still in his wolf form. "No sign of her yet?"

"None, but we've got the house surrounded and lookouts on the roof."

"And the alpha?" I asked.

Argyle smiled. I hadn't noticed before how much he looked like Vex. Were they related? And why in the bloody hell was I wondering that *now*? "He's surly and pissed off because I refused to let him come down."

That was undoubtedly an understatement. "How did you stop him?"

"I told him MacGreggor wasn't ready to be alpha, and that you weren't ready to be a widow."

I swallowed. No, I certainly wasn't. And I didn't think Ethan was itching to take over. "Good job."

"How did you know it's coming here?"

My gaze drifted around the property as I strained my ears. No sound or sight of her yet. "She appeared to be tracking something on the footage we saw. I assumed, given the direction she was headed, that she was coming to Mayfair. Coming to finish what she'd started."

The Scot's mouth thinned. "She'll not get the opportunity."

"No, she won't."

A noise above made me lift my head so fast it felt as though something had snapped in my neck. Vex stood on the balcony in his black robe. He looked a little bit better than he had earlier, but he was still pretty rough. His expression was stern as his gaze met mine, but I read the message in his eyes loud and clear. He didn't like being left out, and he really wasn't keen on me being in the thick of things while he wasn't.

Ophelia was above him on the roof, a rifle in her hands. It was a huge thing – double-barrelled and long. She held it pointing downward, hands loose and relaxed, but I knew she would have the butt against her shoulder and a deadly shot off before I could blink.

My sister nodded at me. I saluted her. She had my back, and I felt a little bit safer knowing she was up there with a rifle full of silver shot tipped with tetracycline.

I just hoped my twin had the same weaknesses as the rest of us.

"She's coming!" a voice called out – another rooftop sentinel.

I turned to look up the street. In the distance, I saw some-one with hair the same candy red as mine. My heart gave a little thump. It was her, the creature that had single-handedly taken on not only Vex but some of his pack, and got away vic-torious. A monster that could tear through metal like tissue paper.

Since finding out that I was a goblin, I hadn't worried too much about my own safety, but when I saw her coming towards me . . . Was this it? Was I going to die tonight?

I didn't want to die.

Above my head, I heard Ophelia with her rifle. I didn't have to look to know that she had raised it and was following the doppelgänger as she drew closer.

"Everyone at the ready!" Ethan shouted, his voice a rough growl in his wolf form.

"She's coming," Ophelia announced.

I nodded. "She is. Goblins up front." As soon as I spoke, my furry followers came forward, putting themselves between the doppelgänger and the pack.

"This is our fight," Ethan informed me. Fang me, was he all bent out of joint because the gobs were going to be what she hit first? Was he hatters? It was the smart move to make, regardless of what his fragile ego might think.

"She looks exactly like me," I reminded him. "She almost killed the man I love. I'd say the fight is mine, but I don't mind sharing."

"Fair enough," he replied, and then, "Full bloods behind the goblins. Halfies in the back."

I looked up. Vex was still on the balcony. We stared at each other a moment before I looked away and went to stand beside William, slightly in front of the six goblins we had with us.

They all wore dark glasses, but I had no doubt they could see perfectly.

My twin reached the gate. She stopped at the wrought iron and wrapped her fingers around the rungs as she peered inside at us. She looked curious – young. Even though our physical forms were almost exactly the same, she had a naïve quality that I was pretty certain I'd lost a long time ago, if I'd ever had it at all.

She glanced up at Vex and Fee, cocking her head to one side in an oddly canine gesture. Had she no concept of danger? No understanding of behavioural cause and effect? I suspected that she didn't know much at all outside of instinct.

Then her gaze landed on me.

Her eyes were greener than mine – more like mine used to be before my goblin nature fully took hold – and I watched them widen to a size I thought somewhat impossible. But if my face could change when I gobbed out, then I supposed hers could as well.

After that, it all went tits up. She ripped the gate right off its hinges and tossed it aside like it was cardboard. The electrical defence kicked in then, but she seemed unfazed as she came up the path, bolts of electrical energy nipping at her heels.

I wasn't surprised. I knew she had to be incredibly, stupidly strong to have even made it this far. She stared at me in much the same way I imagined I looked at her – as though she couldn't believe there was another version of herself in the world.

Her strides lengthened and quickened. I pulled the dagger from my corset. She might be unbelievably strong, but a knife to the heart was not a pleasant experience, and immortal or not, there was no guarantee that she'd heal from it before I dealt the killing blow. I wasn't unsympathetic to her plight: being constructed for whatever purpose, treated like a lab rat. I got it that she was ill equipped to handle the world.

But she'd hurt Vex.

I altered my stance for a fight, fingers gripped tight around the dagger. She ran straight at me. I braced myself for impact, for the fight I was sure to lose if someone didn't back me up.

My doppelgänger made a strange noise as she grabbed me. It was laughter. "Found you!" she cried.

Ophelia opened fire.

CHAPTER 5

LOYALTY IS THE VIRTUE
OF FAITHFULNESS

Instinct had me take her to ground as soon as I heard the shot. I covered her dirty, sinewy body with my own. Shouts filled the air.

"Be still," I whispered in her ear. "They won't hurt you."

Her green gaze turned to mine, wild and full of panic. Trusting. I didn't know what had happened, what made me suddenly decide to protect her, but I had changed my mind.

She ... wasn't *right*. She seemed more child than adult, more animal than person. More dangerous than I'd originally thought. She wasn't ruled by right or wrong, conscience or morality. She was ruled by instinct, and instinct was little more than self-preservation.

She'd do whatever was necessary to survive. Something else we had in common.

And now that I'd seen her up close and personal for myself,

I wanted to know how they'd done it, and just what the bloody hell she really was.

She clung to me like a child to its mother. *Found you!* Was that why she hadn't killed Vex, because she had smelled me on him?

I couldn't dismiss it as a foolish leap in logic. It was as certain to me as my own name, because her scent was familiar to me as well. She had tracked Vex to find me. Had the circumstances been reversed, I would have gone looking for her too. Whatever she was, why ever she'd been born/created, she and I were linked. There were no coincidences, and the same thing that made me suddenly protective of a creature I'd vowed to destroy was what had made her look for me in the first place.

Maybe I was full of shit, but that was what my gut told me, and since she had yet to take a bite out of me, or disembowel me with her claws, it was the best theory I had.

"It's going to be okay," I told her, not sure if it was a promise I could keep.

Shouts rang out around us. Footsteps thundered closer, voices rose in an incoherent babble. One cut through.

"Xandra!" It was Vex. I tore my gaze away from my doppelgänger to look up at my wolf running towards me on bare feet, robe flapping around his knees. He had lovely legs when they weren't covered in fur, as they were now. He was changing.

Beneath me, my twin growled.

"Stop!" I cried to Vex. He did. I watched as he regained control of his feral half, and returned to looking how I preferred him. The partial transformation appeared to have aided his healing, and the injuries to his face were less angry than before.

"She's afraid." I looked around at the assembled creatures

in various states of feral and human form, all ready to kill for me. "I need everyone to back off."

Vex didn't like it, but he didn't question me. That was one of the very many reasons I loved him. He either trusted my judgement or he was willing to let me dig my own grave – it didn't matter which. When I needed him, he'd come to my rescue – no questions and no recriminations.

I met his gaze. "She was scared at the lab and she's afraid now. If she feels threatened, she'll fight."

He understood. I think it helped that he knew I'd be the first one she'd try to rip apart.

"Stand down," he commanded his pack, and they did. No one argued, disagreed or grumbled. He was alpha. His word was law, and all obeyed.

Except for Fee, who stood on the roof of the mansion with the rifle butt against her shoulder – just in case. Her first shot had missed by millimetres. Her second one wouldn't miss at all.

I glanced down at that face that was so like my own. I didn't think I'd ever looked so frightened, though. Or quite so unhinged. "You're safe," I told her as I slowly lifted myself off her. Her grip on me tightened, hauling me close once more – so tight and close that I thought she might snap my ribs.

"You're hurting me, sweetie." *Sweetie?* What the fuck? "You have to let go. It's all right. No one is going to harm you. I've got you. We have to get up." The smell of blood on her made my stomach growl despite the other less pleasant odours clinging to her skin and awful clothes.

She laughed at the gurgle, and I had to smile. Her joy reminded me of childhood in Courtesan House, playing with all the halfie kids. It was the unbridled emotion of a kid with no idea how knobbed-up the world really was.

This time when I got up, she let me go. I rose to my knees and offered her my hand. Dirty fingers entwined with mine. Even our hands were practically identical. Only hers felt stronger.

She didn't need my help to rise, but she held tight to my hand. We stood up together, her so close to me I could feel her trembling. She was terrified. This creature I'd seen rip the roof off a motor carriage and eviscerate its driver – who had terribly wounded the UK alpha – was terrified.

This was not good. I was right to liken her to an animal, and I did not want her going feral any time soon. God only knew the damage she could do – and the damage that would be done in kind. Vex would be ready for her this time. We all would. We would not allow her to walk away.

And I realised that I did not want her to be killed. No more than I would wish it on someone I loved, which made this situation even more ridiculous.

She stared at Vex, her gaze hard. "He tried to hurt me at the doctor place."

"The lab," Vex needlessly supplied. I knew what she meant.

"He wasn't trying to hurt you, dearest." I ignored the fact that I'd called her the pet name I used for my siblings. "He was trying to help you. Those people weren't nice."

Wide eyes turned to mine. "They were nice to me."

Fuck. How did I explain to her that her very existence proved just how not-nice they were? Of course they were good to her – they knew what she could do if they weren't.

This wasn't a conversation I wanted to have out here, in the heart of aristo territory. Anyone might pass by and hear. Anyone might pass by and see her. It wasn't just the Yard looking to find her, but the people responsible for her as well. And the Human League, though any spies they had in Mayfair would have to get fairly close to know what was going on, and we'd smell them. Humans working in Mayfair were closely monitored.

"I'm glad they treated you well. Vex thought they were hurting you and he wanted to save you from that. No one wanted to harm you."

She looked at my wolf again, this time with less dislike and fear, but still with a hearty degree of wariness. "I'm sorry I tried to eat you." Fang me, she sounded like a child – such innocent sincerity.

Vex nodded. His posture was relaxed, but I knew he was ready to attack if necessary. I really didn't want that to happen. He wasn't fully healed, and both of them could get very badly hurt.

William approached. He didn't look the least bit afraid, or even wary, and that said a lot about him. He was perhaps the only one of us I'd wager on to take her down.

"Smells of plague," the goblin said, a slight growl to his tone.

"She's goblin?" For a second, I wondered if maybe the gobs would want her as their queen instead of me. She was certainly more like them than I was. Odd. After months of denying my place among them, I was suddenly loath to lose it.

William nodded his shaggy head, his one eye narrow. "Some and more than that, lady. Another thing altogether."

Relief washed over me despite the ominous proclamation, and I couldn't even feel the least remorseful or foolish for it. I liked being queen. I liked having a purpose that had nothing to do with being bred to protect aristos.

"What do you mean, another thing?" Vex asked.

"We should go inside," I suggested, glancing around the yard. It felt so wide open and vulnerable. Plus, my goblins were extremely sensitive to light, and even though it was dark out, the lights around us could hurt their eyes and give them headaches.

Vex looked at me, and I saw something in his eyes that I'd never seen before: refusal. He was not about to allow my doppelgänger in his house.

It stung, but I couldn't be angry. He had a responsibility to his pack, just as I did to the goblins. He had to think of his people, and this was one of those times when pack safety had to be more important than me.

"William, send those from the plague back to the den, please." I'd always thought the fact that the goblins referred to their pack as "the plague" was a little over the top, but it suited them – us.

He bowed his head. "As she wishes." He walked away, leaving me facing Vex.

"I'll take her to the den," I told him. "She needs to be somewhere she can feel safe." What I didn't add was that we needed to keep her where she could do the least amount of harm.

My doppelgänger stroked my hair. "Pretty." Then she held out a hank of her own matted mess and smiled. She had raw meat caught in her teeth. "Same. We match."

Like insane bookends.

"I'm coming with you," Vex insisted.

"That's not a good idea," I countered. Plus, I was still peevish that he wouldn't take her in – despite knowing logically that he had every reason not to. "She's afraid enough as it is, and you're not healed yet. I don't want you to get hurt, and I don't want her to get antsy."

Oh, I could tell it pissed him off that there was actually a creature that could do so much damage to him – and that I was rubbing his face in it, especially in front of his people.

"I love you." I didn't care who heard it, only that he understood. "Your pack needs you whole and so do I. She'll be safe with the goblins, and everyone else will be safe if she's with the goblins." She might be a match for one of them, but there was no way she could take on all of them.

"I love you too, and I think you're fucking mental."

I smiled. "You say the sweetest things. You know I'm right. Besides, the den is the only place coppers won't look for her. And they will be looking for her after what she did."

Yes, they would. She'd murdered someone. She'd done so much damage, and here I was, about to hide her. Albert's fangs, Val would be looking for her. I was not only hiding her from the aristos that had created her; I was going to hide her from the police – from my own brother.

The "fucking mental" part of it was that I knew all of this, and the possible ramifications, and I didn't care. My only thought was to put her somewhere safe – for everyone involved.

My doppelgänger – did she have a name? – turned to me, eyes wide. "Did I do something wrong?"

Lovely, she really didn't understand. Well done, aristos, you made yourselves an ignorant monster, because *that* always ends well, doesn't it?

I wasn't going to lie to her. "You know when you ate the man in the car?"

Her expression turned blank, so I tried again. "You have his blood on your face."

She lit up like a Christmas tree. "Breakfast. He was delicious!"

"I've no doubt." Fang me, but she was nuttier than a walnut pudding. "We don't feed like that, though. We try not to kill humans."

She cocked her head to one side. My father had a corgi that did the exact same thing. "But that's what the meat is for. We eat it. I eat it."

Vex barked – literally – with laughter, and not the what-a-jolly-day-this-is sort. He had to be thinking the same thing I'd been – that they'd fed her humans in the lab. Live ones.

This just got better and better.

"Humans have been around a lot longer than us," I told her. "Thousands of years."

She frowned as though she found the idea distasteful. "But we're better than them."

"Indeed, though they think they're better than us."

She laughed. I didn't blame her. It was ridiculous when you thought about it. We of aristocratic descent were faster, stronger, just *more* overall. The fact that we ate humans was proof that we were top of the food chain. I could spout that we all had rights, but that would lead to even more discussion and questions, and I wasn't prepared to play matron tonight.

Her laughter stopped abruptly, and I could see the tips of her ears perking up through her hair – they were pointed, more like a goblin's than human. It was a little disconcerting, like those hairless cats.

I heard it then as well – the distant wail of a siren, drawing closer. Special Branch.

Val was part of Special Branch, and I'd got into trouble before with his colleagues. I'd also caused him enough problems recently. "Come . . . " I didn't even know her name, or if she had one.

Her fingers took mine once again. "They called me Alexis."

My heart twitched. My full name was Alexandra. Coincidence? Not very bloody likely. How had they managed to make her?

Were there more?

I couldn't think about that right now. The sirens were definitely closer, almost to the Mayfair gates. They'd be let through almost instantly. I shot Vex a meaningful glance before running for the nearest underside access, Alexis in tow.

She followed me without question, as though instinct told her I could be trusted. Well, yay for her, because my instinct was screaming that this was going to get very messy very quickly.

Victoria just might have to get in line if she decided she wanted my head. And I had a feeling the line was about to get a lot longer.

William gave Alexis a room of her own in the den. There was a comfortable little bed tucked into it, and it wasn't far from one of the bathrooms – yes, there was civilised plumbing – but it was a good distance from the regular goblin sleeping space. That was where I took our guest upon our arrival. Dozens of pairs of amber eyes watched us – some in awe, some in suspicion. I think others were downright frightened.

I couldn't say I blamed them. I wasn't quite certain how to feel about my doppelgänger, who was becoming less of a doppelgänger with every new difference between us I noted. Her pointy ears were just one. Her joyous, unhinged naïveté was hopefully another.

The room held a faint scent of opium, and I noticed small vents against each wall near the floor. Were they there to clear the air, or to pump smoke into the room? I suspected the latter, and applauded my prince's thinking. They just might be able to get Alexis stoned enough to keep her relatively calm. Hopefully she wouldn't get the munchies.

Again I questioned my judgement in bringing her here, in hiding her. It seemed the right decision, but now ... Was I putting my goblins in danger? Was I asking too much of them? I should have waited for the Yard and let them take her, but she probably would have killed them all, and then Ophelia would have shot her.

And I'd have been no closer to the truth. It wasn't enough to know about the labs and shut them down. I wanted to know what they were doing, why they were doing it – and what part I played in it. Was it really about breeding? Because Alexis didn't strike me as the maternal type.

I asked one of the younger goblins to run up to my house and collect clean clothes, then I ran water into one of the large copper tubs in the large Roman-tiled bath, added some fragrant oil, and helped Alexis out of her gore-soaked clothes. I threw them on the fire in the hearth nearby. It hissed as it consumed the fabric, smoking dark and thick for a few moments. I could almost imagine the flames cursing me for feeding them such disgusting filth.

She didn't need help getting into the tub, but she did need a little encouragement.

"It's called a bath," I informed her. "It makes you clean and it feels good."

Alexis slid a dubious look in my direction. "It's wet. And hot. It stinks of flowers."

It did not stink. "Well, yeah. It's a bath. Look, it's only water."

Suddenly her face brightened. "Water?" She threw herself into the tub, creating a tsunami I only just managed to avoid with a quick duck and dive. Good thing the tiled floor here sloped gently towards a centre drain. Alexis breached the surface with a delighted squeal.

I scrubbed her back with a sponge and soap that smelled of jasmine. Her skin looked different wet, almost like . . .velvet. Actually, it was exactly like velvet. I ran my hand against the nap in amazement.

She had *fur*. It was very, very short and the exact same shade of ivory as my skin. Astonishing. There also wasn't a mark on it. That didn't mean much. I had to assume that she healed just as fast if not faster than me or any aristo, so they might have beaten her on a regular basis for all I knew. That didn't fit with her personality, however.

"Ali, the people who . . . looked after you, did they treat you well?" I asked as I shampooed her hair.

She shrugged. "I suppose. Not like you. I enjoy this bath thing. No one's bathed me before."

Disgusting. Poor mite.

She giggled. "Then again, I'm only three weeks old."

I dropped the bottle of shampoo on my foot. Bloody hell. How had they done this? Wolves, vampires, even goblins had average gestational periods that were similar in duration to humans, though a little shorter. None of us gave birth to a creature that reached maturity in three weeks. Unless . . .

Goblin babies were very much like puppies when born, and within a few weeks were walking, running and behaving like toddlers.

I didn't know how the lab had managed to engineer her, or for what purpose, but at least I had a slightly better understanding of her. No wonder she had such little impulse control; she was basically a toddler. I'd just treat her like some of the little ones I'd known during my time at Courtesan House, only with a bit more caution considering she could rip out my spleen and have it for tea.

"You're very young," I commented when I remembered myself.

"How old are you?"

"I'll be three and twenty next month." I hadn't realised it was so close already.

She tilted her head back and grinned up at me. "You're old."

"I am not!" I smiled along with my mock outrage, just to make certain she knew I was joking. Albert's fangs, what was I going to do with her? Cross my fingers and hope for the best? I couldn't keep her down here for ever. I also couldn't let her leave, not when she looked so much like me and had a habit of eating motorists.

I couldn't set her free on the world and I couldn't allow the world to unleash itself on her. Neither would be prepared for the assault.

And there was the fact that she had hurt Vex. I should despise her for that, but I couldn't, any more than I would blame a frightened dog for biting.

But I wouldn't want to bring the pooch home with me, would I? All right, perhaps I would, in order to save it, but I didn't kid myself into believing I could save Alexis.

Still, I had to try.

Could I stop her if she decided to go? I'd only known about being a goblin for a few months, and I still had yet to realise just what I was capable of. I was strong – very strong – and a good fighter, but was I better than Vex? Could I hold my own with William? I hadn't really tested either question. I would have to be at least Vex's equal to survive a scrap with my feral twin – William's if I wanted to subdue her.

I reckoned I ought to figure that out just in case. I wasn't naïve enough to believe this was going to end well. Too many people were going to want her dead, on both the human and aristo sides. She was simply too dangerous – a child with a monster's urges, and the strength to act on them and no moral code to stop her. Even if I could help her, she was freak enough to go through the rest of her life with a target on her back.

"I'm in trouble, aren't I?" she asked.

Would I feel so much for her if she didn't have my face? Would I want to protect her if I didn't feel a freak-to-freak kinship with her? It didn't really matter. I was going to help her – if I could.

"A little." Such a gross understatement. "But you didn't know you were doing anything bad."

"I hurt your friend." She wrapped her arms around the knees bent to her chest. "I didn't mean to hurt him, but I was scared and hungry. I thought he was going to hurt me like he hurt the vampires."

Right. She would have seen Vex and the others brutally attack the only guardians she'd ever known. How could she not react to that?

I massaged conditioner into her hair. What a tangled mess it was. "It was right of you to protect your loved ones."

She tilted her head to glance at me. "I didn't love them. They fed me, taught me, but they didn't love me. They punished me for trying to eat the meat they brought. They said it was special and I couldn't have it. It was *infected*. What does that mean?"

Infected? With what? "It means sick. The mea— the person wasn't well."

She made a face. "Ew. The others were sick too. I wouldn't want to eat them."

"Others?"

"Other meats."

Had they tried to feed her diseased humans? No, because she said she wouldn't want to eat them. "What was wrong with them?"

My furry twin looked at me as though I was the one born only three weeks ago. "They were sick."

Served me right for asking. How could I expect her to know the answer? But it was something worth bringing up with Vex.

"How much do you normally eat in one day, Ali?" I was all polite interest as I gently worked the tangles out of her hair with a comb.

She shrugged. "It depended on who fed me. Some gave me more than others – I was quite hungry."

"Take a guess."

"Maybe one and a half."

"Meals?"

She blinked. "Bodies."

Fang me, that was a lot of meat. Where were her handlers getting it all?

At least that answered my earlier question about how many there were like her out there. There couldn't be too many – any – if they all ate like her. That many missing people attracted attention, and humans being the viable food source they were, most aristos wanted to keep them quiet and complacent.

"You're going to be eating less from now on," I told her. "You can't kill someone whenever you're hungry."

An angry pout was my reward. "Why not?"

"Because humans call that murder and they will want to punish you for it."

The pout turned to a threatening scowl. "Then I'll eat them too."

"They'll kill you." No point in sugar-coating it.

"Humans?" She snorted. "They'll never catch me."

I rinsed the conditioner from her hair. "Sweetie, humans are only one group. There are those among the aristocrats who would hurt you as well."

"They won't catch me either. My makers made certain." It was such a cheerfully ominous statement that it sent a shiver down my spine.

"What did your makers do?" It certainly had nothing to do with scent, because I now knew hers as well as she knew mine.

The bones of her face shifted. Startled, I jumped back, almost knocking over my chair. I watched as her face changed – as her entire form shifted, melted and then came back together with terrible slipping and cracking noises.

She went from a double of me to a double of Rye, then to someone I didn't recognise, then to William, and then she morphed into a face I couldn't stand to see on another's body.

Dede. She turned into a perfect copy of my poor mad baby sister, right down to her copper hair. She rose out of the tub, and stood there naked and dripping, holding her arms out to her sides. "See? I can be anything."

"Change," I commanded between clenched teeth. Any fear

of what she was capable of disappeared as rage overtook me. How had she done that? It would be impossible to use DNA from that many people, wouldn't it? Was she able to copy anyone she'd seen? Smelled? It didn't matter. She could run around with my face, which I assumed was her default, but Dede was not an option.

She tilted her head, regarding me curiously.

My goblin rose up inside me. I felt the bones of my own face shift as I took on a more feral countenance. "I said, change your fucking face. You don't ever wear *her* face!"

Abruptly she dropped back into the water, drawing arms and legs around herself in an almost protective manner. I watched as she cowered, hair returning to my barley-sugar red. The tips of her canine ears bowed.

"I'm sorry," came her tiny voice.

I was such a bitch. Sighing, I forced myself to return to my own normal form before I crouched beside the tub. "I didn't mean to scare you. Do you know why I got angry?"

She shook her head, but didn't raise it.

I stroked her wet hair. She must be getting chilled. "That face – that person you became – was my sister Dede. She was murdered a few months ago. It hurt very badly to see you look like her."

Green eyes peered at me from between the damp strands of her hair. Wider and more gullible than I hoped my own had ever been. "Someone killed her?"

I nodded. Just thinking of Dede hurt more than I could put into words. She was my baby sister, a fragile little thing that I'd loved as much as I could love anyone. Churchill had killed her just to hurt me. "Please don't become her again."

"I won't."

I forced a smile. It wasn't her fault. "How are you able to change like that?"

She shrugged. "I just do it. At home they would show me pictures and tell me to become whatever I saw, and then I would."

Scary. I would probably be much more scared if I wasn't so angry. No, furious. Consumed by rage. Why had they shown her photos of Dede? And how pathetic was it that she referred to a laboratory as "home"?

"Come on, let's get you dried off and into some clean clothes."

She stood up as I fetched a towel from a rack in front of the fire. As I wrapped it around her, she twined her arms around my neck and hugged me hard. "I didn't mean to upset you. I'll never look like Aunt Dede again."

I frowned. "*Aunt* Dede?"

Ali pulled back enough to look me dead in the eye. She smiled slightly – hesitantly, as though she was afraid of me, which was a joke. "Of course she would be my aunt. You're my mother."

CHAPTER 6

YOU CANNOT ESCAPE THE RESPONSIBILITY OF TOMORROW

Fuck. There was no other response lying about in the great blank chasm of my brain.

"I'm not your mother, Ali. Not in the proper sense." Bloody hell, I could barely look after myself, let alone offspring.

She looked crestfallen. "You're not?" I knew that expression. I'd worn it enough myself. It was the look of someone who thought she knew the truth about herself, only to find she was wrong.

That she was alone.

Had the bastards who made her not taken any sort of responsibility? Did they think she'd just appear and know immediately how the world worked? They'd thrown words and concepts at her, but no meanings and certainly no consequences.

If she'd been brought about using the eggs taken from me

in the Tower, then technically – genetically – she *was* my daughter. Who was her father?

"No." I didn't bother trying to explain, because I thought it would only complicate things even more – for both of us.

She cocked her head. "Can I be your sister, then?"

That was a knife to the heart. "Sure," I rasped around the lump in my throat. "Sisters."

A smile as bright as the noonday sun spread across her face. Her teeth were white and pointed – like a wolf's. She really was the oddest little murderous hybrid. I wanted to protect and coddle her even though instinct told me to rip her throat out. "Yay!"

I smiled – it felt strained – and held out fresh clothes. "Let's get you dressed."

Fortunately she was fairly adept at dressing herself, and once she had the light ankle-length bloomers and long-sleeved shirt on, I took her back to her little cell.

"Where are you going to sleep?" she asked.

"At my own house." At her stricken look I continued, "You're safe here, and I'll see you when you wake up."

"Promise?"

"Promise." I pointed to the bed. "Go to sleep now."

She crawled between the linen sheets without protest, pulling the wool blanket up to her ears. "Thanks, Xandra."

At least the bastards had taught her manners.

I left word with young goblin George to notify me if anything happened, but I was fairly confident all would be fine. Ali would be safe here – and more importantly, *feel* safe here. And if she went hatters and managed to bust through the lock on her door, there were more than enough goblins to subdue her. She had a chamber pot and a little food and water. She'd be fine for several hours.

Bloody hell, I was exhausted, but I knew before I crossed the threshold into my house that sleep would be a long time coming. I knew it as soon as I caught a sniff of my visitors.

I walked in, down the hall and into the back kitchen/dining area. Normally it was gauche to have the dining room so close to the kitchen, but I liked it, and since I didn't have a staff of servants, it made my life easier.

Sitting at the heavy, polished oak table that had been left behind in the house were William, my brother Val, and Vex, who had healed even more during our brief time apart that night.

"You look good," I said.

He turned to me. One eye was still a little swollen and the wounds were still angry-looking scars, but he was beautiful to me. "I fed."

"Ah." Blood was important to all aristo races, but like goblins, weres tended to react better to meat. Human was preferable, but not necessary.

There was a bottle of Scotch from Vex's distillery in Scotland on the table, and each of them had a glass. I got one for myself and sat down at the head of the table, pouring myself a glass so full it was vulgar. I took a healthy swallow.

"What brings you here, Fetch?" I used my brother's family nickname in the hope of softening him up.

Val – Valentine – was a year older than me and a chief inspector at Scotland Yard, Special Branch. Of course Ali would be his case.

His green eyes narrowed – suspicion brought out our family resemblance. He looked tense and tired.

"You wouldn't know anything about a hatters redhead running around eating people, would you?" He slid a photograph towards me. It was a little grainy, but I could see it well enough. It was a creature who looked an awful lot like me, eating a man she'd just pulled out of the hole she'd made in his motor carriage. Victoria had been right – the man had been alive while she did it.

"I need a sandwich," I said, about to get up.

Vex handed me a plate with cold cuts, cheese and bread on it. He knew me too well. He also knew when I was stalling. I didn't want to do this, but whining about it was just so unattractive.

"Talk," he instructed. Vex was not the sort of man to boss a woman about. He had a vast well of patience, and he was protective to a fault, but not in a possessive sort of way. Some might think he was too good to be true, but he wasn't perfect; he was just old. He'd had over a century to develop patience and understanding, and a will of iron. If he was being curt with me, and telling me what to do, then there was probably a very good reason for it.

And I would no doubt do well to listen.

"No," I replied. "I've nothing to say."

"*Xandra.*"

"No, Vex." I forced myself to meet his gaze, not because I was afraid, but because I needed him to understand. "Have you all conveniently forgotten what happens to people I involve in the melodrama that is my life? Simon was murdered. Dede was murdered. Val was kidnapped. Vex, you were attacked. I know I'm not responsible for these things, but they happened because of me. I'm not prepared to be that afraid for people I love, not again. None of you are getting involved in this."

William looked at me, and I knew what he was thinking as

clearly as if he'd said it. If I was so concerned about my loved ones, why had I left a monster in the den?

Vex crossed his forearms on the table and leaned forward. "Caring about us is all the more reason to include us. Dammit, we don't want to lose you either." Then his eyes flashed with gold. "She's not a pet, sweetheart. She's not a child. She's not Dede."

My heart squeezed tight. I opened my mouth to rail against him – to tell him to fuck right off – but closed it again. If I couldn't even convince myself he was wrong, there was no point in arguing. "I know that."

"You can't save her."

This was one of those times that I hated his age and wisdom. I also hated that he knew me so well. "I can try," I protested weakly.

My wolf smiled slightly as he reached across and placed his hand over mine. The skin around his knuckles was still a little raw from his tango with Alexis. No, she certainly wasn't Dede. If she had succeeded in killing Vex, would I be so sympathetic towards her? No. I'd want her head on a platter, regardless of the fact that we shared some genes.

"She killed someone very publicly." He said this while looking deep into my eyes, as if trying to ram the point of this into my brain through my retinas. "Hiding her makes you an accomplice to that crime. That will make life very difficult not just for you, but for me, your goblins – who will be without a queen if you are incarcerated – and your family, a member of which is very much involved in the investigation. This is not just about you any more. This affects all of us."

I wish I could say that his tone was condescending, but it wasn't. It was nothing more than a shopping list of facts. A gentle nudge into the land of common sense.

Sighing, I turned to Val. "If I tell you where she is, do you promise you won't harm her?"

My brother scowled. "*If* you tell me where she is? Do you think I'm deficient? I already know you've got her in the den."

My head whipped around so I could shoot an accusatory gaze at William. "Did you tell him?"

Even though his face was furred, I saw him lift a haughty brow. Before he could speak, Val stepped in, "Of course he didn't. Fang me, Xandy, it doesn't take a genius to figure that one out. It's the safest place to put her for all involved."

I was such a prat. I turned to William. "Apologies, my friend. I should have known you'd never betray me."

"Betraying his lady or his plague is not what your prince intends. If the lady-creature is a danger to our people, I will end her."

I had no doubt that he would do just that, whether I liked it or not. I had to respect him for it. And I had to admit that perhaps people I loved had got hurt in the past because I always tried to do everything on my own. Maybe it was time for me to stop keeping secrets.

"What do you want to do with her?" I asked Val.

"Take her in, charge her with murder and lock her up." He said this as though I was slow.

"Can the cells at the Yard contain a goblin?" I asked.

My brother shrugged. "I don't know. They're supposed to, but we've never had one in custody."

"She's strong, Val. If you can't contain a goblin, you won't be able to contain her. She can't be on the streets. No one will be safe if she's allowed to run loose. She's like a child, and has difficulty determining wrong from right. If she feels threatened or backed into a corner, she will fight, and she will kill you. I can't lose you too."

That got him – at least temporarily. It was a shoddy remark, but it was true. I couldn't bear it if I lost him so soon after Dede. When he'd been kidnapped, I was frantic. I would have done anything to find him and bring him home.

I was not going to put him in harm's way. I'd rather go to Newgate for obstructing the commission of an investigation than be responsible for Val getting hurt.

"You're not going to lose me," he insisted, "but there's a fine line between confidence and hubris. And there's an even finer line between protecting someone and harbouring a known criminal."

And it wouldn't look good for him if anyone found out I was hiding Ali.

I looked around the table. If my sisters, Avery and Fee, had been there, around this table would be everyone I trusted most in this world. I did not want to let any of them down.

"I promised to protect her."

"I don't want to hurt her," my brother assured me. "But I have a job to do. This isn't something you can sweep under the rug and hope no one notices. It's already been on the box that she killed someone. The Human League is calling for justice and her head."

News travelled fast in London, especially when it was the nightmarishly bad sort. "Her head, or mine?" I asked. "Do people think it's me? Is that why you want me to give her up?"

My brother leaned his weight over the forearm he had braced on the table. "Did you take a blow to the skull? You're thick, but not normally this thick. Of course there are people who think it was you. She *looks* just like you. It can't appear as though I'm protecting you, Xandy, and it sure as hell cannot appear as though you are protecting her – not unless you want a full on riot on your hands."

No, I didn't want that. "She didn't ask for this. I don't want her to suffer because of what she is."

Vex turned to me. Hell, so did Val and William. I realised then just what I'd said. Could I be any more transparent? Was I so desperate to not be the only super-freak in London that I'd tuck my wing about a creature that had tried to kill the man I loved? Even I couldn't be that hatters.

My brother was sympathetic, but unrelenting. "You don't want anyone else to suffer because of what she is either."

He was right, of course. There was no point arguing. The three of them had staged this little intervention to make me feel as though I was in control and calling the shots, but I wasn't. They'd already decided what had to be done. It stung a bit, but I wasn't so enamoured of myself that I couldn't see the truth. In a way, it was a relief not having to make the hard decisions.

I turned to Val. "I'm coming along wherever you take her. I won't let her think I betrayed her."

But I was going to betray her, because Vex, Val and William were more important to me. I felt for Ali – she'd never asked to be a monster, just as I had never asked – but it was completely knobbed up to endanger those I loved because I felt responsible for her.

And if I were honest, I had to admit that she scared me a little. More than a little.

I took a deep breath, and told my conscience I was doing the right thing. "Right, let's—" The ring of my house phone cut me off. The four of us shared a glance before I jumped out of my chair. The house phone had been installed for one purpose only – because my rotary reception was spotty in the tunnels.

Only the goblins had my number – and Vex, of course.

I grabbed the handset. "Hello?"

"My lady?" It was George. "We need your help." His voice was high, and "help" sounded like a yip. My heart hit hard against my ribs.

"On my way." I dropped the phone and ran for the door, yelling at the others, "Trouble in the den!"

There was the screech of chair legs on hardwood, and the clatter of footsteps chasing after me. Then, a subtle shift in the air, a sound like the brush of velvet or the tearing of thick paper, and suddenly a huge wolf bolted past me, with William behind it on all fours.

Show-offs.

I picked up the pace, Val bringing up the rear. At least he had a weapon to protect himself with. I should have known better than to take Ali to the den. Bloody stupid saviour complex.

Please don't let her have hurt anyone.

We made no pretence of stealth as we frantically worked our way deeper and deeper under Down Street. When we finally burst into the goblin great hall, we found the plague gathered. The number of them always surprised me; there seemed to be more than I thought there ought to be. Humans would be terrified if they knew how many.

The goblins stood in a ring, growling, hackles raised. The hair on the back of my neck rose, and my skin stretched over my bones as my goblin tried to come to the surface to join its pack. At the centre of the ring stood Ali. She looked feral and gaunt – like her skin had shrunk since I put her to bed.

She had baby Alexandra in her arms.

My namesake was a couple of months old now – the size of a human toddler, with the energy of a large, clumsy puppy. I loved her to bits, and seeing her struggle against my laboratory offspring's hold made me realise that I did *not* love Ali – at least not as much.

There was one too many bitches named after me in this den.

"Put her down," I commanded.

Ali's head whipped around. She sniffed at the air and stared at me with wild eyes – eyes that were mismatched. One was bright green and the other blue, and her ears weren't pointed any more. She didn't look so much like me as she had done . . .

"*Duncan.*" Vex's hoarse whisper sent a shiver down my spine. This was too hatters to be real, but there she was with my hair and build and a face that looked like a more feminine version of the young man I'd seen photographs of.

"Where am I?" she demanded. Gone was the girlish voice she'd first spoken to me with. She had a bit of a brogue, and her tone was lower. Had her naïve demeanour from earlier been an act?

"You're in goblin territory," I told her. "Put the child down."

Ali glanced at the fur ball in her arms – Alexandra had reverted to an almost completely canine form in her fear. As she got older, it would become increasingly difficult for her to make such drastic shifts without expending a huge amount of energy. I watched as Ali bared her fangs, the teeth growing larger and longer as saliva beaded on the sharp point of each.

Alexandra's mother made a sound of distress. The tension amongst the goblins grew, but no one moved. No one was willing to endanger the pup any more than they had to. Ali lifted the child closer to her mouth.

A growl tore from my throat – the kind that drew attention. Seriously, I'd never made a noise like it before, and I hoped I never did again, brilliant as it was.

Long, clawed fingers dropped Alexandra to the dirt floor. The pup wasn't stupid; she clambered to her feet and tore off towards her mother, leaping into the safety of her arms and reverting to her normal form.

I faced the monster that, not even an hour ago, had called me her mother. She looked grotesque. Her hair was a mix of red and purple. Her eyes were still different colours, but her nose was like mine and her mouth like Vex's, only both were exaggerated. Her shoulders were broad, her breasts non-existent. Her waist was small, her hips lean, and her legs bulged with muscle. By the time I'd acknowledged these changes, she had shifted again.

"I know you." Her – though she hardly looked feminine – voice was a shredded snarl. "You're the one the mad bitch is in love with. The one she thinks can save us."

Us? Oh, fang me. This couldn't really be happening, could it? Was it possible that the newest freak in town had multiple personalities? When she said "the mad bitch", did she mean herself?

"That's me," I replied, playing the hunch around teeth that were a tad too big for my mouth. "Why don't you toddle off so she and I can talk?"

She laughed. "Yeah, that's not going to happen." She swiped an obscenely long tongue over her lips. "I think I'll just eat you."

Were I not keenly aware that this was real, I might have thought I'd stumbled on to the set of an American horror film. I felt almost obliged to come up with a cheesy comeback.

I crooked my finger at her. "Come and get it, bitch."

I hadn't expected her to actually do it, but she did. She launched herself through the air like a trained ballet dancer. It would have been beautiful if she hadn't been snarling like a feral cat.

Most people would have ducked, or got out of the way. I wasn't most people – not that I'm so terribly brave; I'm not. I am, however, like a rat – when attacked, I attack back.

I let my goblin come, as much as it ever did – fangs lengthened, claws sprouted. I met her in mid-air and we fell to the dirt like an East End bar fight.

Christ, she was strong – too strong. I could barely fend her off. In fact, I couldn't do much more than try to defend myself. She clawed at my face, fangs nipping at my throat. I just managed to shove my forearm between her jaws before she could rip out my jugular. Her teeth closed on bone. I screamed, and sank my own fangs into her shoulder. Her jaw slackened as she roared.

And then she was gone. A great and terrible noise rose from the crowd. I pushed myself up in time to see both William and Vex charge her. Vex wasn't fully healed, and had no business getting in her way again. She kicked William in the head, knocking him back, and then she turned on my wolf.

A shot rang out. Ali's inhuman form jerked back with a screech of pain that threatened to make my ears bleed. Val had shot her with a silver-tipped tetracycline-filled bullet. She'd probably never experienced either before if her howls were any indication.

Another shot. My brother wasn't shooting to subdue; he was shooting to kill if he could. This one grazed her cheek as she jerked to the side. Clutching her shoulder, she bolted for the exit.

Suddenly, I was mobbed. Goblins clustered around me, yipping and whining. Vex and Val came forward wanting to know if I was okay. I cradled my forearm to my chest. "Never mind me, go the fuck after her!"

Val and William and a few goblins gave chase, but Vex stayed with me. He had turned back to his man form and was gloriously naked. The goblins didn't seem to mind, but one of them managed to produce a long black skirt, of all things. It had elastic in the waist so he was able to slip it over his hips. I had to make him put it on. It made me want to snarl when all the goblin females stared at his arse.

Elsbeth, one of the elder females, cleaned and bandaged my arm. Vex wanted to do it, but goblin blood is nasty to those who don't have it running through their veins. It can act as a poison, and Vex wasn't going to be back to one hundred per cent until he got a good day's sleep.

Day . . . shit.

I wasn't surprised to see Val and the goblins return – goblins first. Dawn was breaking, and they had a hard enough time in the city at night; there was no way they could risk the day.

Val swore like a fishwife. "I tracked her west for two blocks, and then she disappeared."

That he knew how much ground he'd covered when he was in the catacombs impressed me. "There are a lot of places to hide down here."

My brother laughed – humourlessly, of course. "She didn't stay down here. She went up."

Up? At dawn? Brilliant. Just one more advantage she had over other aristos. And of course, she inherited it from me. I could go out into the daylight without it burning my sensitive skin or blinding me, and I didn't have to feed right beforehand to do it.

So she was gone, then. Not my problem any more – unless she came back. Time to set up better security, perhaps. I glanced down at the bandage on my arm. The scratches on my face were beginning to heal, and some blood would help them along. I was going to need more than a bag of blood if Ali crossed my path again. I was going to need to brush-up on my fighting skills, and a gun. Something that packed a punch and fired bullets that could take down a goblin the size of an elephant.

"All right," I said, my gaze skimming over Val and Vex and the assembled goblins. William stood with Elsbeth, who fussed over him even though Ali's kick hadn't hurt him. The pup Alexandra was in her mother's embrace, seemingly unfazed by what had transpired, but the sight of her in Ali's arms would haunt me for a long time. "I owe you all an apology for bringing her here. I'm supposed to protect you, not put you in danger, and for that I am sorry."

William's hand brushed my hair. "Good-hearted. Too much."

That was a laugh. I was too selfish, that was what I was. Too cocky and reckless by far. And right now I was heartily ashamed of myself. "Everyone get some rest, we've got a big night ahead of us."

"Hunting the abomination, lady?" William asked, a little gleefully.

I nodded. "We're going to need help on this one, my friends."

"You've got the pack," Vex said.

"And Special Branch," Val offered, holding up his rotary.

"Tactical teams are being called out to search for her now. I'm going to join them."

I took Vex's hand and rose to my feet, holding my injured arm against my chest. "Good. I'm going to need Ophelia and her ... friends." Val didn't know about the insurgent hideout at Bedlam, and I wasn't going to tell him. The longer he believed that place was nothing more than an asylum for damaged halfies, the better. "She has human connections."

"And the leeches?" William asked, lip curled.

I gave him a grim smile. "Leave the vampires to me." One of them owed me a favour – a big one.

My father.

CHAPTER 7

THE SUDDEN DISAPPOINTMENT OF HOPE LEAVES A SCAR

If he'd been fully healed and topped up on blood, Vex could have braved the dawn and joined the search for Ali. Instead, he chose to sleep with me. I didn't allow it to go straight to my ego, however. I reminded myself that my place was the most logical should Ali return. It would keep her from the pack and give us the added backup of the goblins. Although I had to admit that strategical advantage aside, I wanted him to stay with me, and I think he wanted to stay as well.

And since I'd been ordered to stay out of Special Branch's way while they conducted their search, I had nothing else to do. I'd rather be out there looking for my daughter – for all my protesting that's what she was – but Val thought it would make things worse, and then there was the chance I might get shot by someone thinking I was her. Good point, I guess.

Ali was a monster, but she was mine, and I'd always got

abnormally attached to things I thought of as mine. I couldn't get attached to her. I couldn't save her, and I doubted there was much I could do to help her, but I could stop her.

"You should take some of my blood," Vex suggested as we took the lift back to my place. "It will help you heal."

My arm was beginning to itch, signifying that it was already on the mend. "I'm fine. I have steaks in the ice box."

His stomach growled at the same time mine did, and we shared a smile.

He touched my hair. "Are you certain she didn't hurt you worse?"

I shook my head as the metal gate of the lift rattled open. "Just the bite to my arm. She would have got my throat if I hadn't anticipated where she was going to strike." I stepped into the vestibule that led to my door. "She's strong, Vex."

He shot me a glance. "Yeah, I found that out first hand. Or did you think I let her use me as a chew toy?"

I opened my mouth to make a smart-arse reply, and stopped. He'd been mauled, had seen his dead son's face on someone else's body, and had just watched me bleed. And then the person responsible for all three had got away from us. Of course he was in a foul state. So was I.

Instead of saying something, I turned to him, put my arms around his waist and pressed myself against him, my head resting on his shoulder. The feel and the warmth of him did more for my mood than any drug could have. His arms closed over my back.

"Tell me you don't blame me for this." Knowing it in my heart and hearing it from him were two different things.

"You're not to blame for any of it," he replied. I could feel the rumble of his voice in his chest. "You were born an exception to the rule and have been exploited for most of your life. The only difference now is that you're aware of it."

That was true. If this kind of rubbish had been going on and I didn't know I was a goblin, I'd be as confused as hell, but it would still go on, because the aristos behind these labs had known about me since before I was born.

When that were attacked my mother while she was pregnant with me, he couldn't have known what his bite would do to her unborn child. He changed my plague-carrying mother into a wolf like himself because she was susceptible to the Prometheus protein, and when those genes got up close and personal with the vampire ones I'd inherited from my father, I became a goblin. As far as I know, I'm the first one to ever walk in the daylight and have no fur or snout. I had heard a rumour about another queen before me, however. And there was that odd and ancient-looking crown in the plague den.

Speaking of queens ... "How much of this do we have to tell Victoria?"

Vex chuckled, and directed me towards the darkened kitchen – insulated blinds kept my flat fairly lightless. "She probably knows as much as we do by now. She's got eyes everywhere, the news on the box, and Special Branch on rapid-dial."

I should have known. "Brilliant." I sighed and began pulling ingredients out of the ice box and cupboards for a meal before bed. The steaks were thick and beautifully marbled. They were beef, but had been marinating in a mixture of garlic, human blood, herbs and spices for almost twenty-four hours. The blood made the meat taste practically human, though there was nothing quite like the real thing.

"At least she won't be able to accuse you of harbouring a murderer."

"Not any more." I began cutting up cold potatoes to fry as he took care of the meat. I paused. "She's a rutting mess, isn't she? Ali, I mean."

Vex smiled slightly as he popped some butter into the frying pan for the potatoes. "I know who you meant. I'm afraid so. Although it would help if we knew for exactly what purpose she was created. I'm still inclined to see her as a weapon."

"Against humans?" I dumped the slices into the crackling butter. "Bit of overkill, don't you think?"

"No." His tone was soft. "Not against humans."

If glances could be sharp, he'd be bleeding all over my sideboard. "Against me?" The fact that I hadn't already gone there in a paranoid rush was unsettling.

"Most likely – and any other freak, goblin or were who gets in their way."

I didn't bristle at his use of the word "freak". I knew how he meant it, even if modern connotations were more insulting. His son was included under that term, so it wasn't a slur, and I was too tired to correct him.

"They'd be taking a huge risk thinking they can control her."

"She wouldn't be alive if they couldn't, and she certainly wouldn't have been kept where anyone could find her."

"Or maybe they're getting too cocky."

He shot me a look I couldn't quite decipher. "You don't want to think of her as a weapon, do you? Especially not one to be used against you."

"Don't be ridiculous," I scoffed, but my heart gave a hard thump in my chest. How could I tell him that she was my daughter? And worse, that I feared the rest of her might have come from his son, who had been able to shift.

I couldn't tell him she was his granddaughter – not until I had proof.

"You've become attached. Already."

I scraped potato from the bottom of the pan with my spatula. Those crispy bits were the best part – and it kept me from having to look at him. "Of course I feel for her. Who wouldn't?"

"Me. William. Valentine. Ophelia. Victoria. You want me to keep going?"

"No. That's quite all right." I sighed. "You're right, of course, but when I'm standing right in front of her – and she's not trying to kill me or someone I love – I do feel responsible for her." Fang me, I felt ridiculous making that absurd statement.

Vex smiled gently. "You feel responsible for people you don't even know. You take this queen business entirely too seriously."

I chuckled at his teasing tone. "Since you included her in your list, I gather you don't reckon V's behind the labs?"

"No, she's too smart for that – and probably too afraid of human retaliation to support something so overt. But vampires are involved, whether she knows it or not, and you know what I think of them."

Indeed. The only thing worse than a vampire was an English vampire, according to my prejudiced wolf. I suppose he had reasons for his dislike; God knows, there were several vamps I wouldn't trust with postage. But my father was one – an English one – so there was at least a very small part of me that wanted to insist they weren't all bad.

But who would I be trying to kid?

I flipped the sizzling, golden potatoes. "There's nothing we can do for her at all." I had to say it out loud to make it stick.

"Not a bloody thing." He stuck a fork in each steak he was pan-frying and turned them over. Perfect.

"I just hope she ... is ended before too many people have to get hurt." I knew it was a lame hope, though. She'd probably already killed again. Special Branch was out hunting her, so that was good. Val would make certain they had the sort of weapons that could take her down.

She'd torn into me like I was nothing. I couldn't even stop her from taking a huge bite. Would my blood be toxic to her? Or did my DNA give her immunity, just like any other goblin?

"A creature like her can't hide for ever," Vex commented.

If I'd done the right thing earlier, instead of taking her to the den, we wouldn't be having this discussion. Or perhaps she would have eaten her way through most of Special Branch by this point. Maybe her makers would have tracked her down.

"Wait." I pointed the pepper mill at Vex. "All halfies have trackers implanted in them, yeah?" It was a rhetorical question, because I'd had one of the devices under my own skin until just a few months ago.

He took the pepper and twisted it over the frying pan. "You reckon they put one in her too?"

"It would be smart, wouldn't it? Regardless of what their intentions for her were."

Vex set the mill aside and folded his arms over his chest. "Go on, Inspector."

I smiled absently. "We know Church was involved in these labs, and we know he was behind the assassination attempt on Victoria." But I saved her life that night. I ruined his plans.

He leaned his hip against the counter. "All right."

"Let's say you're right about why they made her. They started out studying me because they wanted to increase the aristo birth rate, but Church took it in another direction. What's the deadliest creature on the planet?"

"Goblin. Although your bunch kind of take all the wind out of that sail, you know. They're a pretty tame lot."

I stared at him. He hadn't seen what they'd done to Church. What *I'*d done to Church. "There's a difference between civilised and tamed. Listen, the one weakness goblins have is their sensitivity to sunlight, which I don't have. More importantly, Ali doesn't have it. What she does have is the ability to change her appearance to avoid detection." As good as the aristo sense of smell was, most of us ignored it unless we had need of it. No one expecting me to show up on their doorstep would think of sniffing me when they saw me.

Fuck. I really hoped they'd put a tracker in her. We needed to find her, and soon.

Vex was frowning. "Woman, you talk a lot and say nothing."

I would have laughed if I wasn't so preoccupied with my shiny new theory. "You think she was meant to be used against me – us – but if that was the case I don't think her default form would be to look so much like me. Really, if you want to make some drastic change in human and aristo relations, you don't kill the freaky goblin. If you want to knob things up, you kill the one person whose death could incite fear and uncertainty." This wasn't about me – well, I reckoned they were going to pin the blame on me. It had never been about me, not in the way I'd thought.

Vex's pale eyes widened. "They're going to kill Victoria."

I nodded grimly, turning off the burner. The potatoes were done. "And they're going to make it look like I did it."

After food – not even dastardly theories could hamper my appetite – Vex and I had a drink of that delicious Scotch of his and then off to bed. I was still thinking about Ali and my suspicions. I knew there were a lot of jumps in my logic, but it felt right.

Prince Albert had supported aristo–human brotherhood. Maybe Victoria had as well – at the time. Church himself had told me that his particular affiliations believed it was time for change – time for aristos to take over. That included increasing their numbers, and getting rid of Victoria, who wanted things to remain as they had been a century earlier, who was afraid.

Church would have succeeded with his plan if I hadn't jumped in front of that bullet.

Vex and I slipped between the sheets with full bellies and heavy heads, too tired to do anything other than snog and snuggle. That was fine by me.

He pulled me close. "Tomorrow we start training. You have to be at your best. We both do."

I nodded, stifling a yawn. "Right."

"And you will *never* give sanctuary to someone who has hurt me or mine again. I don't ask for much, Xandra, but I will have your complete loyalty."

I went still, my eyes opening. *Shit*. "Vex, I never . . . "

"I know." He tugged me closer, his breath warm against my ear. "I know." He kissed my neck. A few moments later, he was asleep.

I could have lain there and felt sorry for myself or beaten myself up, but I was too exhausted, and there was no point.

I slept deep and dreamless, waking up just before two that afternoon, when I heard something hit my window. These shorter days were lovely for nocturnals, as was the dreary weather that rolled in while I was dead to the world. Temperature didn't bother me much either way, but overcast skies made it easier for Vex to be up and about during daylight hours.

I slipped out of bed and went to the window that faced south, peering through the light-blocking curtains.

A man stared back through the rain-spattered glass. "There she is!" he cried. He raised a camera and took a photo. Thank God I'd only peeked my face out. He had a camera for filming as well, and he stuck that one up to the window.

"Fuck!" I jumped back, heart hammering.

How the hell . . . ? He was in one of those crane baskets – the kind workers used to clear tree branches and do elevated work. The truck was parked on the other side of the Mayfair wall, allowing him to extend the basket arm across to my window.

Why hadn't the alarm gone off? Just as I thought it, a wail cut through the air. The man glanced nervously behind him, then back to me. I wanted to watch him get arrested. Bastard had scared me, and I hated him for inspiring so much fear. He was a measly human, and I was terrified.

"Lady Xandra, how do you respond to allegations that you killed a man last night?"

I glared at him. First thought was to tell him to get lost, but that would hardly be helpful, no matter how satisfying. "It wasn't me," I said.

"How do you explain that the murderer looks just like you?"

A low growl came from behind me. I felt rather than heard Vex approach – he was that stealthy. The reporter's eyes widened.

"Look again," Vex told him with a fierce scowl before yanking the drapes closed once more.

"I want to watch them nab him," I said, and turned to peek. I had to grin when Vex joined me.

The reporter didn't even make it back to his truck before he was grabbed by Special Branch. That was when my rotary trilled out in greeting.

It was Avery. "Fang me and chew the wound, you're live on the box. Didn't you ever learn not to talk to the press? Vex looks yummy in the morning, by the way."

I was going to make a lesbian crack, but I hadn't any wit about me. "I'm well, Avery, and how are you?"

She chuckled. Then seriously, "Val filled me in. I'm here if you need me."

That brought an unexpected lump to my throat. "Thanks. I'll talk to you later, okay?"

I'd just disconnected when it rang again. It was my mother. Huh. I hadn't heard from her in weeks. Whatever she had to say, I wasn't keen on hearing it. She really only ever rang when she wanted something. I hit the mute switch and didn't answer. I needed coffee, blood and food, and not necessarily in that order.

The blood truck had been by earlier, leaving the day's delivery. The donation of blood was mandatory for healthy humans living in the British Empire, but that was softened by it also providing tax relief. A robust human could save several hundred quid a year just by bleeding a pint or two every couple of months to keep aristos sated and placid.

There were two scheduled deliveries a week. I ordered extra for the second drop, just in case Vex stayed over. Today was one of those days, as luck would have it. I went down to the front door in my bare feet. I was wearing a camisole and short bloomers that provided no protection from the rain as I grabbed the package and darted back inside. If I hadn't been wide awake before, I was now.

Bertie's face was on the front page of the paper I'd snatched up at the same time. It was a bit archaic in this modern age to get the rags delivered, but this was Mayfair, and very few residents knew what a computer was, let alone owned one.

PRINCE OF WALES ASKS FOR DIALOGUE
NOT VIOLENCE.

I tossed the paper aside. "Good luck with that, Bertie."

I sipped a glass of blood – I never drank it from the bag if I could help it – while I poured boiling water over the grounds in the cafetière. The freshly ground beans smelled so good.

I showered while the coffee brewed, and returned to the kitchen to find Vex at the hob cooking breakfast. I admit, it was one of my favourite sights. He wore navy pyjama trousers low on his hips, and that was it. His thick hair curled around his nape. I liked it shaggy – especially after he'd run his hands through it a few times.

His wounds had almost completely healed. One of two of the deeper cuts remained as thin scars, but the rest had faded. Only a bit of bruising remained around his ribs and jaw.

Ali had done that. God, she was strong. I wanted to hate her for it, and part of me did. Another part of me was in awe of her strength, proud almost. But mostly I was just sad, because she had to be stopped, and I had a feeling I was going to play a large part in that. It didn't matter that she hadn't asked to be born, or that she was a victim. Something as volatile and unstable as she was couldn't be allowed to roam about.

"You going to stare at my back all day, or are you going to make the coffee?"

I smiled. Vex's voice was like velvet, and that Scottish accent made it even lovelier.

He held up his rotary as I approached. "Her Majesty commands our presence at seven thirty this evening."

Well, fuck. I'd suspected she'd want to yak again after finding out we'd had Ali and then lost her, but I wasn't looking forward to it. "Huh. Did you see the paper?" I asked.

"Not a good photo of Bertie, but they made him sound sincere in his quest for peace."

I got two mugs out of the cupboard. "You don't believe it?"

He shrugged those wide shoulders of his. "I think people who say all the right things have been trained to say them."

For some reason his words made me think of Church. He'd always seemed to know exactly what to say.

"And you might want to watch the programme paused on the box." Vex gestured to the small appliance further down the counter. It had been his idea to install one in the kitchen.

"It's not this morning's reporter playing Romeo to my Juliet, is it?"

"They did run a bit of that – they edited most of me out, the wankers."

I smiled and pressed "Play" on the digital recorder. A news

announcer's face appeared. She looked slightly drunk, if there was such a thing. "This just in – Scotland Yard says the West End man attacked in his car early last evening was *not* killed by goblin queen Alexandra Vardan. While Queen Alexandra has yet to issue any sort of official statement, there are murmurs from Buckingham Palace that she was in a meeting with Her Majesty Queen Victoria at the time of the attack. The Human League has set up camp outside the palace and the gates of Mayfair demanding answers – and action."

The image cut to the Mayfair gates, where a few dozen humans protested with signs, banners and shouting. The halfies guarding the gate were dressed in protective armour, and were armed to the teeth.

"Fang me," I murmured. This was bad. Ali was enough to worry about without throwing a bunch of bloodthirsty humans into the fray.

"Wait," Vex said drily. "It gets better."

The image cut back to the announcer. "Shortly before dawn this morning, VBC's Magda Taylor-Tate sat down with anti-aristocrat advocate Juliet Claire."

"*Fuck off.*" I couldn't believe it. Really? After more than a decade of hiding, she was coming out into the open? She couldn't send me a birthday card for fear of her own safety, and yet she could do a ruddy interview?

And then there she was – my mother. Sitting primly in an extremely uncomfortable-looking overstuffed chair, she was a vision of angelic beauty. She was well into her forties, but she looked to be mid to late twenties. The wolf-bite had slowed down the ageing process. She had golden-blonde hair and bright blue eyes. Toss in a peaches-and-cream complexion and she could be a cosmetics advert. She looked non-threatening and almost delicate in a coral-coloured gown with a high neck and corseted waist.

"Ms Claire," the woman across from her began. She was as dark as Mum was fair – they made a very striking pair. "You are technically an aristocrat, are you not? Yet you are here to publicly protest against the monarchy."

My mother flashed a serene smile. I had to hand it to her, she was really selling the whole "gentle" thing. She could rip that reporter's arms off, yet she allowed the woman to be alpha – or to at least *think* she was alpha.

"Please, Magda, call me Juliet. I was born one of those privileged plague-carriers chosen to be courtesans. While the sexual aspect of the vocation was repugnant – I wouldn't have willingly chosen an aristocratic mate – it enabled me to care for my family and gave me several beautiful children."

"One of those children is Xandra Vardan, the recently appointed goblin queen."

My mother kept her smile plastered on, but even from here I could see that her gaze became shuttered. "I was pregnant with Xandra when I was attacked by a werewolf. The bite—"

"You were *attacked*?"

Juliet arched a brow. "Yes. The matron of the house had banned him from the establishment because he didn't behave properly with the girls. He went feral and I was in his way."

This was more than I knew about it.

"So you were a victim of aristocratic cruelty?"

"Oh yes. It was a most vicious attack – I begged for the life of my child." Had she really? I was under the impression she'd had quite a different thought. "I was saved by the wolf's alpha, but not before I was bitten."

I glanced at Vex. He nodded at the box for me to keep watching.

"Doesn't protocol require an abortion in cases where the birth might result in a goblin?"

God, that was so cruel. I understood, and at one time I'd supported it, but now ... well, things had changed.

"It does, Magda." My mother really knew how to ingratiate herself. "I didn't want to lose my child, but I knew what had to be done. However, I was stopped by Xandra's father, the Duke of Vardan. He told me to continue the pregnancy so that we could see what came out of it."

Magda was suitably horrified. How many times had she practised that expression? "Forced by the very vampire whose offspring was slowly mutating in your womb to carry a child that might very well turn out to be a monster. Did he not worry for your health?"

She made it sound like I really was a monster, that my father was as well. All right, I *was* a monster, but not in the way she made it sound! And my father was never going to win any parental accolades, but he had been good to all of us, for the most part.

"Oh, he quite doted on me. He believed Xandra was going to be special, and of course, he was right."

I shook my head. "Fang me, she's actually pulling off the proud mama pretence."

Vex took bacon from the pan and began cracking eggs. "She does love you; it's just become ... skewed along the way."

I made a wry face. "You're such a politician."

"But Xandra isn't my only child to have suffered at the hands of aristocrats," Juliet went on. "My daughter Ophelia was imprisoned in one of the laboratories we're now hearing about. Unspeakable things were done to her there, and I know of other former courtesans whose children experienced similar interments. I myself was incarcerated when I refused to do as I was told. That's why I'm here with you. I want the aristocrats to know that we're not going to accept this treatment of our children. These labs have to be shut down and the people behind them punished. Queen Victoria needs to abdicate the throne or be removed from it. Aristocratic tyranny must be eradicated."

"Amazing. She's really going for it, isn't she?" I ran a hand through my wet hair. "First time out in public in years, and she's calling for the end of the monarchy."

Vex shrugged. "She always did have a flair for the dramatic. That's where you get it from."

"That's it, compare me to a lunatic." I was only half as peevish as I sounded.

The interviewer went on. "But your daughter Xandra is an aristocrat now, for lack of a better term. Surely you don't want any harm to befall her?"

Another beatific smile. "Xandra never should have happened, but she was and is a gift to me. Of course I don't want to see her harmed in any way, but I'm sure she'd stand beside me and agree that it is time for the current body of power to be overturned. It's time to stop ruling by fear and intimidation, and to make the empire a place of equality."

All right, so she wasn't calling for complete death and destruction, but she had still climbed on her soapbox and committed treason by calling for Victoria's removal from the throne. And she made it sound as though I was already in her corner.

"And who would lead this new empire, I wonder?" Vex asked, shoving bacon, eggs and fried bread on to my plate.

I took the food from him, my gaze still riveted on the box, and my mother's beautiful face. "Notice she always smiles with her mouth closed?" No flashing the canines for her.

"The better to fool you with, my dear." He filled his own plate. "Juliet's an ambitious woman."

I turned the box off and sat down at the table. "Do you really think she wants to take over?"

A cup of hot coffee appeared before me, then another at Vex's usual place. A few seconds later, he plopped himself down with a loaded plate. "Aye, I do. Your mother's crafty, and she wants revenge on the aristocracy."

"Revenge?" I bit into some bacon. "That's a little extreme, don't you think?"

His gaze locked with mine. "Xandra, I was the one who saved her from that attack. She cursed me for not letting him kill her. She did not want to continue the pregnancy – understandably – and she blamed every last aristo for making her go through with it."

It was like a punch to the stomach, even though I already knew most of that myself. "Does she hate me?"

"Of course not, but she's not going to win any Mum of the Year awards, is she? All those years out of your life, and now suddenly she's back and declaring her love for you on the box? You're not just her daughter, you're a political platform."

He was pissed off – and right. I had to be as well if our suspicions matched. Juliet might actually care for me on some level, but she wanted to use me just like everyone else spoiling for war. Only Vex seemed to want me for who I was, rather than what.

"Maybe I should give my own interview," I mused. "Think anyone would be interested?"

Vex snorted. "No. No one at all." He might as well have rolled his eyes. "I think they'll queue up to have you."

I punctured a yolk with a chunk of fried bread. "It could make more trouble."

He shrugged. "It could also let people know you're not going to be used as a pawn. Talk for yourself rather than letting others do it for you."

And this was why I loved him. I grinned at the prospect of putting a halt to so many plans that seemed to involve me whether I liked it or not. Perhaps taking a public stand was exactly what I needed to do.

Talk for myself, indeed.

"Oh, Ali told me something interesting. She said there was a diseased human at the lab. She said that there had been others. Do you know anything about that?"

Chewing a piece of toast, he nodded. "Mm. Sorry, with all the excitement, I forgot to tell you."

He called almost getting killed "excitement"? He was more hatters than I'd thought. "So you saw the body?"

"We took it. Nasty-looking thing. It didn't look like anything I'd ever seen, but it had already started to decompose, so it was difficult to tell just what was wrong with it. We thought it was tied to the experiments, so we took it to our own lab to be examined."

The pack didn't actually have a laboratory, but there were members who worked for one.

"In fact . . . " Vex consulted his rotary, "she should have sent the results by now. Ah, there she is."

I watched as he read the message, his brow creasing into a deep frown. "Christ."

"What?" I demanded, vaguely panicked. You'd think I

would be accustomed to things getting progressively worse. "What is it?"

Vex met my gaze over the top of his rotary. His expression was grim. "The human died from the plague."

That was it? Oh, goo—

"A mutated and extremely virulent strain of plague no one's ever seen before."

Fuck.

CHAPTER 8

YOU CANNOT BE A **HERO** WITHOUT BEING A COWARD

A new strain of the plague? After all these years? What did that mean? And did Ali have it?

I called Val and told him what Vex's connection had found out. Vex sent the test results to him from his rotary.

"The motorist she attacked showed no trace of plague," my brother informed us, "but I'll have our people check again. No reports of anyone coming down with anything remotely like it, and I'm not going to risk complete panic until I have to. The last thing we need is humans losing their minds and coming after us in plague-crazed fear."

"Sounds good. Any sign of Ali?"

"None."

Bloody hell. She needed to be found. My feelings for her were so all over the place, but I knew that she had to be stopped to protect people – to protect *her*. Maybe she had managed to get through the remainder of the night, and into today without killing anyone.

At least we knew she hadn't killed Victoria, because Her Nibs had demanded a meeting earlier. But where was she? She could make herself look like anyone, and if she could control her hunger, we might never find her.

Would that be so bad? If she learned to control herself, what would be the harm in letting her live?

Perhaps now was the time to admit, if only to myself, that my judgement was not what it ought to be where my daughter was concerned.

My *daughter*. Couldn't wrap my head around that.

Vex had to return to the pack and get the halfies who had joined him on the raid tested for plague infection, so I decided to go out and do a little searching for Ali on my own before meeting him for "training". Did I tell him what I was doing? Um, no. Did I have a good reason? No to that as well, though I told myself he had enough to worry about. I had nothing but the ego-overinflating thought that I was the only one who could flush her out, that she would reveal herself to me and no one else.

Bollocks.

And I still hadn't told him my suspicion that Ali was his granddaughter. I couldn't drop something like that on him without proper confirmation. Meanwhile, it was better if only one of us was uncertain of what needed to be done about her.

Val sent me an update that said Ali had been allegedly spotted in Covent Garden earlier, so that was where I decided to go. It was probably a hoax, but it was worth looking into, and it gave me a place to start.

There were a lot more protesters around today, despite the

dodgy weather. The gates of Mayfair were crowded with humans carrying signs that proclaimed aristos "unnatural" and declared that humans had been here first. It was the usual drivel, but there was a decidedly intimidating vibe to the whole thing that spoke to something feral deep inside me.

I wasn't the brightest of bulbs, nor was I what you'd call careful, but even I knew better than to parade myself in front of that lot. They were even bothering the crew stringing a length of wire along the top of the Mayfair fence. That hadn't taken long – one intrepid reporter and suddenly the neighbourhood was installing better security. I reckoned the electrical charge that would run through that wire once installed would be enough to deter most humans.

Maybe even Ali, as well. Anyway, it was all a little disconcerting, seeing Mayfair being turned into more and more of a prison rather than a haven, so I dragged the Butler inside and on to the lift. If you've never ridden a motorrad through the catacombs beneath London, you're missing out. Of course, you had to know the Met schedule fairly well, but there were enough tunnels and disused track underside that made it easy enough to avoid collision. You just had to have a decent sense of direction, which I did. It was about the only sense I had at all, really, being frightfully deficient in the "common" category.

I rode east, towards Covent Garden, where I came cobbleside. I pulled a knitted hat over my head and tucked my very noticeable hair inside. With my collar up against the chill, and thick-soled boots, I looked like any other young Londoner out and about. Maybe my tailor-made black frock coat was a bit posh, but you could buy similar styles on the high street. With my chin down, I felt confident that no one would take special notice of me.

This was a halfie- and aristo-friendly part of town, but there were papers tacked around, flapping in the wind, that advertised public meetings and spouted anti-aristo propaganda. There were more of them than usual, more than there had been when my house in Leicester Square had been torched. However, there were a lot of posters calling for peace and equality as well. Even a few full of what could only be called aristo propaganda, because they held aristos up as more evolved creatures.

If the humans rose up again – really rose up – we were going to be in for it. There was going to be bloodshed. I had killed before, killed to protect myself, but this wouldn't be self-defence. It would be war.

If Ali had been here, no trace of her remained. The colder months were often a blessing for those of us with a keen sense of smell – winter was like a vacuum of scent. It made it easy to focus on one smell, but hard to pick out a faint trace. Maybe it was just me, but all I could smell was cold and food. All I could hear was chatter and traffic.

What was I doing? Had I expected her to build me a fucking snow angel? Maybe leave a trail of blood splatter for me to follow like breadcrumbs?

My rotary rang. A quick glance at the flip screen told me it was Val. I picked up. "Hullo?"

"Tell me you're in Covent Garden."

I glanced around, suddenly cautious. "Are you spying on me?"

"TrackNav on your phone," my brother explained curtly. "Look, are you there?"

"You're the one with fucking TrackNav." Bloody coppers.

"Xandra!"

"Okay!" I lowered my head and my voice. "What the fuck, Val?"

He paused. That was when I heard the siren kick in – both over the connection and in the distance. "How quickly can you get to Freak Show?" he demanded.

"Couple of minutes if I walk."

"Run. Penny says there's trouble. And Xandy – be careful." Then he was gone – he'd disconnected.

Rotary gripped tightly in my fingers, I took off at a run. What was that smell? My nose tingled.

Freak Show was a club where Val's sister Penny worked, and where Vex and I had first got together. It was weird and fun, and …

On fire. That was what I smelled. I watched in horror as flames licked up the sides of the pinkish stucco walls. There was a crowd gathered, and for a moment I thought they were trying to help; then I saw three bottles fly toward the building – bottles with flaming scraps of fabric in their necks.

The explosions made my heart jump. Heat pulsed. Someone screamed. The crowd cheered. Fire roared as the sirens closed in. They were still a way off.

I spotted Penny – she and the rest of the staff were out front as well. There were three half-bloods including her, and four humans. The humans formed a barrier between the halfies and the protesters.

"Penny!" I ran up to her.

Penny was a little thing, but she was slightly taller than me in her towering heels. The bright orange wig she wore made her seem even taller. She'd been born male, but no one who knew her thought of her as such. She was Penny Dreadful, and I loved her to bits.

She grabbed my arms. "Is Val on his way?"

I nodded. "Sirens blaring." She hadn't called me by name, and I appreciated it. If this crowd figured out who I was . . .

"Oh, shit," came a voice behind me.

I glanced over my shoulder. A halfie I recognised as another waitress was staring at the burning building. I turned to look. Penny gasped. Someone else screamed.

And in an upstairs window of Freak Show, a young human girl bawled her guts out in fear. The crowd of humans cried for help. And still the sirens approached. How long before the fire brigade got here?

Where was that reporter with his fucking bucket?

Weren't the humans all contrite and in a panic now? Not so smug and proud now that one of their own was in danger. Pricks.

"Xandra," Penny rasped. One of the humans and two of the halfies turned to look at me when she said my name. So much for keeping a low profile. "You have to help her."

My shoulders sagged. Was I in one of those true-life box dramas that were so popular in the States? Was there a film crew I didn't know about following me around, arranging shit for me to wade into?

Fang me, but that would make so much sense. However, I knew I wasn't that lucky.

Sighing, I took off my coat, but not my hat. No need to draw even more attention. I shoved the garment into Penny's hands and jogged down the alley that ran alongside and behind the club. Val had been abducted from here a few months ago, and I'd accidentally killed a plague-riddled betty on the wet cobblestones. There were humans who treated the plague like a drug and injected themselves with altered aristo blood to make themselves stronger and generally "more". It never ended well.

I could climb relatively unseen back here, and that was higher on my list than unpleasant memories. I took off at a run, jumped one foot up on to the back steps, then up to the rail, off the top of the door frame. I pushed up, the muscles in my legs easily propelling me into the air. I grabbed the edge of a second-storey window and used it to haul myself higher. Then I used fingers and toes to scale up to and over the roof. I'd always been a good climber, but my goblin genes had given me an extra boost that was pretty amazing.

As soon as I poked my head up on the other side of the roof, the crowd below noticed me. People began pointing and shouting. They didn't know who I was.

From where I stood, I could see the flashing lights of police cars, and further back, the familiar red of the fire engine. They'd be here soon, but I was already on the roof and my conscience had kicked in.

I peered down at the smoke billowing out of the window where the girl had been. Why wasn't there a fire escape on this part of the building? Why hadn't this girl got out with the others? And why the bloody hell did I have to be her fucking rescuer?

Sighing, I gathered up what bollocks I had and lowered myself over the edge of the roof. It took a few creative manoeuvres – much to the appreciation of the crowd, I might add – but I soon managed to swing into the open window, hitting the floor in the smoke-filled room. The curtains were on fire, as was part of the carpet and a sofa.

I coughed. "Where are you?"

Out of the corner of my eye I spied movement. The girl

came up out of the smoke – she must have been down on the floor like they taught us at the Academy.

One of the firebombs had landed by the door – explaining why she hadn't been able to get out with the others. The exit was completely blocked by flames.

"Come on then," I said. My eyes were beginning to water – badly.

"How are we getting down?" she asked, coughing.

I peered out of the window. "I reckon I'll jump."

She stared at me as if I was hatters. "I can't jump – I'll be killed!"

Killed? I snorted, but it made me cough, choking on smoke. "I'm the one doing the jumping. Now come on!"

When she didn't immediately leap into my arms, I reached for her. She tried to pull away.

"Please don't make me knock you witless," I asked. She looked at me as sweat trickled down my brow. She was like a frightened little rabbit, with her reddened eyes and quivering chin.

"Trust me," I said, this time with some gentleness in my tone. I nonchalantly stomped out a flame that was licking at the hem of her long skirt.

She took my hand and I led her the short distance to the window. This was going to put paid to all my effort to remain at least partially inconspicuous. No human could make this jump without sustaining some sort of injury. Maybe they'd think I was just a halfie.

I sat on the windowsill, legs dangling outside, smoke pluming out around me. The girl eased her front half out of the room, clinging to me for dear life. I put my arms around her, held her tight, took one last look down and then, oblivious to the noisy crowd and the flashing lights, I jumped.

I landed in a crouch, the impact hitting my heels and ankles like a slap. Tingled a bit, but other than that I was fine.

A firewoman ran forward to take the girl from me, wrapping a blanket around her shoulders. People milled around me; lights flashed in my stinging eyes. It was so bright, so freaking noisy . . .

Familiar hands grabbed my shoulders. Val. "Are you all right?" he demanded.

I nodded, blinking back the tears. The cold air was a mercy on my eyes and nose – all my senses, really. And oh, so nice and refreshing. "I'm good." Smoke came out of my mouth as I spoke.

Suddenly Penny was there too, as the fire brigade went to work. We were shuffled along with the crowd, Val's presence as a police officer keeping us on the edge. His mates were talking to the crowd. A couple of humans were already in cuffs.

Flashes went off around us, and then there was a film crew. Again. I contemplated moving somewhere that technology didn't exist. A microphone was shoved in my face.

"And here's the hero of the night!" the woman shrilled at the camera. "What's your name, miss?"

I had opened my mouth to say "no comment" when Penny yanked off my hat. "Xandra Vardan," she crowed. "Goblin queen."

Fuck.

I'm not sure what I expected, but Vex laughing wasn't it.

"I'm glad you find this amusing," I snapped.

He sat sprawled on the large sofa in his study – one arm over the back, legs splayed. Normally I might have crawled in there and straddled his lean hips, but right now I wanted to kick him in the shin. "It's not funny."

He grinned at me. "You're right. It's fabulous. You did something wonderful today – and the whole world knows it. The big scary goblin queen saved a human's life, and at risk to your own. You couldn't have asked for better publicity if you paid for it."

"It felt like it was just handed to me." I plopped down on the sofa beside him. "It was the kind of thing you'd see on the box. I just happened to be in the area at the right time."

He patted my thigh. "Your inability to avoid trouble came in handy."

Our gazes met, and I couldn't help but laugh. I leaned my head back. At least I didn't smell like smoke – I'd showered and changed before I came over. "It was pretty brilliant, wasn't it?"

"When Penny pulled off your hat and outed you, I thought you were going to eat someone's spleen. Do you want to see the look on your face? Because I recorded it."

I glanced at him. "Really?"

"Really." He was still smiling. God, he was gorgeous. "You just accidentally did more for the aristocratic race than Bertie and his whole campaign for peace has done in the last six months. It could have gone badly, but Christ, I don't see how it could have gone any better."

We sat there quietly for a moment, smiling.

"Are your halfies okay?" I asked.

"They seem to be. I ordered blood work just in case. It's doubtful they'll get sick." The plague in their blood gave them some resistance, but the human part of them was still vulnerable.

"Do you trust Bertie?" I asked after a moment of silence, returning to our former topic.

Vex propped his arm on the back of the sofa and braced his head with his hand. "With my life? No. To give me the name of a decent tailor, yes. What are you asking me exactly, love?"

I shrugged. "I'm not sure. He sort of came out of nowhere, didn't he?"

Vex frowned. "No, not really. He's followed in his father's path for years, but the last decade or so he's spent most of his time in Russia with his sister, and in France. He's always been something of a diplomat. Spent some time in the Americas as well. Though he has been a bit high-profile since his return."

This was where my youth was a disadvantage. I didn't have history with these people, hadn't had the benefit of knowing them for decades – or a century.

"I don't know him. I need a liaison with the vampires that I know."

"Why do you need a liaison with the vampires?"

"It's us against them, isn't it? If we're not united against humanity, we're screwed. I know you and William. And while I'm surprised by my mother's sudden public revelations, I feel that I know her as well. I don't know Bertie."

"Vardan's the one who handles most of the political goings-on while Bertie's away."

My father. Of course. I'd meant to see him anyway, but hadn't had the opportunity. He was the one vampire I reckoned I could trust when so many of them seemed to be in league with the labs. There weren't that many vampires in London, for God's sake. Maybe they were all rotten. "I always thought Church was higher in the ranks."

"Churchill had his uses." That cryptic remark was so dry, sand fell from my wolf's lips. "But he was half American, and that made him an outsider."

It wasn't such a big deal now, but back when Church had been born, it was a scandal. His mother was not only from America and "new money", but there was talk that she'd been pregnant when she married Church's father.

Well, I supposed back then if you were going to marry an American heiress you had to know beforehand that she could carry an aristo child. Turned out that Church's mum was full-blooded, a fact she'd hidden from American society. She infused fresh blood into the aristocracy.

But it was American blood. New blood.

And that was what had made Church so eager to prove himself. And why he'd got involved with the labs and experiments. My father claimed not to have known anything about them, and I believed him. He hadn't faked his anguish at finding out his wife was involved. He might have been aware of things, but he hadn't been included, and that was enough reason to trust him right there. If he wasn't trusted by those bastards in the vampire ranks, then he was good enough for me.

"I'm going to go and see him," I announced. "I want him involved."

Vex arched a brow. "You're going to step on Bertie's toes."

"Bertie doesn't know me any more than I know him. And he certainly doesn't know what's been going on in this country for the last decade. My father does, and no one's going to think it odd for me to want my daddy at my side." Well, someone who didn't know me wouldn't think it was odd.

"You really want him involved?"

No. I nodded. "I feel like it's the right thing." That was true – as much as I didn't like it. "How long before we have to be at the palace?"

Vex checked his pocket watch. "Hour and a half."

"Plenty of time to pop by Vardan's."

A long, strong finger hooked itself into the waistband of my skirt and tugged. Smiling, I let myself be pulled in close. Vex smelled like sweetness and spice to me – exotic and delicious. He was absolutely the best man I'd ever known. I respected him, and I didn't respect too many people.

He liked me for who I was, faults and all.

I rose and swung my leg over his lap, straddling him like I'd thought about a little earlier. When he touched me, I sighed and gave myself over to him completely, lowering my head to his to lose myself in his kiss. After the craziness of the day, this was the first thing that felt real and worth hanging on to. This was what really mattered.

So I didn't care that I'd have less than an hour to get to my father's and then to the palace afterwards. My father, the Queen and the entire bloody country could wait.

CHAPTER 9

PEACE CANNOT BE ACHIEVED THROUGH VIOLENCE

My father was a top-shelf bastard, but he was still my father, and right now he had a more sympathetic light cast on him than my mother. Though that wasn't saying much.

I couldn't turn on the box or pick up a rag without seeing my mother's angelic face grinning back at me. And in every interview she mentioned me, how she'd been forced to have me. It was as though she was trying to grab the title of being the first laboratory for aristo experiments, which wasn't true.

I understood my mother's dislike of aristos. But for years she'd carried on her fight out of the spotlight, and now that she'd stepped it up, I didn't like her using me – or those poor pathetic creatures I'd seen in the cellar of Bedlam – as a marketing tool. Those battered halfies deserved better, and there she was chatting about the work they were doing in Bedlam to help them.

She hadn't been part of my life for more than a decade, and she could have been. She'd secretly recruited Dede, but ignored me until I became news, and that stung. We were a platform for her now, and she was standing on my fucking face.

Even Vardan treated me better than that.

I'd realised years ago that aristo men often viewed their children by courtesans as both shameful and a sign of potency, which was terribly important to a race that had a hard time flourishing. But courtesans weren't the only ones that could breed with them; halfies could too. My sister Dede had given birth to a full-blooded child that was being raised by the father and his wife to protect it from being poked and prodded like the rest of us who were "different".

My father used that same defence against me – that he only wanted to protect me. Right. Maybe there was some truth to it.

My father's house was a typical Mayfair great house. It had been built in the 1700s by his great-great-grandfather. Originally my ancestor had had to rent the land he built on, as it was part of a privately owned parcel. All that changed after the Great Insurrection, when the Crown seized the land, declaring it a sanctuary for aristocrats.

Luckily the Vardan Mayfair estate had received only super-ficial damage during that horrific night when many aristocratic lines ended for ever. There were still scorch marks on some of the outside stones – reminders that my father chose to retain rather than conceal or destroy.

I was shown to my father's study. He'd redecorated since my last visit. It did seem manlier, with heavier furniture, plush and comfortable, a more understated carpet, and richly coloured Pre-Raphaelite paintings. The duchess's influence was gone.

He rose from behind the desk when I was shown in. He stubbed out a cigar and came around to greet me. "Xandra. It is so wonderful to see you."

He sounded sincere, but it was hard to tell. He was such a *very* good liar, and the last time we'd had any sort of one-on-one time, we'd said some awful things. Well, if I was fair, most of the awfulness came from me. I'd reached the point where I was ready to kill him. I wasn't certain that urge had completely passed.

"Hello, Vardan." He kissed both my cheeks. "You look well." That wasn't a lie – not really. He did look much better than he had shortly after the funeral. Losing Dede, Val's abduction, my own drama and the duchess's murder had taken a toll on him.

"I feel well, thank you." He took a step back, hands curved around my shoulders. "You are the very picture of health and vitality. Look at you! Your skin positively glows. What's your secret?"

"Clean living," I replied drily, to which he chuckled. Actually, I had a feeling my improved looks had more to do with being a goblin than anything else. Maybe beneath all that fur, goblins had perfect skin.

"Sit, sit." He gestured towards the sofa. "Would you like tea?"

"No thank you."

"Ah." His expression changed to one of disappointment as he sat on the chair closest to me. "This is not a social call."

I was a horrible daughter. "Not entirely, no. But first, how are you getting on?" It wouldn't hurt me to wait a little longer to mention the favour I needed.

He went on to tell me about the things he was doing to

occupy his time and his mind. The more he talked, the more animated he became, and the more guilty I grew. He was a lonely, regretful man.

Life would be so much easier if people weren't complicated. If I could just be a monster and my father could just be a bastard, everything would be as it should. Dede might still be alive if she'd been simply the fragile little waif everyone believed.

Someday it might not hurt to think of her. She had deserved so much more than this world. Dramatic, but true. She'd been conceived to be a servant to the aristocrats, bred for specific skills and trained to protect. She hadn't had a choice – none of us had, not really.

"I saw your mother on the box," Vardan said, filling the silence.

I couldn't hide my surprise. "You have a box?"

He chuckled and nodded. "I'm not a complete Luddite." His mirth faded. "I was a little surprised by how much she still hates me after all these years."

I spoke before thinking. "I don't think she hates you nearly as much as she loves the attention saying so gets her."

"Fair enough." A smile lingered on his lips. "I saw you on the box too. Well done with the rescue. You're setting yourself up as quite a champion for humankind."

I made a face. Was he mocking me? "Hardly." I hated that I was all over the news – again. "I was simply in the wrong place at the wrong time."

Tilting his head, he watched me carefully. No, he wasn't taking the piss. "You saved a life."

"It looked like a bloody public-relations bid." The only thing worse than the country thinking I was a human-lover was the country thinking I *wanted* it to think of me as a human-lover.

"Ah." He crossed his legs. "I see. Don't want to look like a defector?"

I arched a brow. "Don't want to look like a politician."

My father laughed. "Now I understand. But you are a politician, my dear. You became one when you agreed to be the goblins' queen."

"Yeah, I reckon I did." I glanced away, then back again.

Vardan folded his hands over his stomach. "If this isn't a social call, I'm going to assume you need something from me."

I flinched – just a little. Hard to be offended when he was right. "If you've been watching the box, then you know the League is firing people up, and my mother has added fuel to that."

"She most certainly has. I wonder who persuaded her to come out into the world after all these years? I always fancied she'd end up like Victoria, forever closed off."

I stared at him. "Well, you did have her committed."

"For her own good. I thought she was going to harm you."

"You thought she might out me as a goblin."

A slight smile tugged at his lips. "That's the same thing. I won't lie to you, not any more. There was a time when I wanted her as far from me as I could put her, and if she had died in that place I wouldn't have mourned her. She . . . could be difficult."

"Did you love her?" I couldn't stop the words from tumbling out of my mouth.

"It would be more romantic and self-flattering to say yes, but the answer is no. I didn't love her, but I was obsessed with her – to the point that I made myself an object of ridicule amongst my set. When she . . . threatened me, I panicked. Not one of my proudest moments, I assure you."

"So you had her locked up."

He nodded. "I'd do it all over again if it meant the world not finding out about you. With hindsight, I should have killed her."

"For wanting to tell me that I was a goblin?"

He stared at me as though I was speaking gibberish. "My dear girl, she wanted to take you out of Courtesan House and *give* you to the goblins. She said you were a danger to the other children, but the pills I gave you made certain that you weren't."

"Back up a tick." My brain was squirming trying to figure this out. "Juliet wanted to give me to the goblins as a child?"

"Yes, but then you went on that class trip, and the prince realised what you were and approached you. Churchill shooting the prince in the eye put an end to talk of simply handing you over. I was worried they'd eat you."

I smiled slightly. "They wouldn't have."

"No." He frowned slightly. "I realise now Churchill didn't want to let you go, even back then."

That wasn't a topic open to discussion. Just the thought of it sent a slither of unease down my spine. "Why are you telling me this now?"

"I know how much you loved your mother. No little girl should find out that her mummy wanted to give her away. That would have been cruel. I've been selfish and underhanded at times where my children are concerned, but I like to think I've never been cruel."

"No," I allowed. "You rarely were."

Was that a flinch? Would he be happier if I lied and said that he was *never* cruel? No matter. We were well beyond all that history now.

"I don't want to dredge up the past," I confessed. "I want to secure the future."

He raised his hands and regarded me over steepled fingers. "How do you propose to do that?"

I launched into my spiel, "We all know that we're on the brink of war with the humans."

Vardan waved a hand in the air. "This sort of nonsense has been going on in Ireland for years."

I stared at him. "The IFA has killed four aristos and a dozen half-bloods in the past two years. And they've destroyed several aristo properties." There were aristos in London who had fled the Irish Freedom Army's wrath with nothing left but their clothing.

My father smiled gently. "You're so young. There's always been hatred and violence, Alexandra. There always will be."

I shook my head. "I refuse to believe that."

"You?" Vardan looked surprised. "My child, who once looked down her nose at humans as little more than ants beneath her feet, is suddenly concerned about civil unrest?"

"They're big fucking ants," I responded hotly. "They outnumber us to a frightening degree, and they have weapons that are very effective against us. It would be stupid not to be concerned. If any of you left this bloody compound you'd see that. Look out of your window, for pity's sake!" The house across from him was one of the ones destroyed in the Great Insurrection.

All trace of humour faded from his expression. "Very well. What is it you want from me?"

"If we're going to avoid another insurrection, we need to stand together – the aristocratic factions. We need to provide a united front, and we need to do something about these labs and the things coming out of them."

He arched a dark brow, reminding me of where I had got the habit. "You *have* become a politician after all. The last time we spoke, I got the impression you would rather chew off your own tongue than become involved with aristocrat problems – or speak to me again."

I fought a cringe. "I don't *want* to be political, but I don't see us having much choice if the humans decide to attack. We have to show them that not all aristocrats devalue humanity, that not all of us are monsters."

"Nice sidestepping of our own issues, but I suppose those pale next to this."

"You're my father, I'm your daughter," I told him. "What else do we need to say? I think you're an arse and you think I'm ungrateful, but at the end of the day *you – are – my – father*. I came to you, and no one else, because I trust you." And it was true, at least where politics were concerned.

His eyes – the same green mine used to be – lit up, and I won't lie, my chest tightened at the sight. My whole life I'd wanted his love, and hating him at times hadn't changed that.

"What would my role in this be?" he asked.

"To make sure every vampire you trust is on board, with all of us standing together to quell the human threat. Make this look like your idea, not mine."

"I can dredge up the sympathy vote, believe me, but you could easily do the same yourself."

"Yeah, but I can't poke around and ask the right people the

right questions." Here was the hard part. "Your wife was one of them. There have to be some people who are in on the experiments and labs who would want to recruit you."

A flicker of pain lit his eyes and was gone in a flash. "You have a higher estimation of my worth than I. As the father of three *special* children who have had dealings with these labs, I don't think they'll trust me."

"Special." Such a pretty word for freak.

"They will if you put the thought in their head that you support the research." I took a breath. "That *I* support it. That maybe I'd be willing to work with them."

His eyes widened. "They'd never believe it."

"That creature that got free and killed the motorist is my daughter."

If I'd punched him in the face he couldn't have looked more stricken. "No."

"Um, yeah. She was created using my DNA, and I'm pretty sure the rest came from Vex's son, who was killed a few years ago. Charming, what?"

Vardan was obviously shocked. "My God."

"Vex doesn't know, and you're not going to tell him."

"No, of course not. Xandra, I'm so sorry."

I shrugged. "It's not like I gave birth to her." I locked my gaze to his. "I understand now why you conspired to hide Dede's baby. It was the right decision."

I think he understood just how much it pained me to say it, but if those bastards had found out that my baby sister could give birth to full-blooded children, they would have nabbed her too.

"Anyway . . ." I cleared my throat, "if you can sell that I've met my kid, that I'm concerned about her, that I'm open to the

idea of working with them, maybe they'll reach out to me."
And I could reach back and rip out their throats.

"I don't like it." His expression was pained. "You'd be putting yourself in so much danger. Those people managed to sneak into my house and kill my wife right under my nose."

"I know." I reached out and took his hand. "That's why we have to stop them. If you help me, you'll be putting yourself in danger as well."

He frowned. "I'm not afraid of being ended."

I was. "They're not going to end either of us. We're useful."

"How did you arrive at that conclusion?"

"They have to know the abnormalities in our family come from you."

"They only know about you."

Now I raised a brow. "You don't think someone heard Dede's rants about having a son with Ainsley? Even with his records doctored they have to have wondered about the kid. Why do you think they took Val? Hell, they're probably just waiting to get their hands on Avery. In reproduction or monster-making, our genes are desirable."

"Fang me."

"Amen," I muttered. We were more valuable dead than alive. Hell, if Church hadn't decided to kill her, Dede would probably still be here, albeit in a lab. And there was Vex, protecting Ophelia and other traitors to the Crown. His son had been special as well – and was killed.

Christ, they had to be practically wanking off at the prospect of Vex and me producing offspring. I mean, look what happened when they combined me with his son.

"I think they're going to use my doppelgänger to kill Victoria."

"And frame you?"

I shrugged. "I doubt it. I think looking like me is just supposed to get her close enough to do the job. Hell, maybe they plan to have her pose as Victoria afterwards." That might be a far-fetched theory, but it was less fantastic than some things that had already happened.

"Can she change into other people?"

He was definitely out of the loop. "Yeah. She says they showed her pictures and she turned into those people."

"Extraordinary."

"Scary." I ran a hand through the tangle of my hair. "She turned into Dede."

He stiffened. "That must have been painful."

"It was." And then, because I didn't want to discuss it, "They already tried to kill Victoria once, but I thwarted them. I don't know what the end game is – start a war, have an impostor take her place on the throne, both. I do know this country is headed for trouble if we don't try to stop it. Stop them."

He nodded. "Yes. There have been mutterings for years – anarchists wanting to destroy the Crown completely, who feel Victoria's isolation is cowardice. They want a leader who isn't afraid of humans."

"Do they have anyone in mind?" I asked.

My father paused. "Not that I know of. Bertie is the heir, of course, but he's always followed in his father's footsteps."

"Yes, equality for all." I didn't really buy it. Mostly because for all his charm, Bertie struck me as the sort who thought himself without equal. Kind of like his mother.

"Bertie's not really much of a threat. Could be they'll want to overturn the monarchy altogether, start a new government."

And that would get mental very quickly. "The deeper I dig into this thing, the blurrier it gets."

My father rose to his feet. "I have something to show you. I had debated what to do with this, but my conscience tells me you'll know." He beckoned me to accompany him from the room.

We walked upstairs to where the family rooms were, entering the one that had belonged to the duchess. My father went to a large painting on the wall and opened it like a door. Behind it looked like the rest of the wall, until I saw him press a tiny switch in the painting's back. "I discovered this shortly after she ... died."

The wall popped open, revealing a safe. A rather battered-looking safe.

"I had some trouble accessing it," Vardan confessed with the hint of a blush. He turned the handle and opened the door. Inside were a few jewellery boxes, some letters and a stack of journals. It was the journals my father removed.

"They seem to be written in a kind of code," he told me, handing them over. "The entries range from short to ponderous, but there are drawings and such that lead me to believe that they have something to do with those horrid laboratories, like the one she put you in. Maybe you'll find some names in them."

I watched as his face twisted with emotion. He'd actually loved her, I think. He knew she didn't like his children, but now he knew just how much, and it hurt him. He was never going to be a brilliant father, but at least he got some of it right.

I held the books to my chest. I'd crack them if I had to dig the bitch up and make her corpse translate. "Thank you. I'll do what I can with them."

He nodded. "I don't doubt it. There's a meeting of some of the higher-ranking vampires in two nights' time. I'll make a point of raising the human issue."

"Human issue." What an understatement that was. "Thank you. Vex is going to gather the weres as well."

"What about the half-bloods?"

"Val was going to take care of that." Better him than me. Some halfies didn't take too kindly to me any more, given my change in species, and besides, I had to convince the goblins that siding with the "leeches" as well as the wolves was a sound idea. Plus, I had to prepare for my first broadcast inter-view. Just the thought made my mouth taste like bile, but it had been the only way I could get the vultures to stop pecking at me after the Freak Show debacle.

Fucking Penny. She thought she was being smart outing me. Maybe it had made me look good to the humans, or maybe it made me look like a fraud. How many people – human, aristo and whatever else might be out there – thought I'd orchestrated the whole thing? More than I wanted to know, I was sure.

Vardan walked me downstairs as I tucked the journals into my cross-body bag. He hugged me before I opened the door. I hugged him back.

"Xandra," he said as I stepped out into the darkening gloom. I turned. "Be careful. Whoever is behind this is very powerful if they had both Churchill and my duchess working for them. God knows how far this goes. No matter how valuable you think you are, if you threaten them, they will kill you without a thought."

"Oh, they'll think about it," I said with a small smile. "Just before I eat their liver."

To my surprise, he smiled. "That's my girl."

Vex was tense when I met him at Down Street to go on to the palace.

"What's wrong?" I asked, eyeing the south wall at the end of the street. In addition to the new electric fence at the top, there were an extra two feet of barbed wire, and another three of strong-looking mesh. That should keep people – and projectiles – out of my garden for a bit.

His jaw was tight as he looked at me. "We're going underground tonight."

I shrugged. "I thought we were anyway. It's the easiest route to the palace."

"And the safest. There are one hundred and fourteen humans gathered at the Mayfair gates. They've had to close the shutters, and the halfies on guard are inside – wearing full armour."

My heart skipped a beat. "Fang me."

"Exactly." He dragged a hand through his hair. "Some fucking half-bloods thought they needed payback for the fire at Freak Show. They started trouble at a coffee house, got a real brawl going. Two humans ended up in hospital because of their injuries."

My shoulders sagged. "And now the humans are out for plagued blood."

"Of course they are." He was really pissed off. "Somebody's going to get killed."

He didn't mean one of us. He meant a human. That was when everything would go to hell.

My rotary rang. It was Val. "Special Branch and riot coppers are en route to Mayfair. Stay underside if you need to travel."

"I will. Are you part of the crowd control?"

"No, I'm still working on the fire. Be careful, Xandy."

"You too." I hung up and sent a quick digigram to Avery telling her to stick close to home. Then Vex and I joined William underside.

"How'd it go with your father?" Vex asked. He still sounded like he was talking through clenched teeth.

"Fine," I replied. "Surprisingly fine. He's in."

"Good. No word on Ali?"

Him using her name made her less monstrous. "No." I wanted to tell him my suspicions, but it would hurt him so badly if I was wrong. Hell, it would hurt him even more if I was right.

"I suppose we ought to be thankful for that."

William glanced over his shoulder as we started through the tunnel, his one eye glowing amber in the dark. "She will have to feed eventually."

And with that hanging over our heads, we moved on towards Buckingham Palace.

Maybe it was the discussion that I'd had with Vardan, the mention of Church that made me think about the night my mentor and I had fought in these tunnels. The weight of him as I dragged him by the foot into the den was something I would always remember. Sometimes I heard his screams still ringing in my ears. I remembered the taste of his heart.

And if I felt the least bit remorse, I made myself remember

Dede dying on the ground in front of Buckingham Palace, and my former mentor's smug pleasure at my pain.

If I could bring him back to life, I would, just so I could kill him all over again.

"Are you all right?" Vex whispered.

I glanced at him. "Sure. Why?"

He lifted the hand that was entwined with mine. "You're holding on a bit tight."

"Sorry!" I instantly loosened my grip, feeling foolish.

He smiled. "No harm done. Anything you want to talk about?"

I shook my head. "Just bad memories."

He didn't press. I'm sure he realised I'd been thinking about Church. He knew more about that night than anyone else, but even he didn't know all of it. I didn't know if I'd ever be able to tell him.

Finally we reached our destination. As we walked up the steps and filed out through that slightly concealed door into the damp night, I turned my head towards the palace gates.

"Fang me," I murmured. Of course, my companions heard it – they both had excellent hearing. They also paused to survey the chaos.

Halfies in protective armour, armed with weapons to shock, maim or kill, somehow managed to hold back the dozens upon dozens of humans shouting and raging beyond the fortified walls. The humans wouldn't get in, even if they killed the guards. There was an electric fence on top of the wall, guards with sniper rifles on the roof of the palace, and more halfies stationed inside the gates. If by some miracle they did get in, the moment they tried to breach the palace they'd be killed by poisonous gas.

Victoria didn't fuck around when it came to personal security – not after she'd been shot at in her own house.

A ball of flame whisked through the air. I reached up and snatched it before it could land. It was a bottle of something flammable with a ragged old wick stuffed into it. A crude but effective bomb – just like the ones used at Freak Show.

"Xandra." Vex's voice held a touch of warning. He knew me too well, the bastard. I was tempted to throw the bottle back, let it light up the Human League when it smashed to the ground.

Instead, I tossed it far enough away not to hurt us and to give the spectators a bit of a jolt.

I couldn't help but reflect on the fact that it was always the humans who started the violence between our kind and theirs. Yes, some halfies retaliated, but that was just it – retaliation. We never attacked first, though we certainly could. Maybe it was because we needed humans as a food source, or perhaps we weren't as afraid of them as they were of us.

Or maybe we were just sneakier. We weren't any better for it, I knew that. There was no convincing myself that I was on some moral high ground. Not any more.

"Fucking goblin!" someone shouted. Then a shot rang out.

I barely had time to react, but William was faster. He dived in front of me as the bullet sliced through the air, and took the shot to his chest.

"William!" I cried, dropping to my knees with him as he fell to the ground. I'd tried to catch him but he slid from my grasp, gasping for breath.

The bullet was probably silver, laced with tetracycline. It was particularly effective against us – goblins. It had missed his heart, but I was worried it had nicked a lung.

My friend looked up at me with his one eye. I took his hand. "You better not fuck off on me."

He smiled, but I could see the pain in his gaze. "Fine is your prince, lady. Couldn't let the cun— bugger hurt my queen."

I might have smiled at his sudden censorship, but I was too scared and too angry. First Vex had got hurt, and now William. They were my invincibles, the things to which I clung.

No one was taking either of them from me.

I lifted my head and saw the human running away. He tossed the rifle aside and bolted. Instinct demanded that I chase, even as palace snipers fired upon him.

So I did. I raised my face and sniffed, catching the scent of his exhilaration and fear – his sweat. In the cold and damp, the heat of him might as well have been a cake fresh from the oven right under my sensitive nose.

Yum.

"Xandra," Vex said as I started to move. "Xandra!"

I didn't stop. I didn't listen. I ran towards the fence, veering left to take me further away from the crowd. They saw me coming – the shouts became louder and more guttural, violent. Flash blubs went off, but I kept my focus on the runner and managed to avoid being blinded.

If any of those humans came within five feet of me, I was going to snap. I think they figured that out as the bones of my face shifted. It hurt – more than usual. The teeth forcing their way into my mouth felt bigger, sharper. It had to be the adrenalin.

I spotted my prey through a line of perfectly aligned trees that gave the palace a bit more privacy but weren't really thick enough to hide in. He was a good runner, my delicious little cake-man, but he couldn't outrun me.

A few feet from the fence, I jumped, clearing the electrified barrier and landing on the other side. I crouched as my feet struck, then sprang upright into a full sprint. I wanted to dive forward, hit the ground on all fours and take him down with my jaws around his neck, but I couldn't do that; I wasn't William. I growled low in my throat, and my prey glanced behind him.

As he hit the street, and traffic, he began screaming for help – fucking coward. I almost laughed as he ran towards a horse-drawn carriage. Did the idiot realise that he was running up Constitution Hill *towards* Mayfair, rather than away from it? He had probably gone this way to use the trees lining the street as cover from the snipers. It would have been a smart ploy if not for the neighbourhood.

He tried to flag someone – anyone – down to help him, but no one stopped. I couldn't blame them. First of all, he looked like a madman, and secondly, I was hot on his heels, and I certainly wouldn't stop if I saw me coming.

I didn't even tackle him, though I wanted to. Instead, I just reached, grabbed a handful of hair on the back of his head and jerked him backwards off his feet, so that I could turn around him in a strange – but graceful, I must say – dance that left us face to face. I held his hair tight, pulling his head back and keeping him up on his toes. We were pretty much eye to eye.

"You shot my friend," I said. Fang me, was that my voice? It sounded like it came from a cold, dark pit. It was the growl of something terrible and awful.

I liked it.

My companion did not share my enthusiasm, if the wet patch spreading across the front of his trousers was any indication.

Why did they always piss themselves? Books, films, on the box – whenever someone was supposed to be terrified, they pissed their pants. Mostly it happened to men. I always thought it happened much more on screen than in real life.

It was nasty and unappetising.

"What shall I do with you, eh?" I gave him a little shake. "Fucking human, calling us monsters and then shooting one of us with silver and poison with absolutely no provocation."

"It *is* a monster. It shouldn't be allowed to live!" He struggled against my hold. He was going to scalp himself if he wasn't careful. "It would kill me if given the chance. You all would, you fucking mutants. Abominations!"

"That's a big word for such a little fellow as yourself." I tightened my grip, yanking his head back further, and pulling down so that his knees buckled. Now I stared down into his pale face. "He would only kill you if he was hungry. Is that what you planned to do to him? Eat him?"

"Of course not!"

"Then who's the monster, you little cunt? You'd kill him just to watch him die!" My control was slipping. My heart pounded wildly in my chest, and I could feel the familiar ache of claws extending from my nail beds. I was one big itching ache of bloodthirstiness, and I wanted this little shit's heart between my teeth while it was still beating inside his chest.

Sirens cut through the roaring in my ears, the bright lights washing the area in blood red.

"Special Branch just saved your life," I whispered near his ear. I didn't add that in doing so they'd probably done me a good turn as well.

"Xandy?"

Fabulous. This night couldn't get any worse. I sighed and

turned. There in front of me was the last person I wanted to see me threatening someone. The last person I wanted to see me like this.

"Hey, Val."

CHAPTER 10

WHEN ANGER RISES, THINK
OF THE CONSEQUENCES

There's something humbling about looking into your brother's face and seeing his expression turn to horror.

"Fang me," he muttered. "Just relax, all right? You can't look like that when the vultures show up."

The press. Of course there would be press. I could hear them nearby, along with police, shouting humans and the whinny of horses. Tabloid reporters loved this kind of shit, as did box news teams. At least the VBC ones would try to slant the story in our favour.

Had I not got myself plastered on enough rags and box screens these last couple of days? When I'd left my father earlier, Vardan jokingly accused me of becoming the face of the aristocracy. I didn't want to be the face of anything.

I took a deep breath as Val relieved me of my prey. With the stink of urine and sweat gone, I was able to compose myself rather quickly, so when a bright light shone upon me I squinted, but didn't look like something out of a nightmare.

At least I didn't think I did.

"Perhaps you could shine that somewhere other than my eyes," I suggested, blinded by the glare. My eyes weren't as sensitive as other goblins', but lights like that stung like hell.

Someone muttered an apology and the light moved – marginally. "Lady Xandra, can you tell us what happened here tonight?" a woman asked.

I peered around the light, holding up my hand to better protect my eyes. I pulled a pair of dark spectacles from my coat pocket and slipped them on. There, that was better. "A human shot a goblin in the grounds of Buckingham Palace." I needed to get back there to check on William. He was more important than standing here defending my actions. If a human had chased one of us for attacking someone, they'd be handing out medals right now.

"Can you tell us the circumstances surrounding the alleged incident?"

"Alleged?" I drew my shoulders up straight. "There's nothing 'alleged' about the hole in my friend's chest. Bottom line is this: we were at the palace to discuss what to do about these unsanctioned research laboratories, how to assure the humans of London that they are safe, and how to protect ourselves against growing Human League violence. In short, we were meeting to discuss making the empire safer for *all* of its citizens, when one of the protesters – who were throwing bombs, I might add – pulled a gun. If he'd shot another human, you'd have him in Newgate by now."

"But a goblin isn't human. Goblins are much more difficult to kill."

Nice of her to remind me of that. "It was a silver and tetracycline bullet. That man – and some, if not all of his companions – came here tonight with the express purpose of injuring – *killing* – someone of plagued blood."

"And now that man will face assault charges."

I looked at her – hard. "Attempted murder. He'll face attempted murder charges, because that was the crime he committed. Did you see his face?"

"Yes." There was an edge of confusion in her tone. "We arrived on the scene just as he was being led away."

"Did you see any bruises or lacerations? Any injury? No, of course you didn't, because other than grabbing him to stop him, I did him no harm whatsoever. Yet he calls me the monster. He doesn't even know me and he would like to see me dead. I understand that humans fear us, but if the Great Insurrection taught us anything, it was that hatred and violence bring nothing but death and suffering to all sides. The only way to make this empire great once more is to work together – not end each other."

"*Child killer!*" someone shouted. The gathered crowd made a sound that was a mix of booing and cheering.

I turned my attention to them. "Do any of you know anyone who has been harmed by a goblin, vampire or werewolf? Anyone?"

Not one of them raised their hand or said a word. They just stood there and traded glances.

I walked towards them, and the cameras followed me. The humans drew back a bit, inching closer together. "My brother has been shot, stabbed and beaten by humans in his work for Special Branch. My sister almost died in a fire set by humans. I've been shot, stabbed, threatened . . . every time by humans. That's three people right there that have been victims of human violence. You call us monsters. No goblin has ever beaten or abused their children. Children are special to aristocrats, sacred, while humans often breed with abandon and indiscretion."

I let that sink in, my gaze roaming the crowd. A couple more film crews had joined us. "No goblin has ever bombed a human establishment. No goblin has ever beaten their spouse or killed out of greed or compulsion. During the months I've spent with them, not one human has died to feed the pack. Yes, we're capable of awful things, but I've never met a goblin or aristocrat as cruel or indiscriminately violent as a human."

All right, so that was a little over the top, but it was also true. If a goblin attacked me, I'd know it wanted to eat me. A human would just want to watch me die.

Silence lingered uncomfortably. My point had been made. "Now, if you'll excuse me, I have a friend to check up on and a meeting to attend."

The reporter called after me, but I turned on my heel and bolted for the palace once more. They could give chase in their vehicles if they wanted, but once I cleared the main fence, they'd have to admit defeat.

Vex met me in the palace foyer, just after I was cleared by security.

"How is he?" I demanded, first thing.

"Fine." Vex looked me up and down. "He's going to be fine. You?"

Tension radiated from him. He paced like he was in a cage. I took a step back. "Caught the bastard and gave him over to Special Branch. No blood spilled. Although I might be on the box again tonight." Might? I don't think there was any *might* about it.

He laughed – a harsh bark. "Of course."

"Vex, I—"

"*No*." Gold flashed in his eyes. "Save it. I don't want to hear it."

The breath literally caught in my throat. *What?*

His eyes were really yellow now. "You were reckless and stupid taking off like that. He could have shot you too. He could have led you into a trap. Or you could have killed him."

"None of that happened."

"Because you've got more luck than sense!" He raked a hand through his hair. "Do you ever think of consequences, Xandra? Do you ever wonder how your actions might affect those who love you? Did you stop for one *fucking moment* and think about how much I worry about you? How afraid I was that you would be hurt? How concerned William was? Or do you honestly walk about with your head so far up your own arse that you think no one could ever possibly knock it off your fool shoulders?"

He hadn't raised his voice, but his words echoed like screams in my mind. He'd been almost this angry when I killed the betty at Freak Show, and I'd been half in awe, half scared of him then. I have to admit that at that moment, I wasn't thinking of William or of humans. I was thinking that I had finally pushed Vex to his breaking point. He was going to walk away after this, and who could bloody well blame him? I was not an easy woman to love. Hell, I wasn't particularly easy to like.

"Don't leave me," I whispered, and cringed. Fang me, could I make myself sound any more pathetic?

He scowled, but his shoulders relaxed. "You're my mate."

Odd how he could pack more into three words than I could

ever try to articulate. I closed the distance between us and took his face in my hands. His fingers closed over my wrists, but he didn't push me away.

What could I possibly say to make this better? Tears burned the back of my eyes. Sometimes I was such a *fucking girl*. Gah, it was disgusting.

"I'm sorry," I whispered. "You're right – I don't think. I just act. I ... I'm not used to having to answer to anyone, and I know that's a poor excuse. I just saw William hurt, and after what Ali did to you, I snapped. No one has ever believed in me like the two of you, and I won't let anyone take you away from me."

Vex released my wrists to put his palms on either side of my head, and then he pulled me up on to my toes, pressing a kiss to my mouth that was so hard I thought I heard a tooth crack. I kissed him back with just as much intention.

I'd never been good with disappointing those I looked up to – especially men. I didn't know what that said about me, and at the moment I didn't care. I just made myself a silent vow to do something about it.

"I promise I'll think more," I babbled when he pulled away. "I'll try not to be impulsive. I'll be better—" He silenced me with another kiss.

"Just be you," he said, resting his forehead against mine. "If I have a problem I'll tell you, but I don't want to change you, sweetheart. I just want you to ... pause every now and then."

I laughed. "I can do that."

A lopsided smile slanted his lips. "Good. Now, we have people waiting for us. Victoria's probably having kittens right about now. She's not accustomed to being kept hanging about."

I took his hand and let him lead me further into the palace, thinking about how Her Nibs had kept *me* waiting. "It might do the old girl some good."

"She's not that much older than me, you know."

"And you're ancient."

He chuckled as we approached the stairs. "Brat."

I smiled, but the remark made me think – played on the insecurity I couldn't seem to conquer. What if I wasn't immortal, or as long-lived as him? What if as I got older I started looking more and more like an actual goblin? Would he still love me when I had more facial hair than he did? A difficult woman could get away with a lot if she was cute, but with fangs and a beard . . . not so much.

"You're fretting."

I glanced at him as we reached the top of the stairs. "No I'm not."

"Yes you are." He gave my shoulders a squeeze. "We can talk about it later."

We walked down a crimson-carpeted corridor, towards the room where Victoria had seen me during our previous meeting. I was becoming a regular fixture here at Buck House. Perhaps she'd give me my own key soon.

Her Nibs was there when we walked in, as was my father. I hadn't expected Vardan to act so fast, but then I had to get my impulsiveness from one of my parents.

Or maybe I got it from my mother, who was sitting on a little antique chair like she owned the place. This was a turn I had not seen coming, I had to admit.

"What's she doing here?" I demanded, turning to Victoria.

The tiny woman smiled sourly. "Apparently Miss Claire and the Prince of Wales have become allies in their quest to make the world a better place for all mankind."

If sarcasm had mass, an anvil would have just fallen on to my head. I turned to my mother. "I thought you wanted to abolish the monarchy, not rub elbows with it."

Juliet smiled at me, serene as a freaking madonna. "All I want is peace, Alexandra. You know that."

I arched a brow and turned away. Seriously, were there hidden cameras watching us? I was rapidly beginning to wonder if I was like that bloke in the American film whose entire life was a box show. I turned back, struck by a sudden thought. Was Bertie the person whom Ophelia had heard on the telephone with Juliet? Was he the one wanting to tour Bedlam?

The Prince of Wales' blue gaze roved over me. "You are in fine looks tonight, Lady Xandra."

I had to try very hard not to frown. "Thank you, Your Highness. As are you." What the hell was I supposed to say?

Bertie smiled. "You obviously take after your mother." He nodded at Juliet, who actually blushed. That was disconcerting. "Why, the two of you could be sisters."

"Indeed," I replied, because it was more polite than "fuck off". Pieces of a puzzle were falling together in my head. Somehow Bertie had got my mother to change her mind about the aristocracy – or had at least bought her about-turn.

"Let me guess, Bedlam just received a large endorsement from one of His Royal Highness's charitable accounts?"

My mother had the grace to blush, but Bertie was the picture of innocence. "As heir to the throne, I take a great interest in helping those subjects who are unable to care for themselves."

I smiled – and didn't care that it was so obviously insincere. "You obviously take after *your* mother."

For a moment – not even a second – dislike flashed in the prince's bright blue gaze, but it disappeared so fast it was just a blink. "Thank you. I take it as a compliment to be compared to either of my parents." He smiled, all grace and charm once more. "That is a rather splendid coat. You must give me the name of your tailor."

"Bertie, do stop flirting." His mother spoke in a monotone, clearly bored. "You're wasting your words on Alexandra."

Her son didn't appear the least bit chastised. In fact the only one who looked at all put out was my mother. Stealing her thunder, was I?

But more important than my mother or flirting, or the cut of my coat, was William. He was stretched out on the sofa. Someone had taken his coat off, and there was a square of white linen covering part of his very furry chest.

I went to him and knelt on the carpet by his side. This should have been the first thing I did upon entering the room, instead of caring about my mother's presence there. I took his hand in mine and petted it. "Are you all right, my friend?"

His wide mouth curved up one side of his muzzle, revealing a glimpse of ivory fang. "The wolf took the silver, drew the poison. I will heal. Did you eat his liver?"

He meant the shooter, not Vex. I hoped. "Special Branch has him."

William scowled. "Not dead?"

"Believe me, I wanted to rip his heart out and bring it back to you, I did, but there were reporters there. Gawkers."

"All the better," he rasped.

I arched a brow. "Really? You honestly think that me ripping a man apart on every box in every household in the empire would be good public relations?"

He growled. "Perhaps not. I have honour, lady."

"He pissed himself," I chirped. "Does that help?"

"Oh, good lord," Victoria lamented, pouring herself a glass of sherry.

William grinned. At that moment I could have sworn that I never saw anything that made me happier. "Indeed."

I pushed up my sleeve and offered him my wrist. "Now, drink."

Once William was back on his feet – though still a little wobbly – we began the meeting.

As we all moved to congregate in the area around the tea table – which actually had tea and sandwiches on it – Victoria stopped me.

"What you did tonight, letting the human live, tending to the needs of one of yours, those were the decisions of a leader. You went against your instinct to protect those who look to you as their queen. You've already come to understand that sometimes to be strong we must be seen as weak. Well done, Alexandra. Well done."

I stared at her. It had been that sort of evening.

She shook her head. "Close your mouth, girl. It's unseemly."

Just when I thought I had a notion of what she was all about, she surprised me. A good tactic to adopt when trying to keep people on their toes. After all, predictability was akin to vulnerability.

Of course, she changed her approach as soon as we were all gathered around the table. "Someone tell me what the bloody hell is being done about the freak running round the city ripping out human gullets like they were meat pies!"

I flinched. She was shrill as a damn shrew. "It was only one human," I heard myself say. That we knew of. Like the actual number mattered.

Those cold blue eyes drilled into me. "And what were you about keeping it in the plague den?"

"She doesn't know what she's doing," I replied. Only then did I realise how utterly stupid I'd been. "I thought I could help her."

Victoria snorted – not very ladylike at all. "You thought you could be a hero, that's what you thought. Queen Xandra saves the day. *Again.* You do realise that because of your actions, we have a monster with a taste for human meat running loose in the city?"

I nodded, duly chastised. "I do."

"Well?" she demanded when I said nothing more. "What are you going to do about it, you who must fix everything and everyone whether they want it or not?"

My temper flared. "You're putting this on me? I'm not the one people want to kill."

"Oh, of course you are!" she snapped back. "You have power, and everyone who has power has a target on their fucking forehead! She'll come for me and she'll come for you. Stop whining about it and tell me how we're going to fix this!"

We stared at one another. Vex, bless him, ate a sandwich. I'd no doubt he was simply waiting for this pissing competition to end.

Bertie cleared his throat. He sat beside my mother, who was strangely quiet, watching Victoria and me with barely concealed amusement. "Pardon me, Xandra, but what did you mean when you insinuated that people want Mother dead?"

I glanced at him, then immediately back at Victoria. Taking my attention off her was as intelligent as ignoring a poisonous snake. "At the jubilee, when I took a bullet for *Her Majesty*" – it didn't hurt to remind her of that fact – "the assassination attempt was orchestrated by Churchill. He was also involved with the group behind the laboratories. I got the sense that he wasn't the only one who wanted you gone."

Victoria arched a brow. "It took you months to come to that conclusion?"

William bristled. "Respect, leech."

I put my hand on his arm and scowled at the tiny woman. "Oh, come on. You're not so out of touch that you don't know people would dance at your funeral."

Her other brow joined the first. "Touché. But what has that to do with the killing machine running amok?"

I crossed my legs and leaned forward. "What if these experiments haven't been about me?"

"Oh no. Surely it has *all* been about you."

Bitch. I drew a deep breath. "I think it started out as a reproductive issue, but then it quickly turned into a lesson in building the perfect monster. Why? To kill you. Now, who would want to kill someone as revered and adored as you?" If sarcasm were saliva, I'd be frothing at the mouth.

She was unmoved. "Why now?"

"Why not?" Vex retorted, finally joining in. He leaned back in his chair, arm draped over the back. "While you're busy dealing with a new queen" – he gestured at me – "and trouble from the Human League, you'd be distracted just enough for someone to take your head and blame it on the humans."

"So." I jumped back in. "Who has the most to gain by wanting you dead?"

We all turned our heads. My mother gave a little jump. Guilty conscience? I frowned.

Bertie placed his hand over his chest. "Me? Is that the best you can come up with?"

I shrugged, my attention taken from my mother. "You'd be king."

"Yes, and then someone would want to kill me too! You'd have to be insane to want to rule this cluster fuck of an empire. No offence, Mother."

The royal family were much coarser than I'd ever thought. Such language.

Victoria inclined her head. "None taken, dear boy." Then to me, "There seems to be someone who wants me gone every decade or so. It never comes to anything, so why should I expect otherwise now?"

I stared at her. "Because now they've engineered a being capable of doing it without raising any alarms."

"You truly believe it was made to be my assassin? I have trouble believing that. It seems a little ... much, don't you think?"

Bertie nodded. "True. If these aristocrats with the laboratories wanted Mother dead, they could achieve such an end simply by paying her a visit. I'm certain they could manage it with a bit more civility."

The skin between my brows itched. Civility. Like what they gave the duchess? I glanced at my father to find him watching the Prince of Wales with no expression. His gaze flicked to mine, and I could see he'd had the same thought.

"Maybe they want to put the blame on someone else," Vex suggested, saving my theory so deftly that I could have kissed him.

"The girl – the creature – it has the power to shift," William added. "Could wear any face to spill blood."

When William and Vex were on the same scent, I knew enough to follow. I didn't like where this trail led. There was a heaviness in my stomach when I turned to Victoria. "It's true. She could walk in here looking just like me, or someone else. She could make it look like I killed you." I should have known that wearing my face would serve more of a purpose than getting close.

"She could start a war," Vex announced, putting a fine point on my paranoia with his matter-of-fact tone. "Not just with the humans, but within the factions themselves. And with Hanover connections to most ruling families across Europe, that war wouldn't be limited to just Britain."

We all shared a grave gaze. What would we do if war broke out? Not just civil unrest, but a continental conflict. England hadn't been to war in . . . fang me, a century and a half, maybe two. Wellington had led us to victory, but he was long gone. We had no army, no navy – or at least not much of one. We relied on claw and fang to keep us safe. On half-bloods. We would be no match for armed humans. Oh, we'd kill a few, but they'd drive us underside. And if our aristo factions were set against one another . . .

What if the Americans showed up? From what little I knew about them, they were a well-armed country, determined to preserve their way of life, and that way was *not* our way.

Why would anyone want to instigate such a thing?

"Let's not get ahead of ourselves," Victoria said softly. There was a steely edge to her voice that relieved my anxiety. "We do not know what this creature is about. I do not care what it is about. It is a danger to our way of life, to our safety and to *my* empire. I want it destroyed by any means necessary. I want this contained." Her gimlet gaze slipped to my mother. "I want the humans mollified. I will have order. I will not allow any more bloodshed. Do whatever you must to make certain that happens."

That was a dismissal if ever I heard one. Not much of a meeting, but then she'd only asked for it to let me know I'd been caught hiding Ali and to lay down the law. She might as well have grabbed us all by the back of the neck with her teeth and mounted us, she'd done such a proper job of asserting her dominance.

"One more thing," Vex said, stopping everyone as they began to rise. We sat down again.

"Well?" Victoria snapped, clearly peeved.

The alpha wasn't the least bit cowed. "We discovered a human corpse in the same lab where the creature was held. When I had it examined, I was told that he had died from a previously unknown strain of plague."

I didn't think Victoria could get any paler. Apparently she could. "Are you certain?"

Something about her tone set off warning bells in my head.

"Yes," Vex replied, and from the inside pocket of his coat he withdrew some folded papers – copies of the lab report. He handed them to her.

As she scanned them, Victoria's jaw tightened. "This is the second incident. Three days ago, sanitation workers found a body in the sewers that had died from the same thing. Fortunately their gear saved them from infection."

"Second?" I cried at the same time as everyone else. One infection in a lab was one thing, but a second found outside of a laboratory was unsettling.

I wasn't worried about catching the plague, even if it was a new strain. Those of us of plagued blood had a strange immunity to it even as it changed us into something more. No, I wasn't worried about me, but it might affect halfies and humans, and if it went like last time . . .

We all looked at each other. "What do we do?" I asked. Revealing it to the public would be disastrous – it would drive the populace into a panic – but keeping it a secret was wrong and dangerous.

"We wait," Victoria decreed, voice firm. "If more cases show up, we'll release what we know to the public. Meanwhile, is that corpse at Prince Albert Hospital, MacLaughlin?"

Vex shook his head. "No, but it can be. Just tell me who to deliver it to."

Her Nibs nodded. "Thank you. Another case to study will facilitate our team's search for treatment." She sounded so convinced that I believed her. That was the mark of a strong leader, someone who could inspire such certainty in her people. I might not like her, or really trust her, but there was a lot I could learn from the harpy.

I looked at Juliet to find her watching me with a stricken expression.

"I bid you all good evening," Victoria said, rising. "As you may assume, I have people to whom I need to speak immediately."

We all rose. My mother practically lunged out of her chair towards me, grabbing me by the arm with deceptively strong fingers.

"My children," she said.

I covered her hand with my own, prising her fingers loose with as much care as I could. "Will be fine, I'm certain."

"Ophelia." Juliet glanced away. "She hasn't spoken to me in days. We had ... a disagreement. You will look out for her, won't you? Protect her?"

The more time I spent in this world, the more I came to marvel at the shades of grey from which it was made. No one was completely good nor completely evil, and people I loved proved themselves capable of being monsters, while those who seemed so black astonished me with all their patches of light.

"Yes," I promised. "I will." I meant it too. I would do everything I could to protect my sister.

Juliet's shoulders sagged. For a moment, she almost looked like a frightened mother ought. I watched her leave with a heavy heart. I savoured the sensation, because I was jaded enough to know my sympathy wouldn't last long.

As we were leaving, Victoria asked me to stay for a moment. Vex said he'd wait for me in the foyer.

I stood my ground as the tiny little vampire – the Blood Queen – approached me. "Going to take another round at buggering me?" I asked.

She frowned. "Don't be crass. It's beneath you."

This from the woman who could make a fishwife blush. "I don't know what my mother is up to, so don't ask me. Although I hear she might be getting a little slap and tickle."

Victoria gave me a look that seemed to say "Bitch, please." "Juliet Claire is not half the woman her grandmother was. She's no concern to me."

Now I frowned. "Her grandmother?"

That severe little face slackened in surprise. I'd have taken satisfaction in it if I hadn't had a horrible feeling she was about to deliver some very interesting news.

"Eliza Prentiss. Surely you know the name."

A punch couldn't have taken the breath from my lungs any more effectively. Elizabeth Prentiss had been one of the leaders – if not *the* leader – of the Great Insurrection. A hero amongst humans, a great villain amongst the aristocracy. And she was my great-grandmother.

Albert's fangs. No wonder Victoria distrusted me. No wonder I made the perfect science experiment – the perfect scapegoat. I was just a regular little hodge-podge for everyone. A little rebel, a little aristo, a little goblin. Before, I'd thought predictability was akin to vulnerability. Now, I was convinced it was ignorance of your place in the world that led down the road to having your head cleaved from your shoulders.

"You honestly didn't know?"

I shook my head. "I knew my grandmother was Alyss Claire, that was it."

"Claire was her middle name. I suppose Eliza wanted her daughter to grow up without the scandal hanging over her."

But Alyss was human. Why not raise her to be proud? I glanced at Victoria. "Why didn't you just kill her?"

"Kill an innocent child?" Affront dripped from her words. "That's barbaric. Besides, who blames a child for her mother's mistakes?"

Who indeed. My head was spinning. I needed it to stop, so I shook it. "You didn't keep me here for a genealogy lesson."

Any concern Victoria had for me dissolved from her face as her features became impassive once more. "You have a sister who was formerly Peerage Protectorate, yes?"

I nodded. "Avery. Lady Maplethrope dismissed her last month." It seemed the lady hadn't been aware of my sister's sexual orientation, and when she found out, she decided she didn't want Avery anywhere near her precious daughter. I reckon she was worried that being a lesbian was contagious, and like all aristos, she was bent on seeing her line continue.

Unfortunately, it wasn't against the law for her to dismiss my sister. There weren't many laws at all regarding the rights of half-bloods, and while most would agree that Lady M was a ragged old bint, no one could make her take Avery back into her employ.

More importantly, no one could make Avery go back even if the cow wanted her.

"Is she like you, this Avery?"

I raised a brow. Was that a sneer? "She lacks my charm and grace, but she can hold her own against trouble. She's strong, and she's smart. She's never had an aristo injured under her watch."

"What about her attitude?"

I couldn't help but smile. "She's nicer than I am."

"That's not saying much, though, is it?" Victoria sighed. "You trust her?"

"With my life," I responded without hesitation or condescension. Avery and I had our differences, but we were sisters, and we were always there for one another when it truly counted – even if we were at each other's throats the entire time. We'd had a few moments when we didn't speak, but we always worked it out. Being an only child, Victoria had never known that kind of relationship.

"Tell her to come to me at her earliest convenience. I wish to offer her a position."

"Doing what?" I demanded incredulously.

Bright eyes narrowed at me. "Washing windows." She was so cold, her words had frost on them. "I wish to hire her services as a guard, of course."

"Of course," I repeated – rather dumbly, I might add. "Why?"

Victoria crossed her doll-like arms over her torso. "I haven't lived this long by being stupid, contrary to what your so very young mind might believe. I've felt the ground shifting beneath me for some time, long before you were born. I'm not going to make it easy for my enemies to take what I've worked so hard to build. I need someone I can trust watching my back. I don't much like you, but I have a degree of disconcerting respect for you, and you seem to inspire loyalty in those around you. I need someone from outside my usual stable, someone with a fresh pair of eyes and ears who may see and hear things I cannot. I need someone I know I can trust implicitly."

Fair enough. That was quite a list, but I had no doubt Avery could do all of it while dancing a Highland fling and balancing a teapot on her head. "I'll give her a ring when I get home."

A small smile curved her lips – no fang, of course. "Thank you. Now, please leave before my son takes your hanging about personally and decides to seduce you. He's no shortage of confidence, that one."

"Indeed," I replied before I could think better of it. She didn't appear offended, though. I left her after bidding her a good evening, and joined Vex and William by the palace entrance. My father had gone off for a drink with Bertie, and my mother had left as well.

I wasn't certain that drinking with Bertie was going to earn Vardan points with the vampires we were hoping to attract. After all, the prince made no bones about his hopes that all the races in the empire could learn to live side by side. Of course, it wasn't as though my father could refuse if Bertie had done the inviting. Wouldn't be polite.

The crowd out front had been cleared away by now, and it would have been easy for Juliet to leave. How had she even got in? It didn't matter. Her comings and goings were none of my concern. I was sure she had her ways of skulking about and protecting herself. If she and Bertie had formed an alliance, he'd probably told her a private way to enter the grounds.

Did Ophelia know about our great-grandmother? Of course she did, I thought bitterly. Dede had probably known too, and she hadn't even been related to the old woman.

No one spoke until we were in the safety of the tunnels under London.

"What did she want?" Vex asked.

I told him. Then I asked both of them, "What are we going to do?"

"We look for Ali," Vex replied, ignoring the fact that I was referring to much more than a murderous science experiment. There was so much at stake, so much hanging in the precarious balance. "Take it one catastrophe at a time."

"And then we do what goblins do best," William informed me with a comforting pat on the shoulder. "We watch and wait, pretties. Watch and wait."

CHAPTER II

SEEK AND YE SHALL FIND

Waiting had never really been one of my strong suits, so it was good that looking was still an option. It seemed like forever since Ali had bitten me in the den, but in reality it hadn't been very long ago at all. In fact, my bone was still a tiny bit tender where her teeth had scraped against it.

"Do you reckon she has enough goblin in her to not be poisoned by my blood?" I had wondered this before.

Both Vex and William paused as we walked back to the den.

"I don't know," Vex said, turning to the prince.

William shrugged. "First of her kind."

A lot of help the two of them were. I tried to remember if she'd seemed sick after biting me, but it was all a jumble of insanity in my head. Everything had happened so fast. Probably safe to assume she wouldn't have been affected, but if she had ...

"If she was, she couldn't have got far. She went cobbleside just west of the den, yeah?" God, how could I not have had this particular thought earlier?

Vex nodded. "That's what your brother said. He chased her two blocks cobbleside."

"I'm going to have a look," I announced. It probably wouldn't do any good – Special Branch had been combing the city for her, and Val had already given chase.

But Val was a halfie, as was the entirety of SB. They had good eyes and a good sense of smell, but not like full-bloods.

Of course my wolf and my prince came with me. It was around midnight now, and there would be no going to bed for any of us for several hours at the earliest.

It was a crisp night, and the chill felt cleansing on my face. I could almost see it pushing away the scent of the underground from my hair and clothing. Some nights the cold had a dampness to it that made it feel as though it was seeping right down to your bones, but not tonight. It was dry and sharp and just cold enough that it wouldn't snow. You couldn't see them from here, but I'd wager that the sky was clear out in the country, with stars filling the limitless black.

I stood just a moment on the edge of the underground entrance, savouring the moment. For a few seconds there was nothing but me, London and the night. People had begun decorating for Christmas, adding to the array of lights that already lit up the city.

Releasing a sigh, I opened my eyes and drew a deep breath, searching out the scent of my kid. I had to push hard to sort her out from the million other scents that assaulted me, but I finally caught the faint trace of her on the air. It helped that I'd been able to smell her in the underground, so her scent was fresh in my nose. She'd been wounded, so that helped. She'd left her blood here, and that made the scent linger.

It was easier for Vex and me to track out in the open – with a hat, I could pass for human. William had left us to return to the den, where he'd check in with the gobs scouring CCTV footage from across the city. A camera somewhere had to have caught a glimpse of her.

I won't lie, I was nervous sniffing around cobbleside. Humans were so plentiful, so angry and vicious. If Vex and I were set upon ... I pushed the thought away. We wouldn't be long, and there weren't many humans milling about this close to Mayfair.

Vex nudged me with his elbow. "Blood."

I looked down. It was right by my feet. If I hadn't been distracted by fear, I would have smelled it. It was just a drop on the sidewalk, smeared from the weather and feet into a long, thin strand, but it was still there. We were lucky it hadn't snowed or rained heavily.

The meagre trail led us on almost a block past where Val said he'd chased her. That was where we found a bloody handprint on a post, and the trail ended.

I glanced around. "Knightsbridge station is right around here."

"We would have heard about it if she'd gone into a station. No matter what face she wore, someone bleeding profusely from a shoulder wound would attract attention."

"True enough ..." I turned to the post where her smudged handprint was. Why had she stopped here? Had she crossed the street?

A motor carriage roared by. I stepped back, grabbing the post to steady myself. My fingers fitted over Ali's print exactly. Had she moved back from a speeding vehicle?

Or had one stopped for her?

I crouched down. There was a spatter of blood on the edge of the pavement. "Someone picked her up," I called.

Suddenly Vex was there beside me. He glanced up. "There are CCTV cameras. Maybe the goblins saw who stopped."

I stood. "Makes me think she might have a tracker in her after all." I hadn't mentioned the theory at the palace because there'd been no need, and I didn't know Bertie or my mother well enough to reveal all in front of them.

He held out his hand to me and I took it. No sense hanging about any longer. After all, those CCTV cameras could see us as well.

"I have to call Avery," I remarked as we walked – a bit of normal after so much madness. "Victoria offered her a post."

He looked surprised. "Didn't see that coming. All right. Good to have a set of eyes in the palace."

"Always." Our arms brushed. "Hopefully Val will turn up something." I wanted to ask him if he was concerned about the plague cases, but I didn't dare ask with people about.

"What do you suppose is going on with your mother?" he asked. "Odd that she's suddenly in the spotlight."

"I know. I don't trust her."

He grinned at me. "Most people trust their parents and not strangers. You have a habit of trusting strangers more than family."

I stared at him. "Have you met my family?"

He laughed, and let go of my hand to put his arm around me. For all my rushing in and trying to save the day, as Victoria so nicely pointed out, I was more than a little scared of what the future held. Vex was something to cling to. Something safe.

I called Avery once we were underside again. She wanted to know if I was okay, and what the hell I thought I was doing running into burning buildings and chasing down would-be assassins. And then she demanded to know why she had to hear about it on the box and not from me when she'd left me eight Britme messages and two digigrams. I apologised, briefly caught her up on all that had happened, and then dropped the bomb.

"So, Queen Victoria wants you to work for her as her private guard."

Silence. 1 … 2 … 3 …

"You're taking the piss."

I chuckled. "I wish I was." I went on to give her details. "I feel like it's my duty as your sister to try talking you out of it, but you'd make a lovely spy, and she needs someone to watch her back. Someone who knows the real me when she sees me." You know, just in case Ali did try to walk in with my face on and kill Victoria.

"I'll do it. For you, and because I want to see her bedroom."

I didn't even want to know what appeal V's bedroom held for my sapphic sister, so I filled her in on what we were up to, and accepted her offer of assistance.

Meanwhile, Vex made calls of his own. By the time we entered the plague den, we had the most trusted members of the were pack that were still in London as well as my goblins working on finding Ali and whoever had scooped her up. It wasn't much, but it was something new, so we ran with it.

Val rang to say that Special Branch were doing their own sweep as well. They had a couple of leads he was going to follow up before sharing – which annoyed me. I was to notify him if we found Ali or got the plate of the carriage that had picked her up. He didn't specify whether they wanted her alive or dead, but demanded that everyone in our search party should be given his rotary number.

I was going over a map of the city with Ophelia when Avery

and Emma arrived. My jaw dropped at the sight of my younger sister in the goblin den. When she'd offered to help, I didn't think she'd meant right then.

Avery and I looked a fair bit alike, but she had pink hair, and was shorter and curvier. I was surprised to see her in black trousers and a frock coat. Normally she dressed like she was the icing on a birthday cake. Emma wore similar attire, and her black-and-white hair was pulled back from her gorgeous face. Vardan had had a difficult time of it when the two of them started dating. It wasn't the fact that his daughter was a lesbian that bothered him, but rather that her girlfriend was half black. He was from a time when if you wanted to be with a black woman, you went to Jamaica and kept one as your mistress.

Really, the ideas some of these aristos clung to were ridiculous.

Avery hugged me as soon as she was within reach. "I'm so happy that you're not hurt!"

"She smacked me around a bit, but I'm fine."

My sister blinked at me. "Not that. I meant earlier – when you caught that human. No one's sure what to make of you. I thought it was going to get ugly with the League, that they might target you."

"They still might." I knew that wasn't going to reassure her, but lying to her wasn't going to do any good either.

Avery looked at Ophelia. The second she made the connection, her mouth dropped open – just a bit. "Xandy, introduce us."

And of course I had no choice. "Avery, Emma, this is my sister Ophelia."

Poor Fee didn't seem to know what hit her when Avery launched herself at her, grabbing her in a fierce hug.

"It's so wonderful to meet you," Avery enthused.

Fee patted her awkwardly on the back, looking for all the world like she had no idea what to do. "Likewise."

I watched them with a mixture of amusement and trepidation. Should I tell Avery that Fee had known Dede? No, not now. That would only lead to questions I didn't know how to answer. What Avery didn't know couldn't get her into trouble.

Such as the fact that I'd eaten part of my mentor, fed the rest to my goblins and allowed his bones to be used in the construction of my throne, which was right there in the great hall for all to see.

Also, it wasn't my place to out Fee like that.

Vex joined us as my sisters pulled apart. He greeted the newcomers and then informed us it was time to head out to join the search for Ali.

"You are not going by yourself," I heard him say to Fee, as he handed her a dark hat to hide her hair.

My sister protested – same as I probably would have. "I'll be fine. I won't go anywhere near her."

"No," I joined in. "Fee, she hurt Vex and she almost ripped my arm off. You're not going after her alone." If the goblins hadn't already started their own search, I'd ask William to go with her, but he had already left with Elsbeth, his lady friend.

"I'll go with her," came a familiar voice from behind me.

I glanced over my shoulder with a frown. What the hell was Rye doing here?

He looked good – better than he had when I found him, at any rate. He was still a little too lean and had a bit of an unhinged look about his eyes, but at least he didn't look feral and vacant.

And here he was stepping up to fight by the side of my sister if necessary. Had he developed something of a crush while Ophelia helped him back into this world? If so, it appeared he wasn't alone. Fang me, the tension between the two of them was so thick I could practically put my hand through it.

Regardless, I understood that he needed to be involved in this, and we could do with all the help we could get. Rye had been a better fighter than me back at the Academy. Hopefully some of those skills remained. It made me feel better knowing he had Fee's back. "Good."

Fee looked as though she didn't know what to make of this, but realised she had no say in it. If she was going out, she was going with Rye – and vice versa.

Geared and armed, we prepared to leave. The goblins went underside, to search catacombs and tunnels; the rest of us were cobbleside. Everyone was equipped with a small square from the sheets that had been on the bed Ali had slept in during her brief stay in the den. She could change her look, but smell was smell. If we could find her scent and keep hold of it, we'd find her.

"Wouldn't it be easier to just hang about the palace and wait for her to show up?" Avery asked.

"If we weren't trying to save any potential victims in the time it takes her to get there, sure."

An odd expression crossed my sister's face. "The humans. I forgot about the humans." She looked much more upset by the realisation than I ever would have been. I wasn't in favour of human death or suffering by any means, but I wasn't about to forget their penchant for violence, or put their survival above my own.

I patted Avery on the shoulder. "I can't keep it straight if we're supposed to fight against them or for them." It was true.

The inconsistency of my feelings toward humans was as back and forth as my feelings for Ali.

Instinct told me to love and protect her. She was my child and my responsibility. My heart still hoped she could be saved, while the practical side of me knew that wasn't likely. I didn't want to be the one to hurt her, but another part of me wanted retaliation, vengeance against her.

Since I couldn't trust my instincts or feelings, I decided to trust my gut and concentrate on just stopping her rather than saving or ending her.

I turned to Vex. "Any vamps show up?"

He surveyed our gathered ranks from his superior height. "Couple of halfies. Not like we really got the word out though, did we?"

He had a point. It wasn't as though my father could have done much in this short a time anyway, but a few halfies at least had decided to come and check us out. They wouldn't learn anything from us if they were spies. Still, it would have been nice to have a few more fangs in the ranks – if we knew who we could trust. There were too many vampires involved in the labs to know for certain.

Vex frowned over my head. "Well, that's unexpected."

I turned in the direction he was looking – the front door. There at the threshold was Lord Ainsley, Dede's former lover and father of her child. He was pretty much a rotten bastard, but he had my nephew, and he'd given me good information from time to time.

He was also a full-blooded vampire, who knew about the labs. He had two halfies and another vampire with him. The vamp was Viscount Ockham, grandson of the poet Lord Byron.

"Ainsley," Vex said by way of greeting as the blonde vampire drew closer.

"Kintyre," Ainsley replied, using Vex's proper title as a marquess. Then to me, "Your Majesty."

I didn't even wince, though there was something about him that made me feel as though I required a shower. "What are you doing here, Ainsley?"

He looked genuinely surprised. "Vardan said you might appreciate some assistance in finding the creature from the lab. We're here to help."

Vex appeared just as dubious as I felt, but Ainsley fixed me with a steady gaze. "We can't afford a war with the humans, and these laboratories and experiments affect us *all*." He arched a brow.

How could I have been so stupid? Of course he would want to help. He was the father of Dede's son, the son he was now raising as his wife's. If anyone figured out that his pure-blood son actually had a halfie mother, that child could become another victim of these aristos. Even if they didn't harm him, they would want access to him, would want to monitor him, just as they'd monitored me.

I hadn't thought of Vardan's limited involvement with the experiments and other activities as a way of keeping a watchful eye and protecting his child. Then again, I was beginning to learn just how short-sighted I actually was.

I offered him a square of the cut-up sheet and a tracking device. "Here's her scent. Don't engage her. Ring for reinforcements. She can shape-shift, so trust your instincts and your nose."

He paused, holding the items I'd given him. "Shape-shift? You mean into a wolf?"

I wished. "I mean into other people, other forms. I saw her become my sister."

There was no denying the pain in his eyes. I didn't like him, but I think at one time he had loved Dede as much as anyone could love her. I'm not sure any amount of love would have been enough for my baby sister.

"Wellington district," I told him. I had thought Vex and I would search there since it used to be my home neighbourhood, and that Ali might know that, but I'd realised there was a better place to look. In fact, I was ashamed of not thinking of it before this.

"All right!" Vex's voice boomed through the house, immediately quieting our gathering. "The goblins have a head start. You all know where you're going, so go. Be back here an hour before dawn."

It didn't leave us a lot of time, but we still had several hours ahead of us. Someone would surely at least catch a whiff of her somewhere.

The doors opened and our party spilled out into the dark. I waited on the step for Vex to join me. We were the last to leave.

"So, where are we going?" he asked.

I reached out and took his larger hand in mine. "Home," I said. "We're going to the only home she's ever had."

The laboratory looked sinister by moonlight. It was deserted, a gouged-out ruin scattered with broken glass and misshapen metal.

"Did you take the logic engines or did they come back for them?" I asked.

Vex stood beside me with his hands in the pockets of his long wool coat. "We got a few. When I went down, everyone lost focus."

I turned to face him, laying the palm of my hand over his broad chest. "I'm glad they lost focus."

He smiled and covered my fingers with his. "I wasn't about to expire without seeing you again."

I blinked and looked away so he couldn't see just how rattled I really was. Part of me wanted to break up with him – honestly – but it was better to be at his side and afraid than apart and feel just as helpless.

Not a big fan of helpless, not at all.

"I remember when they discovered how halfies were conceived," Vex commented, as though picking up on my train of thought. "It was such an amazing thing. Now, I realise that they must have been experimenting back then. They had to, to figure it out. I know you feel like so much of this is because of you, but it started a long, long time ago."

His words reminded me of what Victoria had said earlier, that this wasn't all about me. I was glad of them, but they also made the world seem so vast, this fight so ... futile, and shamefully less personal.

"Vex, I don't know what I'm doing. I don't know how to stop her if we find her. I don't know how to stop a war. I don't know if we *can* stop a war."

He shrugged, his usual relaxed self. "Your instincts have been dead sharp through all of this. I'd keep listening to them if I were you – minus the mad ones, of course." He smiled.

I stared at him, throat tight. His faith in me was unwavering and undeserved. "I love you."

He pulled me close, kissed me, squeezed me, and then let

me go. Neither of us said another word as we silently picked our way through the rubble. I tried to ignore all the blood. Some of it was Vex's – I could smell it – and it ignited panic deep in my chest. I was overwhelmed by the need to protect him.

"I don't smell her," I said after we'd poked about for a while. "Nothing fresh."

"Agreed." He rubbed a hand over his jaw. "I'm thinking your hunch about someone picking her up is the soundest thing we've got to go on, which means they do have some way of tracking her."

"She wouldn't come back here to be safe, because they've got her somewhere safe already. Somewhere we'd never think to look." I smiled grimly. How could we have missed it? Fucking brilliant. We'd set out to search every neighbourhood but our own.

Vex nodded, expression grim. "She's in Mayfair."

CHAPTER 12

THERE IS NO INSTINCT LIKE THAT OF THE HEART

Ali's scent teased the back of my nose, like a sneeze that refused to come. The smell of her was in the lab, and lingered at the spot where she'd eaten the motorist. It was at Vex's and in the den, and because everyone had a bit of those sheets, the smell of her was all over us too.

It made it very hard to track her in Mayfair.

Maybe they hadn't brought her here, but my gut insisted I was on the right path. Vex told me to trust in my instinct, and I was. They would know how to subdue her. They would know how to care for her – which was why she hadn't killed anyone else. If I could have a corpse delivered, someone else could too – or they were giving her blood. If I thought it would do any good, I'd check with the agency to see who was getting more blood than normal, but they didn't give out that sort of information. Wasn't good for business.

But where would they keep her? It would have to be so very, very secure, and I had to think that there weren't many Mayfair mansions with such facilities inside. After the Great Insurrection, quite a few aristos had built special rooms in their homes in case there was ever another uprising, but those were designed to keep humans out, not aristos in.

So what was the reality of this situation? I reckoned someone wanted Victoria out of the way, but why? Was it to stop a war, or start one? Were her enemies looking to replace her, or demolish the monarchy altogether? Had Ali been made in order to kill Victoria or to increase the aristo population? Or both? And was I supposed to be the one to take the blame? Or did she simply look like me because of her genes, and she was going to kill Her Nibs while wearing someone else's face?

Where the hell was she?

We had returned to Mayfair almost immediately to follow up on my suspicion, and I was beginning to doubt my instincts along with my sanity. We'd traversed the streets following our noses until the scents became muddied and we couldn't tell if we were on the right path or not.

I stood on Vex's doorstep and tasted the air. She was out there. Somewhere.

Then something else hit me. Was that ... blood? Yes, it was. It was familiar too, but then so many scents in Mayfair were. That was the problem, and with so many halfies, vampires and weres out and about, it was extremely difficult to pin down just one.

A few from our search party had already returned, their sectors yielding nothing of use. Rye and Ophelia had come back after catching Ali's scent around the house I once shared with Avery. They followed the trail back to Mayfair, where it dwindled away. It was as though someone had taken pains to ensure we couldn't find her.

As if they knew we were going to organise a search. Did we have a traitor in our midst? Of course we did. Probably more than one. Even if it wasn't intentional, there was no way to keep anything secret with this many people in on it. I should have known the bloody thing was a waste of time. Should have anticipated that our unknown enemies would swoop in to protect their creation and their own arses.

I stood in front of Vex's home and sniffed the crisp air once again. It smelled like snow. Snow and blood.

Vex joined me on the step. "Do you smell that?" he asked.

I nodded. Neither of us said another word as we walked towards the gate together – slowly. Cautiously.

Vex opened the gate, and as we stepped out on to the pavement, a man staggered towards us – he was the source of the blood. Was it all his? He was covered in it. When we got close enough, the fog in my nose cleared – like taking a snort of coffee beans – and his scent hit me like a brick.

My father.

I ran to him just as he fell to his knees on the pavement. He looked like something out of a horror film – slashed and beaten. Chewed. Christ, there were bites taken out of him.

"Vardan?" No response. "Father?" His left eyelid twitched.

Had Ali done this? It had to be her – that would explain the trouble I'd had immediately identifying him when my sense was overwhelmed with the scent of her. He stank of her – just like the rest of Mayfair.

His blood soaked my hands, soaked the ground beneath him. And all I could do was just kneel there, staring at it.

Vex swept the duke up into his arms and ran back to the

house with him. That was the jolt I needed. I jumped up and followed close on his heels. My father was taken to the small infirmary Vex had set up for such occasions.

"He's lost too much blood," Vex said. "He needs to feed. If he can."

I didn't like the look in his eye. My father was on the brink of death, and I couldn't save him. He didn't even have enough blood left in him to heal, and mine would only hurry his death.

"I need a vampire!" Vex yelled. My father could take Vex's blood, but the most beneficial would come from the veins of his own kind.

"Here." It was Ainsley who rushed to help. He bit his own wrist as he prised Vardan's mouth open with his fingers, then shoved the torn flesh of his arm to those dry lips. It was a crude but expedient way of giving blood in an emergency.

I waited, heart pounding, fists clenched. My father's throat convulsed and he began to drink. I think I could have bloody wept at that moment.

Ainsley gave him as much as he could, then Vex donated, then Avery. By the time he had taken from all three of them, Vardan had healed enough that I knew he would survive.

I sat by his side as dawn neared.

"You need blood," Vex said, handing me a cup. He leaned his shoulder against the wall. We were in one of his guest rooms, far away from the chatter going on downstairs, but I could still hear it.

"Thanks." I took a sip. AB neg, slightly warm with a hint of cinnamon. The comfort drink of bloodsuckers.

"William wants to speak with you."

"Now?"

He nodded. "He says it's of some importance."

It probably was. I didn't want to leave Vardan, though. To be honest, I wasn't sure if I was worried about something happening to him, or whether I just wanted to be the one he saw when he opened his eyes. His hero.

He wasn't going to open his eyes any time soon.

I drained the cup, licked my lips and rose to my feet. "I don't know what day it is."

"Thursday. I think."

These last . . . what, two or three days? If that? . . . felt like an eternity. But then, that had become somewhat commonplace in my life ever since Dede first went missing and led me down this twisted path. There were moments of normality, of quiet, but when trouble hit, it threw one hell of a bloody party.

Vex put his arm around me as we walked down the corridor to the stairs. I leaned into him, brazenly taking advantage of his strength. Of course, I was standing on my own by the time we reached the bottom. There were still a few goblins around despite the hour – Vex kept his home sufficiently dark for them – and I didn't want them or anyone else to see me weak.

Avery approached me. I noticed she had her own cup of spiced blood. She needed it after the amount she'd given Vardan. "How is Father?"

"Resting. Did you call Val?"

She nodded. "I told him Father was healing. He'll be here as soon as he can get away from work. Are you okay?"

"Yeah." If I said it with enough conviction, that would make it true. "William wants to see me. Would you mind sitting with Vardan while I speak to him?"

"Of course not. I was going to ask you if it was all right for me to see him."

I hugged her. She could be a proper pain in the arse when she wanted, but I loved her. "Thanks. I'll be up as soon as I can."

"Take your time."

There were people everywhere, though not as many as there had been an hour ago. Most had gone home, Ainsley amongst them. It was just as well he was gone, as I didn't know what to think of him any more. He was pompous and a bit of a knob, but he really had loved Dede, and he had helped save my father, so I had to give him some credit for that.

My life had been so much easier when I saw everything in black and white. Honestly, it seemed as though lately the entire world had been washed in shades of grey. Melodramatic of me, I know, but it fitted my frame of mind at the moment.

My father's attack had been a message. They knew what we were doing, and they knew I'd enlisted his help. This was them telling me to stand the fuck down – just like when Church killed Dede.

Had they learned nothing about me from that? Of course not, because no one knew I'd eaten Church's black heart. They might have thought twice about baiting me in such a manner again if they knew about that.

William was waiting for us in the downstairs loo. He sat cross-legged upon the commode – lid down –reading a copy of *Gentleman's Edition* magazine.

"Looking to see what this season's style of cravat will be?" I enquired.

The goblin didn't miss a beat. "An article on baldness, I was reading. Your prince is thinning in the front."

I smiled at his dry tone. If he was losing fur, then I was turning into a morning person. "What are you doing in here?"

Vex closed the door, shutting the three of us into the small room together. I hopped up on to the vanity while Vex leaned back against the door. With one finger he hooked the switch and turned on the fan. The gentle hum of whirring blades gathered speed above our heads.

"Privacy," the prince said, tossing the magazine into a nearby rack. "A bit at least."

"Why?"

A furry eyebrow rose slightly. "Vardan's blooding. It was done by the abomination."

I already knew that. "I smelled her on him." It was one more reason for me to kill her. I should have done it when I had the chance. My life was full of should haves. When was I going to learn from them?

"Left by her was this." He handed me a piece of paper he withdrew from inside his patched and shabby frock coat.

I took the bloodstained note and opened it. In my father's blood was written in crude letters *THEY MADE ME*.

So I was right. It had been a message. "Didn't take them long to strike."

"It's like they're watching us," Vex remarked. "Responding to our every action before we even finish it." We exchanged a glance, and I knew I wasn't alone in suspecting a traitor.

Worse, I knew he also shared my suspicion that the traitor was pack.

The paper crumpled in my clenched fist. "How can anyone force a creature like her to do anything she doesn't want to do?"

My wolf shrugged. He was scruffy and tired and delicious. "They could have any sort of controls in place. Someone who can design such a creature is going to make certain he or she can control it."

True enough. I hated the idea of someone controlling her, but at the same time I was relieved. It made it much easier not to put all the blame on her. I wanted to make her saveable, even when I knew she wasn't.

"We still don't know who 'they' are, though." I rubbed my forehead. "Anything on CCTV? Was she picked up?"

"Black motor carriage. A Daimler. The licence placard wasn't entirely visible. Val's running it."

"A Daimler? Brilliant. Any aristo or halfie wannabe pretentious arse in the city who wants a fancy outfit owns a bloody black Daimler."

William cleared his throat – it sounded like a growl. "There's more."

"Of course there is." I ground the heel of my hand into my skull. My brain ached. "What is it?"

"Tracked the girl. The scent led to the leech house."

I stopped rubbing and peered at him from beneath the ball of my hand. I didn't care how ridiculous I looked. "Buckingham Palace? You're telling me you tracked her scent to Buckingham fucking Palace?"

He nodded. "There then vanished."

"Could she have gone there to get Victoria?" I looked from him to Vex and back again. Neither of them appeared convinced.

"Inside, she went not," William replied. "Leech queen says she knows naught."

I could hear the distrust in his gravelly voice. I looked to Vex. He shook his head. "I talked to her myself. She insists she's had no visitors. She even called the Royal Guard in to do a sweep."

A few months ago I would have been one of them. "You

think she's been lying to us this entire time?" She was in on it? That made no sense, and yet part of me was ready to believe it.

"No trust for leeches," William remarked. "Never."

I turned to Vex, my voice of reason. "Why would she go through all the trouble of making it look like someone was out to get her?"

He raked a hand through his thick hair. "Buggered if I know. I've known the woman more than a hundred years and she's never been this duplicitous or manipulative."

"She is a Hanover leech!" William jumped to his big feet. "Nothing but manipulative."

I understood the goblins had been dealt a raw deal as far as the aristocracy went, but William's hatred of Victoria always seemed much more personal.

"William, why do you hate her so much?"

One amber eye turned towards me, hard and bright. "Unfair that our lady was named for leech queen. Most unfair."

I scowled. "What the fuck are you talking about?"

To my left, Vex sighed. "She doesn't know, William. Did you not pay attention in your history classes, sweetheart?"

I glanced at him. "Some." True, I hadn't been the most diligent of students, but I had tested well enough, and I was strong – a trait that served me better than intelligence. I'd kick my own arse if I thought it would do any good now.

"Victoria was born Alexandrina Victoria. You were named in her honour."

Bollocks. "I'm not the only one to have been named for her." Neither of them was looking at me any longer; they were looking at each other. "All right, one of you needs to fill in the blanks for me here. I'm in no bloody mind to play games."

"Tell her the rest," Vex demanded, arms folded over his chest. "Or I will."

William growled – a frustrated sound rather than one of aggression. "Do it. I will not." He looked away. "Cannot."

Vex nodded. His gaze was full of sympathy as he looked at the goblin. It was just as sorrowful as he turned to me. "William was born the Duke of Clarence. Does that ring any bells?"

The Duke of Clarence? Of course I knew that title. That was ... Oh. *Fang me.*

"You're her uncle," I blurted.

"The younger brother of George the Fourth," Vex added.

I couldn't believe it. William met my gaze as I stared at him in astonishment. He nodded as my brain struggled to put it together.

"You're the fucking King of England."

CHAPTER 13

WHEN ONE HAS NOT HAD A GOOD FATHER, ONE MUST CREATE ONE

"No." William's voice was low, but there was an edge to it that warned me he wasn't going to discuss this any further. "I am not."

I'd gone and put my foot in it this time. "Apologies, my friend. I didn't mean to upset you."

He raised his hand to my cheek – the pads of his fingers were rough, calloused. "It is not you that upsets your prince." He dropped his hand. "King I never was. King I will never be."

He moved to the door. "Dawn approaches. I must go."

I watched him leave. The door clicked shut behind him.

My spine sagged. "Knobbed that up, didn't I?"

Vex did what he always did when I got my head up my arse – he came over to where I sat on the sink, wrapped his arms around me and kissed my forehead. "He should have told you a long time ago."

"It explains so much." My voice was muffled by his shirt. "I should have figured it out on my own. Albert's fangs, I thought I'd paid attention in history class!"

"To be fair, your professor might have skipped over William. Many tend to. Not good manners to mention the goblin heir to the throne."

Good point. Of course they'd leave him out of the school books.

"He's not the one trying to kill Victoria," Vex said, misinterpreting my silence. "If he wanted to do that, he could have done it a century ago."

I lifted my head to finally meet his concerned gaze. "I know." None of this was the goblin's style. He could be secretive and stealthy, but he wasn't sneaky. He wasn't cruel.

And he never, ever would have let them take me to one of their labs and violate me.

"Other than you, William's the only one I trust implicitly." There were things I would keep from Avery and Val – and had done –but only one thing I kept from Vex, and that was about Church's death. And William? I'd trust him with my life. In fact, I had done just that the night I walked into the den and asked for his help finding my sister.

Vex lowered his head to mine and kissed me. It was better than any pill, any good news. For those few moments I felt as though the world wasn't such a bad spot after all, and that everything was going to be all right in the end.

He pulled back, giving me a lopsided grin. "If we stay in here any longer, I'm going to have my way with you."

I grinned. "Best idea I've heard in forever." Of course, we didn't have time for it. I had to check in on Vardan first, then I'd have to address the fact that Ali might be holed up in Buck

House, and I'm sure there were a dozen other things I needed to do.

I grabbed the front of his shirt and pulled him between my open knees. "Now."

His expression turned suddenly serious, and after relocking the door he helped me out of my trousers and dropped his own. It was quick, intense and wonderful – exactly what I needed. Both of our spines and shoulders were a lot more relaxed afterwards.

We left the loo to some good-natured ribbing – people wondering what we'd been doing in there so long. They hadn't seemed to notice that William had left ahead of us, otherwise I'm sure that would have led to some highly inappropriate jokes.

Halfway through one of my witty comebacks, a scream echoed through the house. "Xandra!"

My heart caught in my chest. "Avery."

I shot forward, Vex right behind me. I practically leaped up the staircase, landing near the top, then ran down the corridor and burst through the door of the room where my sister and father were.

Avery stood over Vardan, trying to quiet his flailing limbs and arching body. He was having some sort of fit.

I immediately joined her, and only just escaped a punch in the face.

"What happened?" I demanded as Vex arrived at my father's feet.

Avery shook her head, eyes wide with terror. "He said he hurt, so I gave him some of the medicine on the night stand."

My head turned so fast my neck made an awful cracking sound. There on the small wooden table was a brown glass bottle with a dropper top, labelled as "pain eliminator".

Eliminator as in the ultimate pain destroyer, death? Because that bottle hadn't been there when I was with him, and I'd only left him for a few minutes, and now bloody froth was spilling out of his mouth.

I'm sure I looked just as terrified as Avery as I turned to Vex. "He's been poisoned. What do we do?"

My wolf slipped off my father's legs. "We have to get it out of him. Sit him up."

Avery and I did as he ordered, holding Vardan so he sat upright. Vex prised open his mouth and stuck a finger inside. Vardan lurched once, then again, and finally retched over the side of the bed on to the carpet. I didn't like the colour of it – blood mixed with something black and oily.

My father sagged forward. Only Avery and me holding his arms kept him from collapsing on to his own legs. I eased him backwards, toward the mountain of pillows. He stiffened, back arching. Bloody and blackened lips parted to emit a horrible sound – like the screaming of a wild animal caught in a trap. The wounds he had suffered returned, slowly tearing open his flesh, exposing raw tissue and muscle beneath. Blood ran from him in tiny rivers, quickly soaking the bed.

And then his head snapped back and a torrent of blood and gore erupted from his mouth. It shot toward the ceiling like a geyser, raining hot wet clots down upon us in a blood storm.

Vex was on his rotary, ringing for medical assistance even as he shouted for help from the pack.

Avery and I were silent, staring at each other through the crimson shower. I held my father with one hand while the other reached behind him and took hold of Avery's. Her wet fingers slipped over mine, but we held fast, blood forming a glue between us.

We didn't have to speak. It was a few minutes to dawn, and we both knew that time was not on our side.

Avery's fingers tightened around mine as the blood pouring out of Vardan lessened to a trickle. The three of us were covered in it – foul-smelling and thick. Our father crumpled like a rag doll against our joined hands. He was a mess – ripped, torn and depleted of blood, yet drenched with it.

My sister bit into her wrist, hard and without a care, and pressed the ruin of her arm to Vardan's mouth. His lips didn't move.

"Drink!" she commanded, practically pouring her life into his mouth. Nothing.

I stroked his throat, trying to make him swallow the fresh blood, but it was too late.

The Duke of Vardan was dead.

Someone called Val – I think it might have been Argyle, Vex's secretary. Argyle was the halfie son of Vex's first cousin, which explained the strong resemblance. This thought occurred to me for no reason as I stood to the side, watching as medical people – the plague doctors – took my father's corpse away in a black, non-porous bag that wouldn't show the stains.

Avery and I had both showered, and I lent her some of my clothes that I kept at Vex's. The garments that were soaked with our father's blood I put in a large plastic sack to be tossed away if they weren't needed for evidence or ... something.

So she and I were standing shoulder to shoulder when our brother finally arrived. He stopped the halfies with the gurney and flashed his badge. He didn't have to do that, but I reckoned he was in shock as much as Avery and I were.

Val paled when one of the halfies opened the bag for him to look inside. It wouldn't be a pretty picture. My brother had seen far too many corpses in his lifetime, but seeing his father's drained all the professional, hard-arsed copper right out of him. He ran his hand across his face, holding it over his mouth for the span of a breath before nodding that they could close the bag again.

He crossed the threshold into the house, and somehow his gaze found Avery and me immediately. His expression softened, and I saw him blink back tears as he came towards us. He was trying so hard to be the strong big brother. He didn't have to do that, at least not with me. I don't think I could have cried if I wanted to. I was numb all over, particularly inside.

I don't think Val grasped the entirety of the situation. With our father dead, he was the new Duke of Vardan. It was rare that halfies inherited titles, but about thirty years ago or so Victoria had decided that they could, as there was a chance they might be able to produce a full-blooded heir. If the halfie failed to do so, at the time of his death the title then went to the closest full-blooded relative.

With the Vardan genes being as they were, I didn't doubt that Val would produce an heir, although who knew what sort of freak it might be. Maybe it would have to be locked away like a shameful secret.

Like William.

"Are you two all right?" Val asked, letting us go.

I nodded, dry-eyed. Avery sniffed, her eyes and nose red, but she held her shoulders back. "I will be."

"Val," I said, "we need to talk."

He nodded, understanding that something had to have happened for our father to be dead. Vampires didn't just die on their own – not that we knew of. It was assumed that their lives were finite, but the world had yet to see a naturally occurring aristo death.

I led both him and Avery to a small upstairs sitting room that Vex had said I could turn into a little study/office for myself when I was at his place. I had a similar room at my house for him. All nice and cosy. Unfortunately, I wasn't able to get my brother into the room before two maids and a footman walked past us on their way to the servants' stairs carrying the blood-soaked bedding.

Val stopped and stared, all colour draining from his face. If it weren't for the fact that I knew he'd seen worse in his line of work, I'd have feared he might empty the contents of his stomach on to my shoes.

"Stop looking," I commanded both siblings and practically shoved them into the room. Call me cold, but I had no desire to dwell on any of this.

I knew I had shut down that part of my brain that reacted to tragedy in a normal fashion. Later, I would no doubt cry and wail and gnash my teeth – or maybe not. My father and I had had a complicated relationship, and my feelings towards him weren't going to change just because he was gone.

However, it was how he came to be gone that actually made me feel something. I believe it was rage.

I closed the door, and turned to face my brother and sister. Avery had composed herself, though that could change at any moment. I loved her dearly, but she could cry at the drop of a hat. To be honest, I was more in awe than angered by it. Avery let her emotion out and then was done with it. Me, I ignored it until it started to fester.

"What happened?" Val asked. "Take a deep breath and start from the beginning."

I scowled at him. "You want to pull out your notebook and take my statement while we're at it?"

He returned the frown. God love him for being like me in that his reaction to anything painful was to fight.

"Stop." Avery's voice was like a slap to the face, knocking reason back into place. "Father is dead, and I will bang your skulls together if either of you makes this about you."

And God love Avery for taking charge. She'd had her cry; now she was going to take control, which suited me just fine.

She jerked her head towards Val. "Go on."

I rubbed my forehead. "All right. It could be coincidence, but I doubt it. I asked Vardan to help me convince the vampires that war with the humans was not in the best interest of those with plagued blood. I also asked him to see if he could find what vamps are involved with the labs. Only a handful of people knew this. Next thing I know, he's dragged himself here to find me after being attacked by Ali – the laboratory escapee."

Val blinked. "Why would she go after Father? He had nothing to do with those labs." There was just enough of a question in his voice to make my chest clench. Neither of us wanted to believe our father was a villain, but we knew him too well to paint him as a hero.

"She was sent after him." I handed him the blood-written note. "I reckon she intentionally left him alive so that he would find me, or I would find him." It wasn't wishful thinking on my part. If she'd wanted him dead, she would have made certain of that before she left him. Maybe it did show a presence of conscience on her part, but she was still a monster.

"Did he die from his wounds when he got here?"

Ah, now the fun part. "No. We gave him blood. He had started to rally."

Val was starting to get a dark glint in his green eyes. I would not want to be someone for whom he got a hate-on. "This isn't a fucking melodrama, Xan. What the fuck happened?"

"He was resting when Vex told me William needed to speak to me. We went downstairs, where I found Avery and asked her to sit with Father. In that short space of time someone snuck into his room and left a bottle of poison disguised as medicine beside his bed."

"I never should have given it to him," Avery whispered. "I should have checked it."

"There was no way you could have known," I reminded her for the third time since Vardan's death.

"Something tried to kill him and you left him alone?" Apparently my brother hadn't taken Avery's warning about smashed skulls seriously.

I refused to rise to the occasion. "He was alone for perhaps a minute or two – in the house of the alpha, I might add. I thought he was safe. He should have been safe."

"So your boyfriend has a traitor in his house, is that what you're telling me?"

Managing to not get defensive took an enormous amount of energy on my part. "There were a lot of people here tonight trying to help us track Ali. It could have been anyone." Just because I suspected it was pack didn't mean we shouldn't look at everyone.

"You should have fetched me." Val's cheeks flushed with anger. "You should have told me everything when you called."

"You were supposedly on your way," I shot back. "What took you so fucking long?"

His lips curled into a faint sneer. "He died on your watch."

I sighed. "You want to blame me, go the fuck to town." I pulled a plastic bag from my pocket; inside it was the bottle of medicine that had been used to kill our father. "But you might want to take a bit of time to have this analysed. I reckon it's got silver, tetracycline and goblin blood in it."

"The holy trinity of poison," Avery remarked. She took the bag when Val wouldn't, and handed it to him. "Grow up, Fetch. Xandra and I both did the best we could. If you're going to blame her, then you have to blame me too. Personally, I had my fill of passing blame when Dede died. We've lost a sister and our father this year, so can we not do this right now?"

"Fine by me," I said, folding my arms over my chest.

Val hesitated – the bastard. Then his shoulders slumped. "Forgive me, both of you." He put the bottle in his coat pocket and wrapped one arm around me and the other around Avery, drawing us in for a tight group hug.

I kissed his cheek and hugged him back. Of course I forgave him. I would always forgive him. It was forgiving myself that was the problem. However, I was not going to forgive Ali. I didn't care if she was forced to do it; we all had free will. And I was definitely not going to forgive whoever had given her the task. In fact I had pretty much decided that I was going to conduct a little experiment of my own on that lucky fellow.

It would be most interesting to see just how much of a person I could tear off with my teeth while they were still alive.

CHAPTER 14

GRIEF CAN TAKE CARE OF ITSELF

By the time everyone left the house, I was beyond knackered. The part of me that had a good rage on wanted to storm Buckingham Palace and maybe chew Victoria's face off, but there was a wee part of me that cautioned me not to be so hasty, and for once, I listened. So instead of racing off like a madwoman, I washed my face, brushed my teeth and went to bed.

Everything would seem better at dusk.

Vex crawled in with me. We were both too tired to do anything but cuddle, and really, shagging a couple of hours after watching my father die just felt ... wrong. Maybe if I'd been more distraught I could have worked up the emotional need, but beneath the tired and weary was nothing but anger and a sense of being fed up.

Was it just me, or was I the only person these anonymous aristocrats liked to fuck with? No, I knew I wasn't the only one – I wasn't that special – but I certainly seemed to be a favourite. Or maybe I just made too much noise for them – stuck my face in their business. They'd been allowed to carry on for far too long because no one had ever pieced it all together before. If it weren't for Dede, Ophelia and William, I would still be in the dark.

And I probably wouldn't have Vex. I snuggled as close to him as I could get in his big bed, wrapping arms and legs around him so tightly he chuckled. "I'm not going anywhere, love."

"Make sure you don't," I muttered into his neck.

His arms tightened around me. "I'm sorry about your dad."

Saying it that way – like Vardan had ever truly been a father – made the back of my eyes prickle. "I'm not about to make a hero out of him, but I think he did the best he could."

Warm fingers stroked my back. "I'm sure he did. You know, he was born in a time when fathers left child-rearing to the mother and the governess. Honestly, I think I turned out all the better for it. My old man had a temper you avoided at all costs – until you discover you're a werewolf and he isn't."

I lifted my head to look at him. It was dark in the room, the curtains keeping out the watery December sun, but I could see Vex's face. "What happened?"

He shrugged. "He raised his hand to me and I . . . bit it."

"Oh no!" I couldn't help but laugh. I covered my mouth with my hand to stifle it. "Was it bad?"

"He required stitches, and he never tried to hit me again."

I ran my fingertip along the line of his jaw. I loved every inch of him right down to my bones. "I can't imagine hitting a child."

"Like I said, those were different times. Did you know there used to be a law stating that a husband had the right to beat his wife provided he used a stick no bigger around than his thumb?"

"You're lying." He had to be, but I was oh-so-grateful for the distraction.

"I swear it on my mother's grave. That's where the phrase 'rule of thumb' comes from." At my dubious look he added with a chuckle, "Look it up if you don't believe me, wench."

"I will." He was a top-notch liar, my wolf, and liked to take the piss out of me whenever he could. This could very well be one of those times, and I would never know the difference unless I looked into it. He'd been right about people emptying chamber pots out of windows into the street, so he might very well be right about this.

It was very educational at times, being involved with an older man.

We resumed our cuddle. Just as I was drifting off, I heard Vex whisper, "I love you."

My lips curved as a rush of strength and peace coursed through me. It was going to be all right. "I love you too."

Four hours later, we were woken up by the ringing of my rotary. I snatched the bloody thing off the night stand and was about to fling it across the room when I saw that it was Avery's number.

"What?" I didn't care if I sounded surly.

"Xandra, you have to come to the funeral home with me."

"Now? Why?"

"Sometime today. The director says there's a problem."

I didn't want to say it, but I'd already figured out that we wouldn't be able to have an open casket. Poor Vardan had looked like a blood-covered chewed-up prune when he finally died.

"Is it an emergency?"

"He didn't say, only that he wanted me to come by. I'm not going alone."

So why did I have to be the one to go with her. "Did you call Val?"

"He's on a case."

"His father just died!"

"I reckon that's the case."

I frowned. "Isn't that a conflict of interest?"

"I don't know and I don't fucking care. Are you coming with me or not?"

"I'm with you, don't get your knicks all in a twist. I'm not going to be ready for another four hours, though."

"Why not?"

"Avery, I need sleep. I'm going to go back to bed for a couple of hours and then I'll come and fetch you. Vardan's not going anywhere. He won't care." A little callous, but true.

She sighed – loudly. "Fine." I could picture her pout perfectly in my mind. Wasn't she exhausted too? And why didn't she take care of this with Emma? She didn't need me with her. Then again, as the oldest, Val and I usually took point on these family issues. Avery had never had to do something like this on her own before.

"I love you. I'll see you in a bit."

"Right." Then she disconnected.

"Cow," I muttered, and flopped back on to the mattress.

Vex merely drew me against his chest. No doubt he'd heard the entire conversation. "Do you want me to go with you?"

"No." Actually I would love it if he came along, but if he did, I couldn't make a stop at Buckingham Palace on my way home. I wanted to talk to Victoria, and I wanted to do it in private. If I accused her of killing my father, and of being behind Ali's creation, I wanted to do it to her face – and I wanted to do it with no one else around so the gossips didn't get wind of it, or just in case I was wrong.

I was reckless, yes. Impulsive too, but I liked to think that I wasn't stupid, at least not entirely.

"What the rutting hell do you mean, our father's body has gone missing?"

The attendant at the Eternal Flame funeral parlour looked as though he might vomit at any moment. I kept my boots out of the splash area just in case, fists clenched at my sides. What I really wanted to do was reach out and grab him by the throat and shake him until his trachea snapped in my hand.

And then I'd rip his heart out of his chest and eat it. I'd smear his blood over my face, lick it from my lips and fingers until they were clean. Then I'd stick my face in the empty cavity of his ribs ...

"Xandra? Xandra!"

I shook my head at Avery's panicked tone. I hadn't moved any closer to the attendant, but he'd backed away from me. Frightened little thing was practically perched on his desk, face as white as one of his ... clients.

Avery didn't have much more colour, but at least she didn't look so terrified. She appeared curiously disgusted as she pointed over my shoulder. I turned my head, and saw my reflection in the mirror.

Fang me. Well, on the plus side, at least I knew why the last few times I'd gobbed out had felt odd.

My eyes were bigger, deeper-set. My cheekbones had

widened and lifted. My nose, mouth and jaw protruded like a short muzzle from which long, curved fangs glistened. Claws had sprouted from my fingertips, slicing into my palms so deep that blood had rushed to the surface and pooled on my skin.

What would have happened if Avery hadn't caught my attention? How much more would I have changed? I looked less animalistic than a goblin, but I was close – minus the fur.

Nature wasn't quite done with me, I reckoned. That realisation made me want to hop up on the desk with the attendant and tremble a little myself.

"Can you fix it?" Avery asked, looking at me like she'd had a shot of vinegar.

"Bugger if I know," I replied. My voice sounded at least two octaves lower and slightly impeded by the size of my fangs. I took a deep breath and visualised returning to my normal self, the way I usually did.

Nothing.

Fuckfuckfuckfuckfuck. Right. Do not freak out. Keep calm. Picture Vex. Lovely Vex, with that little grin of his, talking you off the ledge.

Soft, cool fingers closed around mine, slippery with my blood. It was Avery. She squeezed twice – the way I always used to squeeze her hand when we were children.

It's a bizarre and somewhat painful process, having the bones of your face change composition and shape. It was like an intense muscle cramp that lingered for a little even after you'd walked it off or pressed it against something cold; or like getting punched where there was already a bruise.

Regardless of this uncomfortable procedure, I was able to bring myself back to a state of normality, thanks to my sister providing a little grounding.

When I opened my eyes, not only was Avery watching me –
with a little smile – but so was the attendant and another
morgue employee, a woman with red hair. Human red.

"Apologies," I said, warm-faced. "That happens sometimes."

"You might want to have that looked at," replied the new
person without a hint of sarcasm. She held a clipboard to her
chest like it was a shield. "I'm Dr Quincy, the director. Perhaps
you ladies would join me in my office so we might discuss this
unfortunate situation."

"Unfortunate?" I arched a brow. "That's a bit of an understatement, is it not?"

Her bland expression didn't change. She was good, this
human. "Then would you care to join me in my office to privately discuss this colossal fuck-up?"

I admit, I looked around for hidden cameras. This was starting to border on paranoia.

"Yes," Avery replied. "We would." Still holding my hand,
she pulled me towards the woman. I held on, despite thinking
of how Vardan's blood had stuck our hands together.

The woman's office was a tiny glassed-in closet of a room.
Did all these places come with some sort of prerequisite for
bad lighting? Honestly, my skin looked the colour of an under-
ripe lime.

"Please sit," the woman said. "As I said, I'm Moira Quincy,
director here at Eternal Flame."

"I'm Avery, and this is my sister Alexandra."

"Yes." Dr Quincy seated herself behind the pressboard desk
as Avery and I sat opposite. One of the legs of my chair was
shorter than the others. I resisted the urge to rock it back and
forth until one of them slapped me.

Actually, a slap might be nice.

This was shock, I thought. The thought was followed by the urge to laugh hysterically. You'd think I would have developed a higher threshold for histrionics by now, but no. No matter what happened to me, I inevitably reached a place where I wanted to beat my head against a wall until my brain leaked out of my ears.

I simply didn't want to deal with this, but like all things, I didn't have a choice, so I had to do as Vex often told me: put on my big-girl knickers and do what had to be done.

"Why don't you tell us what happened to our father's body, Dr Quincy?" I made the suggestion so that it wasn't really a suggestion. If I was going to deal with this, I was going to have to be in charge of the situation.

The woman removed her spectacles and sat forward, resting her forearms on the desk's cluttered surface. I'd wager she knew where everything was in that mess. "First of all, I want to apologise to you for this unf— this situation. The duke's body was delivered here and processed as usual. By processed I mean cleaned and examined. We strive to treat our people with the same respect and care that we give the living."

"How lovely." Bitch. Bitch. Bitch. "Obviously someone decided not to respect our father, though, because he's missing."

When a redhead is embarrassed, there's no hiding it, as was the case with the doctor. She flushed a brilliant coral red. "Yes, and I must apologise again—"

"No." I cut her off, leaning forward. "You *mustn't*. What you must do is tell us every fucking detail of how you lost our murdered father."

"Xandra." Avery put a hand on my arm, I flung her off. Wonderful, she'd got blood on my sleeve. I just picked this coat up from the cleaners and now I was going to have to take it in again.

"No. I'm not trying to be a cow, but someone killed our father, and now the only evidence of that has disappeared." I turned to Quincy. "That is what you're saying, yes? That he was taken before you could determine cause of death?"

I hated it when people gave me condescending looks. So rude. "Well, I think it was fairly obvious he died because of his injuries . . ."

"His injuries had started to heal before he was given some 'medicine' that made him vomit out his internal organs like a blender without a lid. Correct me if I'm wrong, but that's unusual, yeah?" Because he was an aristo, Vardan's body would have been brought straight here for examination and preparation for interment.

Oh, she hated me. Can't say that I was all that heartbroken over it. I was somewhat accustomed to getting what I wanted, and this woman wasn't inclined to be generous. I'd been challenged before, but never by someone who had lost my father's corpse.

"It is unusual, yes. Perhaps if I had a blood sample I could at least test that for any toxins." She didn't seem particularly convinced it would work.

"You didn't take a sample when he was brought in?"

She flushed darker. "His injuries and blood loss made it seem a simple case. I'm sure I would have noticed if he'd been poisoned when I examined his stomach and tissue."

Of *course* she would have noticed. "I gave the bottle of poison to my brother to have tested. He's with Special Branch."

Quincy cleared her throat. "Yes, well we spoke to them as

well earlier today. It seems their evidence has also gone missing."

I opened my mouth, but Avery cut me off. "Would a piece of clothing yield anything beneficial?" She reached into her purse and pulled out a bag containing what I assumed was the shirt she'd worn when our father died. It looked like little more than a blood-soaked rag or towel.

"You brought it with you?"

"I thought we might need it."

She was smarter than I ever gave her credit for being. "I was going to throw mine out."

My sister barely met my gaze. "It was Dede's."

Ah. There was that lump in my throat. I'd become rather accustomed to the feeling. I looked at Dr Quincy. "Take care that you don't lose that as well, will you?"

"Of course." She withdrew something that looked like a swab with a plastic cap. She dabbed the swab into the bloody shirt, and then capped it. Then she drained blood from the bag – the top was literally blood-soaked – into a small vial that she also capped and quickly labelled.

Perhaps she wasn't completely incompetent after all. She sealed the bag and gave it back to Avery. "If this is special, I'd rather you hold on to it. I know of a cleaner who is a miracle-worker when it comes to getting blood out of clothing."

Avery smiled – a hopeful, childlike expression that made me wonder if I could hit Quincy hard enough to poke her nose out the other side of her skull. Jealousy was not a good colour for me, but this woman had lost our father. She didn't get to play hero for my sister. Only I got to do that. And Val, of course. I was the one that fixed things, not this ginger bint.

"You were telling us how our father went missing."

"Yes, of course. After cleaning the body in preparation for internal examination, I was told that a very important telephone call had come for me. At the same time someone buzzed that they needed help bringing a body down from one of the upper floors. Jeremy – the boy you frightened so very well – went to assist. I suppose I don't have to tell you that there was no call and no body."

"No," I replied sweetly. "I deduced that one all on my own. I once saw it in a film. Am I also to assume that our father's body was gone when you both came back?"

"Correct." She turned to Avery. I reckoned she was done with me. "I assure you, Lady Avery, that this sort of thing simply doesn't happen here. I have no idea how anyone could have got in here and walked out with a body … er … the duke."

I glanced out of the large window at the bank of refrigerated units along the far wall. "Maybe they were already here, waiting." I pointed through the glass. "Could someone hide in there?"

Dr Quincy recoiled. "I think you watch too many films."

I rolled my eyes. "Could they?"

"Yes, they could, of course, but—"

I pushed my chair back and stood up, ignoring her. I walked out of her office and sniffed.

I sneezed. The chemicals used to clean these places were murder on a sensitive sense of smell. So much bleach. I shook my head and rubbed at my tingling nose. I sniffed again. There it was – a familiar scent.

The smell led me to the refrigerator units. I opened one just right of the middle, about one down. It was empty now, but when I leaned in for a sniff, I knew who had been in it not long ago.

And I knew how she had managed to come and go undetected. I looked over my shoulder. Avery stood on the threshold of the doctor's office, a worried frown on her face. She didn't have to speak. I nodded, and she immediately rubbed her forehead with the ball of her hand, in exactly the same way I did. I didn't blame her – I could have cheerfully slammed the heavy steel door on my own head several times.

Ali had been here, and if my instincts were right, she had worn the face of someone who worked here. They were getting more brazen using her in such a public way. Either she had learned to control her urges, or they had strengthened their control over her.

Either way, my father was missing and we were fucked.

CHAPTER 15

LOVE ALL, TRUST A FEW, DO WRONG TO NONE

It was too much to ask that the bastards who took my father would forget who I was and drop him down a Met tunnel as goblin kibble. At least then I'd know what had happened to him and be able to return his body to the funeral home. But the purpose of taking him had been to make certain no one could prove that he'd been murdered.

Because stealing a body didn't raise suspicions at all. Fucking idiots.

Ripping him up was easy to blame on an out-of-control creature such as Ali. Poison was a bit more . . . personal?

I was never going to get how he died out of my mind. I don't know how Vex was going to get it out of his carpet, or bedclothes, or curtains. My father's blood had seeped into the walls, I'm certain of it.

It had been intentionally cruel to kill him like that. Cruel and unnecessary. A message to sit down, shut my mouth and behave.

Right. Because that always worked so well on me.

I had accompanied Avery back to the house and had coffee with her. I think we both were a little numb, somewhat automatonic. Emma was at work, but my sister had been told to let Victoria know when she felt ready to start at the palace. The position would be held for her.

What a lovely, considerate employer the Queen was. I snorted at the thought, but kept my mouth shut. Avery was paranoid enough without me adding to it. It would be a good paying position and look good on her record. And while my sister might be a little silly at times, she was not stupid.

If Victoria was hiding Ali, Avery would find out. And unlike me, she wouldn't charge in on her own. She'd call for backup.

After leaving Belgrave Square, I returned to my house in Mayfair – cobbleside. Let the Human League take a shot at me at the gates. Let them throw their bombs and bags of shit.

I was disappointed. There weren't many protesters there at all. The gates were shut tight, black wreaths draped on the front in respect for my father. The sight was touching. I walked up and rang the buzzer. The humans there didn't speak to me – didn't utter a sound. They just stared at me. It was unsettling.

One gate opened, and an RG came out. I recognised him from the Academy.

"Morning, Ross."

He actually bowed to me. "Your Highness. The Royal Guard sends you its deepest sympathies."

"Thanks." I cleared my throat of the damn lump. "You need me to give a sample?"

"Unfortunately, with this . . . problem running about, I do." He offered me the small device.

I smiled half-heartedly. "Don't worry about it. I'd rather you do it than not." I poked my finger with the sharp, and the screen on the device immediately popped up with my proper identity displayed.

Ross removed the tip from the device and discarded it. "Have a good day, ma'am."

"Oh, I don't think so, Ross. Thanks, though." I walked through the gates and slowly made the meandering trek home.

It was cold, with the smell of snow on the air. It felt . . . nice.

My house was empty, save for a small platter of fruit on my kitchen table. Dark ripe cherries and fat indigo grapes. The goblins had brought me their equivalent of a casserole.

Unexpected tears burned my eyes. My throat closed as my vision blurred. I sat down at the table with my head in my hands and bawled and snotted until I had nothing left inside me and I'd gone through almost an entire box of tissues.

My eyes burned like coals tossed into snow, and my head felt as heavy as a brick, but my heart . . . my heart was a little lighter, I think.

I went into my bedroom, changed my pumps for a pair of black boots with a sturdy hourglass heel and lacing up the outside, and snatched a hat out of my cupboard. I was already wearing black clothes as a sign of mourning, so I needed nothing else but a little concealer and mascara to make me feel more presentable.

Then I took the lift down to the platform, but I didn't go to the den. Instead, I made my way to one of the tunnels and then made the short walk south to Buckingham Palace.

It was an uneventful walk. Had I expected ninja assassins to wait in the shadows? Did I think the tunnels would be suddenly filled in? That wasn't likely, since they were her only escape route from the palace.

I had to be silent as I emerged cobbleside from the door at the side of the palace. I stuck my head out first to make certain there were no guards too close, and then slipped out into the early evening. The grounds were already lit – another deterrent against human invaders, but I managed to keep to the shadows tight against the base of the building. I leaped on top of a guardhouse, then up on to a windowsill – mindful of the alarm – and from there scaled my way to the roof.

When I broke into Bedlam asylum months ago while looking for Dede, I had discovered that I was a champion climber. So long as there were crevices for my fingertips and toes, I could ascend almost anything. I reckoned goblin strength had a lot to do with that, but I preferred to think that I was simply extremely talented.

I had to have *something*.

The roof of the palace had security measures as well, but those were designed to keep out humans, not someone with enough aristo blood to possess increased agility and vision. They should fix that My sensitive eyes took in the infrared scanners and pressure pads with a quick glance. Rather than walking on the roof itself, I moved along the balustrade that ran the entire perimeter of the building until I reached where I thought I needed to go.

On the front of the place, just beneath the roof, there were three large triangles made of stone. The centre one held the royal crest, while the other two each had circular windows. It would be practically impossible for a human to get into one of these windows, given the angles and the security, but it wasn't difficult for someone like me.

I didn't have to break the glass, the bloody thing actually opened. Perhaps opened was the wrong term – I was *able* to open it with a bit of a tug.

I looked for sensors – none, just as I thought. I slipped into the dark interior and replaced the window.

The attic of Buckingham Palace. It should be a veritable treasure trove, but it was decidedly disappointing. Boxes, trunks, furniture – all the things you might see at your nan's or auntie's, and covered in the appropriate dusty shrouds. I'd probably find some interesting bits and bobs if I went looking, but that wasn't my reason for breaking and entering, so it would have to wait for another time.

I managed to find the door, and had to break the lock in order to get out. It didn't take much, just a sharp twist. Once I entered the deserted corridor, it was a matter of following my nose down some stairs and a little creeping along to find the right room.

I sniffed again. Smelled like she was alone. I opened the door.

"I must commend you on your stealth, Alexandra," she said as she turned from the dressing table to face me. She was adorned in diamonds that sparkled dizzily in the lamplight. "I didn't know you were here until I heard the knob turn."

Was it wrong for me to be impressed with her when I suspected her of killing my father?

"I'll be quieter in the future."

"In the future, I would hope that you would simply call ahead, or send a note if you wish to talk." Then her expression changed. "I am very sorry to hear of your father's passing. Vardan was a good man, and a good friend."

I frowned. She sounded genuinely sorry. I stomped over to her and took a sniff. It was really her. Ali hadn't taken her place. "Don't play games, Victoria. It insults us both."

Now she scowled, and rose to her feet. "Sniff me again and I will bite that keen nose of yours right off. Now, what the devil are you talking about?"

"The other night a few of us with sharp noses decided to track the laboratory escapee. Her trail led here."

The little woman drew herself up in indignation. I hadn't known it was possible for her spine to get any straighter. "I know that. If she came here, then she came of her own accord. I know nothing of it."

"Really? That's all you're going to say?"

"There's nothing else to say, you impertinent baggage! I'm fairly certain it would have made the news if the creature had showed up on my doorstep, or was brought here. Have you noticed the legion of press skulking by the gate?"

"They wouldn't know a thing if you covered it up like you tried to with my father's murder."

Her nose lowered a bit, so she wasn't staring so imperiously down it at me. "Your father's death is a tragedy that affects us all, but why would I seek to conceal any of it?"

"Because he was healing until someone poisoned him."

Her jaw dropped. "What? How?"

"With poison. That's generally how poisoning is done." Yes, I was being a bitch, and it felt good.

"I don't know how you survived this long with that mouth of yours," Victoria remarked. "What manner of poison?"

"I don't know. It disappeared. We do, however, have another

blood sample." I wasn't about to tell her how we got it or where it was.

"When you know for certain, you must tell me."

"No, I mustn't. In case you haven't been listening, I don't trust you. In fact, I just accused you of having been involved in my father's murder."

She waved a hand at me. "You don't believe that. Besides, Special Branch has notified us of their key suspect. That's what this is about, isn't it? Oh, you foolish girl. That woman thinks of you less than I do."

My heart gave a little jump. "A suspect? Who?"

"You haven't heard?" When I shook my head, I could have sworn she said "fuck" under her breath. "Alexandra, do you never watch the news?"

"It started to feel a little narcissistic, what with how often I'm on it."

"Well, so am I, but as queen, I still feel the need to be on top of current events."

"Are you going to lecture me on monarch etiquette right now? Because really, I would just like to know who the fucking suspect is."

Colour bloomed in her cheeks. "Take that tone with me again and I will disembowel you with my bare hands."

She was full of threats today. I had no doubt she meant every one. And this time I didn't kid myself about whether or not I could take her. She was older, crafty, and if she had spent that much time with Church, she knew how to fight.

I swallowed my annoyance, and my pride. "Would you please tell me who the suspect is?"

She didn't pat me on the head or acknowledge my forced politeness. "Your mother."

"What evidence?" I asked a little while later over a plate of chocolate-dipped biscuits and a floral tea that tasted divine. Food was such a driving force in my life. Victoria seemed to share the feeling, as she shovelled the biscuits away as fast as I did.

She'd dropped that little announcement about my mother and then rung for refreshments rather than elaborate. All she would tell me as I growled my frustration was that there was "evidence" against Juliet. Then she'd asked me if I liked chocolate.

Now, however, it seemed she was finally ready to enlighten me. "There was her little appearance on the chat shows a few days ago, for a start. She's been quite vocal of late about her feelings toward the aristocracy – me in particular. Bertie told me that she looks after half-bloods who have been rescued from laboratories, and that she blames aristocrats for their deplorable physical and mental states. She apparently suspected that your father was involved with these horrible crimes. I know Vardan rang her not long before he was attacked, and that his wounds were consistent with a were attack. How much more evidence do you want?"

I paused, and the dunked bit of my biscuit broke off into my cup. Fuck. I hated finding soggy bits at the bottom of my tea. "It's all circumstantial." I didn't mention that I trusted Bertie's word about as much as I trusted Rasputin. "His body disappeared; how could any such information be determined?"

She shrugged her delicate shoulders. She was wearing black – her signature colour – and she looked like a prim little doll. "That is what the examiner said when asked."

Dr Quincy was a stubborn bint. Then again, she was just

covering her arse by sticking with her original assumption. Not like she had a body she could examine.

"It looked like a were attack because it was Ali who attacked him." Her claws could easily be identified as were or goblin. They were pretty bloody sharp.

"And how do you know that?" Victoria demanded in that schoolmarm tone of hers. Sitting here with her, I alternated between comfort, agitation and wariness. She had this odd way of making me feel at home and at ease while simultaneously making herself annoying and frightening. She was very good at it.

"Because I saw the note she wrote in his blood."

"You're certain she wrote it?"

"As certain as I can be. Not like I could have it analysed or anything. Her scent was all over it, so it's a sound assumption."

Her eyes hardened. "That's not good enough."

My teeth clenched. "It's all I've got."

"You should have examined the location of the attack. You should have checked for further evidence."

"Forgive me for being too concerned for my father's life to run back to his house and look for clues as to who attacked him when it was fairly obvious to me who the culprit was."

"I don't understand how you ever got to be Royal Guard."

I sucked in a deep breath. Fuck counting to ten. "Lucky for you I was, or I'd be having this conversation with Bertie and you'd be rolling over in a concrete box."

"You are the most vexing child."

"And you're a cantankerous old crone."

Fang me, was that a hint of a smile? I couldn't tell; it was gone in a flash, replaced by a very guarded expression. "Tell me more about this poison."

Back to that, eh? "I don't know much about it. As I said, it went missing along with my father, but we were able to give Dr Quincy a new blood sample."

Victoria reached out a tiny hand to her right and picked up the handset for a telephone that sat there. "Connect me to the Eternal Flame," she commanded into it.

A switchboard? Really? That was so retro it was positively ancient. And just a little bit cool.

And who the hell named that funeral home? It sounded like the title of a pop song.

A few seconds later she said, "Dr Quincy, please." And then she passed the phone to me.

"What?"

She waggled the handset. "I cannot ask for the results; it will raise speculation."

"Bollocks." But I took the telephone from her regardless. When Dr Quincy announced herself, I let her know who I was and asked if the results were in yet. It would be odd if they were so quickly.

"Actually, those did come back. You caught us at the right time, it seems. The sample you gave me contained high levels of silver, tetracycline, goblin blood, arsenic and laudanum."

Pretty much what we'd expected. "Thanks." I hung up.

"That was rude."

"She's a cow." I grabbed another biscuit. "So, why are you so interested in the poison that killed my father?"

"Tell me what was in it first."

I debated holding out, but if what I told her didn't match her suspicions then it wouldn't matter why she was so interested. If it did match, then I had to trust she'd fill me in. That was the difficult part.

My gaze locked with hers. "Silver. Tetracycline. Laudanum. Arsenic and . . . ?"

Her face was a perfect mask that slowly dissolved into an expression of cold, deep anger. "Goblin blood." There was no hesitation or question to her response.

I set my empty, soggy-bottomed cup aside. "What does that mean to you?"

Victoria drew a deep breath and put her own cup and saucer on the low table between us.

"It means that the poison that killed Vardan was also the same poison that killed my Albert."

CHAPTER 16

ONE OUNCE OF BLOOD IS WORTH MORE THAN A POUND OF FRIENDSHIP

"I thought *she* killed Albert."

Avery set a cup of tea in front of me and sat down at the table. We were at her house, and if it weren't for the general sadness hanging over the place, it would feel like old times.

Val had been made to take some time off work, of course, and he was with us. He hadn't said anything about his inheritance yet, but then I hadn't given him much of an opportunity. He had, however, beaten himself up good and proper for the poison bottle going missing. The only thing he'd said since his arrival was that the Yard had found evidence of Ali being at the morgue, and that they were still looking for her.

I took a sip of Earl Grey. "That was the popular story."

Val dropped a handful of sugar cubes into his cup. Somebody needed a kick of energy. "If Albert didn't die from injuries and if Her Nibs didn't kill him, then who did?"

"Someone with access to the royal family," I said, need-lessly. Then, perhaps not so needlessly, "Someone who still has access to the Buck House set?"

That circle was even smaller than it had been before the Insurrection, understandably. Not only were there fewer aris-tocrats alive, but Victoria's social interactions had been scaled back significantly. Only a handful were granted entrance to the palace on any kind of regular basis. Vardan had been one of them.

"Has to be an aristo," Val insisted. "Vardan's staff was loyal."

"Not just that, but we already know that aristos are involved at a high level." I plucked a piece of cheese from the platter Avery had placed in the centre of the table, and wrapped it in a bit of bread. "The involvement of the duchess and Churchill in the laboratories and experiments proves that."

Val watched me bite into my crusty sandwich. "You still reckon he was killed because you asked him to rally the vamps?"

"No, I think he was killed because he *did* try to rally the vamps." I took another sip of tea. "Also, I think whoever did it was worried he knew something. Probably thought the duchess confessed to him."

"Speaking of that," Avery began, nibbling on a crisp, "did you find anything in the duchess's journals?"

"Not yet." I'd scarcely had time to look at them. "They're written in some code I haven't cracked yet." And I wasn't going to crack it at this rate.

"Want me to take a look?" Val asked. "I've got time, and we did some training in cryptography and cryptanalysis at the Yard."

I leaned over and kissed his cheek. "I love you."

He flushed. "Stop it. I'll come by and get them later."

Avery toyed with another crisp but didn't quite get around to eating it. "Do you think he's . . . all right?"

Of course we knew who she meant – we didn't need our super-sibling powers for that. We'd managed to avoid talking about the body for as long as any of us could.

"He's not there," Val said. "Whatever happens, you need to know that Father is in a better place."

It was on the tip of my tongue to tell him that I hardly thought that being buried in some aristo's dirt cellar – or being Ali's luncheon – was a better place than the Vardan crypt, but I caught myself in time. My brother and sister would not appreciate my particular sense of humour at that moment.

Avery reached over and covered his hand with her own. "Thanks, Fetch."

If it made the two of them feel better to think that Vardan was perched on a cloud, finally able to enjoy the sunshine and plucking away at a golden harp, so be it. Personally, I wasn't going to feel any better until I had his murderer's kidneys in a pie. I would like to then feed said pie to said murderer. That was possible, wasn't it?

Ill-timed levity aside, I would find some satisfaction in delivering my own brand of justice. I might sometimes wake up in a sweat after nightmares about Church, but I didn't regret what I had done. I regretted that he had become such a monster that killing him had become necessary for my own continued existence, but I'd wear his blood on my hands without guilt.

Something had been niggling at the back of my brain, and I finally realised what it was. "Why take the body?"

My siblings turned to me. "To hide the evidence," Val said.

"But a blood sample proved that there was poison in his system. There was blood everywhere – taking his corpse didn't affect that. So if it wasn't to hide the use of poison, why take it?"

Avery paled – even more so than usual. "For tissue samples."

For once, someone other than me had gone the dark route. That it was Avery was perhaps the biggest surprise.

"Elaborate," Val commanded.

She closed her hands around her teacup as if her fingers were chilled. "First, I have to confess something to the two of you."

Aw, fang me. I hated it when conversations started with a confession. Just the word was enough to make my stomach clench. It almost always was a harbinger of horrid news.

"Go ahead," I said.

My sister paused, gathering her thoughts. If I cuffed her around the head would she gather at a more efficient rate?

"A few weeks ago, Emma and I decided to have a baby."

Val and I exchanged startled glances. He reached out to Avery. "Are you . . . ?"

She shook her head. "No, I'm not. Neither is Emma, though if we go through with it, it will definitely be Emma who gets pregnant."

Dread tightened the floor of my stomach. "Why?"

Her gaze – so much like our father's – met mine, and I realised that Vardan would never see his grandchild. "Because I had my blood checked in Paris by a friend. We both did. She told me there was a ninety-seven per cent chance that if I was impregnated by plague-carrying sperm, I would have a full-blood child."

"Just like Dede," I whispered.

She nodded, then turned to Val. "I know you reckon this insanity skipped you – that they didn't find anything when they took you – but go to someone you trust and get checked. The Vardan line is unusual – mutated if you want to go there. This mysterious 'they' didn't take Father to cover up his poisoning; they took him to take everything they can use."

My stomach clenched again. The idea of someone – probably people he knew and thought of as friends – slicing bits off my father was too much. Too cruel.

Unfortunately, it made too much sense to discredit. How could I not have thought of it? Wasn't it obvious that we were an odd bunch? What else would they want Vardan for, except to possibly send a message?

I'd got too close and pissed off the people behind the labs. They thought killing my father would stop me. Church had thought killing my sister would stop me.

I wasn't going to stop. Did they think I'd let them get away with it? Did they honestly believe I would let Dede and Vardan die in vain? They didn't know me very well. They didn't know me at all.

"I need the two of you to leave town," I blurted.

My siblings regarded me with a mixture of annoyance and surprise.

"No," Val said. "Absolutely not."

Avery joined in. "We're not going to leave you to face these bastards on your own."

My brother wore a fierce scowl. "How can you even suggest such a thing? Avery and I are every bit as trained as you are. I'm in Special Branch, and she's newly hired by Victoria herself. Are you really stupid enough to ignore those connections?"

Val rarely sugar-coated anything, so his questioning my intelligence didn't sting.

"In fact," Avery began, "perhaps you should be the one to leave town. You're the one who is the most visible, who has been the most endangered."

If I frowned any harder, my face would fold in half. "Don't be absurd."

She arched a brow, as did Val. Another family trait. Did I look half so smug when I did it? If so, someone should give me a good kicking.

I held up my hands. "Fine. Point made. I'll just worry about the two of you."

Val punched me in the shoulder. It fucking hurt. "And we'd worry about you whether we're here or Italy. At least with us here you'll have people you can trust at your back."

"Yeah, I'm just as capable as Ophelia," Avery added.

I stared at her. "Are you jealous of Fee?"

She crossed her arms over her chest. "No." Of course that meant she was. "But I wager you haven't tried to get her to run away."

I almost said I didn't worry about Fee the same way, but I caught myself. Avery wouldn't see that as a compliment. I certainly wouldn't. Instead I said, "You're right. The three of us ought to stick together. Just promise me you'll be careful and be armed at all times." And then to Val, as I rubbed my shoulder, "And stop hitting me, you great brute."

We talked then about what steps we could take to find Father. I had to admit that finding him took precedence over stopping Ali – at least at that moment and under that roof. Val would use his Yard connections to do what he could, I'd use the goblins' spy network and Avery would keep an eye on the palace and who came and went so we'd have a better list of suspects. I didn't believe Victoria was involved, not after she'd told me that the same poisonous compound had been found in Albert's blood. She'd seemed genuinely distraught, but then she'd had a long time to perfect the act. I'd trust her when I knew she deserved it.

Although I didn't think we'd ever find Vardan. Because no one would ever find Church, and I wasn't nearly as wily as this bunch.

I honestly didn't know what day it was. It felt as though I'd been tracking Ali and dealing with Vardan's death for weeks, but in reality it had been . . . what, a few nights? I shouldn't be surprised that things had spiralled out of control so quickly, but I hoped that I never got to the place where this sort of thing seemed totally run of the mill.

At least no more plagued corpses had popped up. At least Ali hadn't killed anyone else. No one that we knew of at least. I truly hoped they hadn't fed my father to her. That would be the tipping point for me. That would be the moment that I gave myself over completely to the feral. To the madness. Even the thought of him being sliced up and studied was better than that.

My rotary rang in the midst of that cheery thought. I pulled it from my pocket and glanced at the screen. It was Ophelia. Should I take it? Avery might get even more bent out of shape. But Fee might have information. Or Vex might be hurt again. I admit, the latter had more pull than the former.

I answered. "Fee?"

"I need your help," came her reply. She sounded . . . shaken.

I frowned. "Are you all right?" Avery shot a concerned glance in my direction. She was a sucker for anyone in trouble.

"Physically, yes. Emotionally . . . " She chuckled humour-lessly. "Xandra, can you meet me?"

Halfie hearing being what it was, both my companions heard her request, and the tone in which it was delivered. Avery and Val nodded at me, silently giving consent. Sometimes I loved them so bloody much.

"Where are you?" I asked, rising from my chair and steal-ing another sandwich. Was she with Juliet? Had the police found our mother?

"Clarence House."

I halted. "What the ruddy hell are you doing there?" Every person, be they human, aristo or something in between, knew who lived at Clarence House.

The Prince of Wales. And given that Ophelia was a sus-pected criminal, and the daughter of a woman thought capable of murder, I doubt she'd be all that welcome.

"I'll explain when you get here. Hurry up." Fee discon-nected as I slipped out of the door into the chilly night. The smell of snow teased my nostrils, the brusque air making me sneeze.

Bloody right she was going to explain. Dragging my arse out when I should be with Vex, eating, shagging and basically enjoying his company, was cruel. I had too much to concern myself with to worry about what my older sister had got her-self into.

Still, she came when I called her, so I should return the favour.

I didn't have the Butler, as winter conditions often made it difficult to drive the two-wheeled vehicle, but I'd been doing most of my travelling underground anyway. I would have to use that same system to get to Fee.

Not far from the Belgrave Square house was a grate, tucked into a narrow alley between two houses. I didn't know how old it was, or even if it was the work of the city. It might just as easily have been the doing of goblins. Regardless, it led me underside, and once I had my bearings, it was pretty much straight on – with a few twists and turns to access other tunnels. I emerged not far from Clarence House, though it required me poking my head up once or twice to find an appropriate spot. You couldn't just pop up in the middle of traffic, or in a well-lit area where you were likely to be seen. It wasn't that I was worried so much about humans seeing me; more that humans weren't going to feel very secure knowing that the "monsters" could scurry about beneath their feet and their notice. Let them think we were confined to our West End.

Maybe I was being too careful. Clarence House wasn't far from the palace, and therefore not exactly a hub of human activity, especially now. I wasn't certain how to take the fact that the humans seemed to respect that we were in mourning and had backed off. Or maybe it was the fact that Scotland Yard was threatening to arrest troublemakers. Regardless, it was unlikely I'd be seen. Still, I preferred to be stealthy.

Ophelia hadn't given me her location, so I was forced to try sniffing her out. I caught her scent around the back of the mansion, where the shadows were deeper. My rotary vibrated in my pocket. I took it out and glanced down.

Meet me in the gardens. It was from Fee, of course.

I leaped easily over the wall. This place didn't have the same sort of security the palace did. This was a bit more modern, with motion detectors and the like. Fortunately, as Royal Guard I'd been made to study and practically memorise the security detail for every royal residence in the city – and those elsewhere. Unless Bertie had made some significant changes in the past six months, I shouldn't have any problems.

And since Fee had obviously already sneaked in, I was going to go with the assumption that he *hadn't* made any changes.

I caught a scent as I crept closer. *Ali*. She'd been here. Was that why Fee had called? Was the Prince of Wales dead? Eviscerated by my mad doppelgänger? I really hoped not. I'd smelled her at the palace and she hadn't attacked, so perhaps she'd been here doing a little reconnaissance.

You tell yourself that, Vardan, I thought, *if it makes you feel better*.

I kept to the wall, practically on it as I skirted the gardens. Then I avoided lights and sensors by scaling the side of the house, using windowsills and tops for foot- and handholds. The alarms would only sound if I tried to open a window or broke it.

There, suspended from a harness that extended high above her head, was Fee. She was clad entirely in black. Even her hair was covered. The soles of her sturdy black boots were braced against the stucco as she kept herself just out of line of sight from the room on the other side of the glass. A faint glow came from within.

She saw me coming, and placed a finger to her lips for me not to speak – to not make any sound if I could help it. If she was surprised to see me climbing without aid of any kind she didn't show it. Cow. The least she could do was be impressed.

But then she looked decidedly grim. And ... heartbroken. My own heart thumped hard once in response. What the hell had happened?

Slowly, carefully I inched closer to her, taking care not to alert anyone to my presence by scraping my boot across a window frame. It had just begun to snow – big fat flakes falling around us – and the air had taken on that sort of eerie stillness it sometimes did on a snowy night. I had to be extra cautious, as the slightest noise could sound like the crash of thunder in the silence.

When I finally joined Fee, her mouth was set in a grim line, and I saw a sheen of wetness on her eyelashes. She'd been crying.

Since we'd met, I'd always thought of her as having less use for tears than I did, though I'd known her to turn into a watering can at times. Seeing her so upset affected me – made my stomach clench and flutter with anxiety.

She pointed at the window. I followed her gaze.

The room beyond was a bedroom, done rather splendidly in shades of pale blue and cream. It probably hadn't been updated in the last century, but it appeared well cared for and opulent.

But who gave a flying fuck about the room? What Ophelia wanted me to see was Bertie, naked as the day he burst from the womb, going down on a woman on the bed.

I scowled as I looked at my sister, and mouthed, "*What the fuck?*" I hadn't busted my arse to get here, and hang off the side of a building in the cold and the snow, just to see Bertie shag some bird.

Fee clenched her jaw and jabbed her finger at the window once more. Silently, I sighed, and looked again. Whatever she wanted me to see had better be worth the mental scarring Bertie's white arse and raging hard-on was going to leave behind.

The woman, who had her face averted, and mostly obscured

by her blonde hair, writhed and arched on the bed. I could hear her moans with little difficulty. Either Bertie was really good, or this woman was a brilliant actress.

Things followed the normal path, and the woman was soon screaming. I admit, I cringed at the volume. Then Bertie pulled his face from between her thighs, grabbed her hips and flipped her over.

That was when I saw the woman's face – flushed and glassy-eyed, filled with anticipation of what was yet – pardon the pun – to come.

No wonder Fee had cried. Myself, I felt a tad pukish. It was one of those times when I wished my suspicions and paranoia were nothing more than neurosis. I did not want to be right, and I most certainly did *not* want to see proof of it.

The woman giving Bertie what appeared to be the ride of his incredibly long life, and showing no concern for the fact that she was a wanted fugitive, was our mother.

CHAPTER 17

NO SOUL IS EXEMPT FROM A MEASURE OF MADNESS

Of all the hatters, knobbed-up things I'd seen over the course of my near-quarter-century on this planet, this was definitely one of the top five.

My mother – naked and looking far better than a woman her age had the right – was bumping nasties with the Prince of Wales right before my very eyes.

First thought: *Victoria is going to have a haemorrhage.* Second thought: *What the buggering bloody hell is going on?* Our mother had gone on the box practically calling aristos villains. She'd personally attacked Bertie's mum, then invited Bertie into Bedlam, and now here she was bouncing up and down on him like a rubber ball in one of those paint-mixing contraptions.

I had suspected there was something going on between them, but I hadn't imagined it would be quite so … enthusiastic.

I knew my mouth was hanging open like it had come unhinged, because I could taste snow on my tongue. I turned to my sister – who I felt the understandable urge to both hug and slap – and met her gaze. She was not happy about this. Neither was I, but I couldn't sort out my moral outrage at the moment.

Ophelia, though, had had more time to let it sink in. There'd be no unseeing this, no pretending it hadn't happened. She pointed towards the roof and began to slowly walk up the side of the house. I crawled after her, following her to the balustrade at the top – a popular feature of these older buildings – and swung my legs over so I could rise to my feet on the flat roof.

"What the fuck is that?" I hissed, jabbing my finger at the roof as though we could see right through it to the carnal spectacle below.

She shook her head. Snow drifted around her shoulders. "I don't know." She kept her voice low as well. "How could she?"

I shrugged. "Don't ask me. I hardly know the woman. I thought she hated aristos." Being fang-raped by one of them would do that, right?

"She does." Fee frowned. "Or at least, she *did*."

"Yeah, I think it's safe to say her opinion has changed where at least one is concerned." I squinted out at the falling snow. It was coming down more heavily now. It would be nice to have a little white stuff about for a day or two; it made parts of London look so Dickensian.

"What does this mean?" she asked. "Xandra, this makes no sense."

I turned my attention back to her. "No, it doesn't." It explained why Juliet had seemed so odd at Buckingham

Palace, and it explained the coyness Ophelia had told me about, but the rest of it . . .

"It won't look good for her if anyone else finds out. She publicly declared herself anti-aristocracy. The press will disembowel her like William Wallace."

"Who?"

Her gaze narrowed – obviously I was a halfwit. "You've never heard of William Wallace?"

Halfwit might be a tad generous. "No, and what fucking difference does it make? Our mother is shagging Bertie, and there is absolutely no explanation for that that paints her in a flattering light."

"Do you reckon she loves him?"

Her hopeful expression pressed on my chest, even though I wanted to laugh out loud. "I bloody well hope not!"

My outburst only served to make her seem all the more crushed.

"You're really upset by this."

"You fucking think so?" she shot back. Coming out as a whisper, her words lost some of their vehemence. "Can't think of a single fucking reason why I would be fucking upset that my fucking mother is fucking the fucking enemy!"

That was a lot of fucking. Appropriate, given the situation below. "What do you want me to say, Fee?"

Her eyes actually welled up. "I want you to tell me that Bertie is secretly on our side, or that he seduced her. Tell me that my mother hasn't betrayed everything I've been raised – by her! – to believe in. Tell me that she's still who I thought she was."

I stared at her. Ophelia was strong, and I'd always felt that we had a certain coping mechanism in common – the ability to make sport of things and then indulge in anger and vengeance. I tried not to cry if I could help it, especially in front of an audience. Seeing her so vulnerable irked me. I wanted to go into the house and drag my mother out of bed by the ankle and tote her up here so she could see what she'd done to her daughter.

"I'm sorry I told you to follow her. You shouldn't have seen this."

"But I did, and now I know." An odd expression settled over her face. "I know his voice."

"Yeah, he's the Prince of Wales."

She glanced at me. "If you hadn't met him, would you know what he sounds like?"

Actually, no. I only had a dim memory of him speaking at the Academy, and giving the odd holiday broadcast. "So where have you heard him before?"

Fee shook her head. "I'm not sure, but I'll figure it out." She looked away, sighed, and then lifted her gaze to mine again. "This looks very bad, doesn't it?"

Did she honestly require an answer to that? "It does. Not just for Juliet, but for Bertie as well. The press would crucify them." Not just the press, but Victoria as well.

Was that our mother's motivation? Did she want to provoke Victoria into doing something rash? If so, she could have chosen something that wasn't so dangerous to her own health.

No, I didn't believe she had any other motive for bonking Bertie than the fact that she liked bonking him – a fact that boggled my mind. She hadn't been wearing any slutty under-wear, and there were no toys or whips about. Those things would hint at seduction, perhaps even manipulation, but naked, joyous sex with lots of eye contact and smiles was not typically a weapon. At least not for a woman. I couldn't vouch for the opposite sex.

My thoughts were interrupted when a wash of bright red light flashed across the scene. Special Branch. I grabbed Fee and hauled her down to the roof, so that we were lying down, hidden by the balustrade.

"What the hell?" Ophelia whispered.

I put my finger to my lips to shush her, and listened, peeking between the spindles.

Two officers I recognised as Maine and Cooke approached the house. Cooke was all right – bit of a dishcloth – but Maine was a first-class bastard. He'd tried to get me for Church's death, even though Church hadn't been declared dead, and basically made my life difficult for as long as he could.

They rang the bell, showed their credentials to the housekeeper and were taken inside. Soon afterwards, a commotion arose inside. There was a feminine scream, and a few minutes later Cooke and Maine exited the house with Juliet between them. They'd let her put on a dressing gown, and she weaved between them like a drunkard.

They'd shocked her into submission, I reckoned. Nothing like a big bolt of electricity to make one compliant.

Fee stuck her head near mine so she could see as well. Bertie stood on the steps, also in a dressing gown. After putting my mother in a wagon designed to hold those of great strength, Maine came back to the prince.

"Thank you for your call, sir. It must have been difficult."

"She's a lovely woman," Bertie remarked. "But Vardan was a good friend, and he deserves justice. Take care of her, Inspector."

Ophelia stiffened. I glanced at her, only to see that her eyes were wide and black, her face stark white. Surely seeing our mother arrested – forked over by her wanker bonk-buddy – wasn't that distressing. She looked ready to pass out.

"Fee?" I whispered? Below us, Maine returned to his carriage.

"I know where I've heard him before." Her voice was hoarse – strangled. Her creepy gaze turned to me. "The labs. I remember because I was blindfolded, put in a cell. He told one of the guards to 'take care of her', and then the bastard raped me."

Oh fuck. Could it be? She hadn't seen his face. Maybe . . . No, I couldn't do that. Fee deserved more respect than that.

"Are you certain?" I asked. Below us, the door shut. Bertie had gone back in. I doubt he heard us whispering over the carriage, his own conversation and the noises of the night.

She nodded. "I'll never forget that voice."

It made sense in an awful way. Bertie had been Church's mentor. Church had adored him. Would have done anything for him. He had told me that the laboratories, the experiments, all of it was above his rank. The duchess had been killed – or forced to commit suicide – to protect the secret. And whoever was in charge seemed to be one step ahead of us, as if they knew our plans.

Shit.

My father had been a duke, and the only thing that outranked him other than Victoria – who seemed to have no freaking idea what was going on – was a prince.

I only knew two of those, and one was William. The other had shagged my mother, the leader of the Insurrectionists, before having her arrested – but he didn't have her arrested before he'd had a look inside Bedlam and discovered where all his other escaped "experiments" had gone. Travelling all over Europe promoting peace was just his cover. He'd been on the continent collecting samples, and forming alliances for the day he dispatched his mama.

"Who's taking care of things at Bedlam tonight?" I asked, keeping my voice calm.

Ophelia frowned. "The usual security guards, a few halfies and Rye. Why?"

I didn't want to be paranoid, but I had caught Ali's scent around the palace, and I'd caught it here. I thought it was because she was hunting the royals, but now that Fee had recognised Bertie, I knew that wasn't true. The reason we hadn't found her wasn't because she was so good at hiding, but because someone was very good at hiding her from us.

Bertie. And now he'd just taken care of the one person in Bedlam who might be able to stand against him – against Ali. Which inmate did he want? The little halfie girl who had been repeatedly raped by goblins? Or maybe the one with bits of metal in her brain.

"Xandra?" There was fear in my sister's voice.

I swallowed against a lump in my throat the size of a croquet ball. "I think we ought to go to Bedlam. Now."

That was all I needed to say. My sister snatched up all her gear and dropped over the edge of the roof once more. I followed on her heels. Within minutes we'd made it out of the garden and on to the street, where Fee had left a motor carriage a few blocks away.

We were in the North End, and Bedlam was across the river on Lambeth Road. We could get there in decent time if the traffic worked in our favour. Ali was on foot, so we had the advantage there, but she was incredibly fast and had a head start.

Rye might already be dead.

I pulled out my rotary and dialled Vex. I got his Britme service, so I left him a message letting him know what I suspected and that I was with Ophelia en route to Bedlam.

"I hope I'm wrong," I said before disconnecting. "I've been wrong before, right?"

But I knew without a doubt that this was not going to be one of those times.

Bedlam was, well, a madhouse when we got there.

The place had a long history of treating the insane, and was now a front for the Insurrectionists. They still treated patients, however, and that was part of the reason I was anxious. There were halfies in that place that had been so ill-treated, they deserved what peace Bedlam could give them. They didn't need another monster trying to tear them apart.

And quite frankly, Ophelia didn't deserve to see more people she cared about killed.

The front gate – looming iron with the name "Bedlam" above – was intact when we arrived, but wide open. I couldn't say the same about the front door, which had been ripped off its hinges and tossed aside. I ran in, but Ophelia came up short on the threshold. I would have spared her the sight if I'd been able.

The two guards at the hounds had had their throats ripped out. They hadn't even had time to reach for their weapons. The hounds – those lovely scent-detecting machines – looked as though they'd been kicked apart. They crumpled towards the floor, smelling of burnt wire.

"James and Tully," Ophelia whispered, white-faced, as she stared at the dead men. They'd been human. Never stood a chance.

"Come on." I took her by the arm. "You can't help them now."

Thankfully – if there was anything to be thankful for – the trail of blood splatter led to the left. Patients were kept in the opposite wing both above ground and below. It was the ones beneath that I was most concerned about, so I was relieved that it seemed that at least Ali had left them alone.

But the bloody bootprints heading towards the lift suggested that someone else must have gone into the subterranean cells. Fuck, fuck, fuck.

If she had backup and they'd gone below, that meant that Ali was on clean-up, or assassination, detail. The fact that the blood continued down the corridor suggested that she'd been given a scent to track. It became obvious that she hadn't stopped to randomly bust open doors; however, someone *had* opened a door at the end of the corridor, no doubt to see what was going on.

Ali was the last thing the woman saw before her face was torn off.

Ophelia's voice was at the choked-sob phase now. "My God, Xandra. Why would she do this?"

I thought of my father, and the note she'd left. No one could make her rip someone's face off. There were ways to kill that caused less suffering.

"Because someone let her." Ali was childlike, and with that came the ability to be carelessly cruel. Her mind, however, was not always her own, and it seemed that whoever had made her had fixed it so that she could be easily nudged into killer mode.

Bertie, you naughty, naughty bastard. I could try to talk myself out of it, but those instincts I was supposed to trust were screaming that it was him. Why he'd done it didn't matter. There was nothing he could say that would excuse this, or my father. Or Vex. Or Dede. Or Ophelia and Rye. Me. And countless others who had suffered because of him.

"Fee!" cried a voice behind us.

We both whirled around. There, at the end of the corridor, not far from the dead guards, stood two large male halfies. Between them they held a halfie girl who was obviously medicated. She had coral-coloured hair and wide eyes. She looked terrified, poor thing. I didn't need to know her name to realise who she was. One look was all I needed to know that she was the one that had been repeatedly raped by goblins. She had finally found sanctuary, and now this. How could she ever feel safe again?

"Don't hurt her!" Fee moved forward, but stopped abruptly when one of the men pulled a needle out of his pocket. He used his teeth to pull off the cap before jabbing the sharp into the girl's neck.

"No!" screamed my sister, running forward. The men threw the girl towards her, and then ran for the exit.

I let them go – it was not like I would ever forget their faces or their scent. And I knew who they worked for. Right now, that little girl was more important.

"She's alive," Fee said when I reached them.

"Any idea what he gave her?"

She shook her head as she knelt beside the halfie, cradling her bright coral head.

"Right." I glanced down the corridor one way and then the other. When a door behind me opened, I pulled my dagger from my corset and whirled around, ready to fight.

It was one of my mother's half-bloods. Her eyes widened at the sight of me, but even I wasn't scary enough to keep her from Fee and the girl.

"Get her inside," I ordered. "Lock the door. Help is coming."

"She's been injected with something," Fee explained, handing over the unconscious girl. "Take care of her, Gladys."

The halfie nodded. She was pale and frightened, but she was in control. Good. She took the girl into the room with her. The bolt slid into place with a thunk.

Above us, something crashed hard into the floor. The sound of shattering glass and voices raised in panic followed.

And then a roar. It was Ali.

My goblin responded to that roar. Saliva flooded the back of my mouth and my gums began to ache. I ran faster towards the set of stairs partially concealed by the wall at the end of the corridor. Ophelia was close behind me.

As I climbed, more and more of the upstairs hall came into view. One of the doors had been ripped clean off frame and hinges, and lay splintered on the carpet. A swipe of blood marred the wall outside.

"That's Rye's room," Ophelia said. I could hear the fear in her voice. She had feelings for Rye, and she'd already lost one lover because of this nonsense. Although that one had been a spy for Church. If he'd been a better spy, perhaps Bedlam would have been raided long before this, but he'd taken the location to his grave.

Had my mother given Bedlam up? God, she couldn't be that stupid, could she?

It didn't matter. A door down the corridor flew out and smashed against the opposite wall. A tangle of fur and limbs, snarling and bleeding, tumbled out, followed by a number of halfies and humans wielding weapons or wounded. Four halfies were propped up against the wall closest to us. One had a broken arm, one a broken jaw. The third was bleeding badly from the shoulder and the fourth ... the fourth was dead.

The snarling fur monster was Rye and Ali. Both were in wolf form. No wonder Church had wanted Rye to poke and prod at. To take samples from. He could shift just like Vex's son. So many "special" half-bloods running around, and most of us knew nothing about them because they'd been scooped up to be studied and abused.

I smelled Rye's blood, hot and rich – that earthy scent that was uniquely wolf. It was a good thing he could shift. She probably would have killed him by now. I didn't know what they'd done to him in that lab, but he fought like an animal, and that worked to his advantage.

"Rye!" Ophelia's voice cracked as she rushed forward. I stopped her with my arm. Her eyes were wild with fear. There would be no denying her feelings for Rye after this. It was plain to see how much she loved him.

That was reason enough for me to throw myself into the fray.

"Don't be stupid. When I toss him out, I want you to get him as far away from her as possible, understand? Get him to Vex." I had no way of knowing if Vex had received my message or not, and it was too late to call William. I ought to have been smarter than this. Storming Bedlam would probably be the end of me.

Or not, I thought, as I slid my lonsdaelite dagger from its sheath in my leather corset and dived into the middle of the fight. A halfie punched me in the jaw – he'd been aiming for Ali. Good thing he got me instead, because she would have snapped his fist off at the wrist.

I managed to insert myself between Rye and Ali, earning a rake of claws across my back. I hissed, but didn't stop. I planted my foot against Rye's furry belly as he reared up, and pushed him backwards, towards Ophelia. He was wounded and bleeding – one ear was badly torn, and he favoured his front right leg. With treatment and blood he would be fine.

And it was only because of the halfies and humans who fought with him. There were four more dead in the room they'd just busted out of.

With Rye suddenly gone, Ali stopped to take stock of the situation. I took that opportunity to shove the dagger between her ribs. *Fuck!* I missed her heart.

She shifted before me, despite the injury I'd inflicted and those handed out by Rye. Like something liquid, she turned into the form that looked the most like me. Her hair was wild – like blood-soaked candy floss – and she wore the blood of others on her skin. She was completely naked, and I could see the muscles rippling beneath her velvet-textured flesh.

My blade was still in her as she changed. I tightened my grip and yanked it free before she could. Then I backed up – out of arm's reach.

She looked down at the blood running down her side. "That wasn't nice," she said, her voice a mix of child sing-song and goblin growl that made my spine shudder.

"Just a little poke," I said. "You've done worse to the people here."

She looked around, wound apparently forgotten. The bleeding was already starting to slow down. "They got in my way. I wouldn't have hurt them if they'd just given me what I came for."

"Rye," I supplied. Of course, he knew too much about the

labs. "You came for him." Out of the corner of my eye I saw Ophelia leading a still furry Rye down the stairs. At least she'd listened to me. She must really care about him, because she loved a good thrashing almost as much as I did.

Ali frowned. "Yes. He has to die. I don't know why." A wide grin spread across her blood-splattered face. "That rhymes!"

Madder than a bag of cats. "He doesn't have to die at all, Ali. You don't have to kill."

"Yeah, I do," she replied, absently scratching her head. Had no one taught her to brush her damn hair? It was like a bird's nest. "I'm sorry about your father, though. I didn't want to kill him, but I had to. My master was very upset when he found out I hadn't done it properly. He had to get someone else to finish it. I got whipped for the mistake."

Great big eyes lifted to meet my gaze. "I don't want to get whipped again, Xandra."

"The Prince of Wales, that's your master, yes? Bertie?"

Ali frowned, and glanced around distractedly. "Where'd he go? The wolf man? Where is he? I have to kill him. It will stop when I kill him."

"What will stop?" I asked, trying to draw her back to me, to buy Fee more time. I grabbed at Ali's arm, but she shrugged me off.

"The pain," she snarled. "He'll make it stop if I do what he wants."

Well, fuck. This was not good. I thought of the halvies in the underside cells at Bedlam who had all manners of horrors done to them. Things removed, things implanted, terrible torture in the name of science. Had they implanted something in Ali? Some kind of sensors or receivers?

When she moved towards the stairs, one of the halfies broke

a heavy oak chair over her back. Ali stumbled, but soon regained her footing. She had him by the throat in the space of a blink. Arterial spray decorated the walls and ceiling as she bit, ripped and spat globs of meat at the others, who cried out and drew back.

She tossed the halfie to the floor. I watched the light snap out in his eyes. Dead, just like that.

Ali moved again, zipping down the corridor. I bolted after her, catching her in a tackle at the top of the stairs that took both of us arse over appetite down the entire narrow flight.

Falling down stairs is never a treat, especially not when you're trying to keep someone from killing you. Ali snarled and snapped at me as we hit every bloody sharp edge. I was going to be black and blue for a bit later on.

If I lived that long, that was.

At the bottom, I rolled to my feet at the same time she did. We came up in exactly the same stance, except I had my dagger – somehow I'd managed not to drop it – and she had a wickedly clawed hand. She could scoop out my intestines like stew from a pot with those claws.

"I'm not here for you, Xandra. Get out of my way."

I shook my head. "Can't let you kill him, Ali. He's a friend, and he's done nothing wrong."

"He escaped from the lab. He's an anomaly, and he ... " Her gaze met mine, her eyes widening. "He's important to you. That's why I'm supposed to kill him, because he knows too much, and because it would hurt you."

"Do you want to hurt me?"

"No." She rubbed the heel of her hand against her forehead, just like I did when a headache threatened. "I don't, but ... Arggggh!"

She struck her fists against her head as she growled and roared. Someone was jacking up the insanity. Brilliant.

Her eyes glittered when they met mine. A snarl curled her lip, wet with saliva. Whatever had just happened to her, it had put the monster back in control. "Xandra, you need to back off."

I placed myself between her and the end of the corridor – the exit. She was my responsibility whether I wanted it or not. My daughter. I was the only one who stood a chance of taking her down, though I doubted appealing to the little girl in her would work at this moment. "I'm not going to do that, Ali."

Suddenly, she grinned, all fang and spit and crazy fucking eyes. "Good."

She launched herself at me. I barely had time to lift my arm in defence as she took me to the floor. Her fangs bit deep into my forearm, sinking through muscle all the way to bone. This was too much déjà vu. A ragged sound caught between a scream and a growl tore from my throat. Fuck, but that hurt!

I brought up the dagger with my other hand and stabbed her in the shoulder. When she didn't release my arm, I stabbed her again. That was enough to make her break free with a scream. Her claws raked my face as she reared up. I barely managed to pull the blade free.

My cheek burned. I could feel the blood running from the wound, smell it. She'd just missed my eye. She slashed again, this time across my chest, slicing through the boning of my brocade corset like the metal strips were butter, easily shredding the fabric and flesh beneath. I roared in pain and rage. I had to get it together before she killed me. And she would kill me.

It's an odd thing realising you are not the big bad whatever-you-thought-you-were. That there was someone bigger and badder. It was frightening and oddly relieving at the same time. Like I wasn't such a monster.

But I was getting my arse kicked by one. She struck again, and I managed to narrowly avoid those claws ripping into my throat.

With my blood running everywhere, I lifted my arm and shoved the blade up. She pivoted at the last second, so I got her in the ribs again and not the gut. Even creatures like us went down from a stomach wound.

Ali was full-on hatters now. Was it the scent of my blood, or the thrill of the kill? Maybe both. Her face was covered in both dried and fresh blood as she grinned down at me like some sort of grotesque clown.

At least I knew that my blood didn't seem to have much effect on her.

"I'm going back for Vex when I'm done with you," she cackled. "Maybe I'll pretend to be you and fuck him first. Then I'll go visit William, your precious prince. Maybe I'll fuck him too. He'd like to fuck you, you know that, right?"

Where had this come from? One minute she's blubbering about not wanting to kill me and then she spouts this knobbed-up stuff. It didn't matter what Bertie had done to her – she was mental. Completely insane, and there was nothing I could do to save her.

That made everything terribly clear to me at that moment. She wasn't going to go easy on me. The fact that I was her mother meant nothing to her now. She had every intention of killing me, and yet I thought of her as someone to pity. To help, rather than fear. My child. I needed to start fearing, and I needed to do it now, before she ended me.

And before she could hurt William or Vex.

"You almost killed the man I love," I told her.

She cocked her head to one side. "I'll do better next time."

I muttered a silent thanks to whatever was responsible for people making threats at exactly the right moment. It always happened in films and on the box. The villain said just the right thing to send the hero over the edge and come back fighting.

Despite a dearth of witty one-liners, I was the hero in this particular drama. And I was not about to let it become a tragedy.

What I was going to do, I realised as my heart began to thump harder, was fight. I just needed that anger and desperation . . .

Ali was more surprised than I was when I started to change. After all, at this point I had become accustomed to feeling the bones in my face shift around and my fangs come out.

I focused on her threat. Focused on the people I loved and the people I had already lost. I would not lose any more – and I would not allow them to lose me. I couldn't.

My arms tingled. I glanced down and through the blood saw that my skin looked strange. That was because I'd grown fur – short velvety stuff like Ali's. And my hands ached as they lengthened and twisted into claws – again like Ali's.

What the sweet ruddy fuck was going on? And what difference did it make? I could *shift*.

I growled and lurched upright catching her by the shoulder. I dug my fangs in deep, rejoicing as she screamed. If I bit really hard, could I snap the bones there? I wagered I could.

She hit me in the side of the head and I let go, but not before I let my teeth rip a bit. She screamed again and slashed at me with her claws. She caught me on the left side as I pivoted away.

She was stronger than me – larger now too. I didn't know how to make myself like her. I couldn't. All I could do was fight.

So I fought. I don't know how much time passed. I only know that the carpet in the corridor was soaked with our blood as we rolled around like fighting cats. We were both tiring, but me faster than her. I'd landed a few good strikes, but she'd cut me to ribbons. I could feel bits of my skin flapping when I moved, and my lack of agility bespoke torn tendons and serrated muscle.

I was cold. Afraid. Tired.

This was it. This was how I was going to go out – defeated and bloody in Bedlam. It was the sort of thing I used to have nightmares about. Now, it seemed absurd that I should die here, of all places. But then here was where it all began, where Dede opened my eyes. It seemed somehow appropriate that I end here.

I swung the dagger at Ali. She knocked it out of my numb fingers. How long had we been going at this? The blade fell with a thud out of my reach. My vision was blurring and I was so very weak. Everything was covered with a haze of red.

She punched me hard in the face. I felt the bones crunch and splinter, but I didn't make a noise as I fell back against the carpet. I couldn't.

Then I heard a beautiful sound. It was a wolf howl – Vex's howl – followed by William's growl. My cavalry had arrived.

I tried to smile, but my face refused to work. Ali paused in her persistent bashing of me to listen. Slowly she staggered to her feet. At least I'd tired her a bit.

"Now you're for it, bitch," I crowed, but it came out as incoherent gargling moans. There was too much blood in the back of my throat, and my jaw was broken on both sides.

Through the narrow slits of my eyes and that fine haze of red, I saw Vex in wolf form tear through the air at Ali. She turned and ran into the nearest room. She was still pretty fast, the bitch. I thought Vex had given chase until I saw his huge paws in front of me. It must have been William who'd gone after Ali. I heard the crash of glass and a loud popping noise that could only mean that she had gone through a window and taken the bars on the outside of it right out of their moorings.

She was so strong. Why couldn't I be that strong?

"Xandra?"

My eyes fluttered open. Vex had shifted, and was crouched over me in all his naked glory. Too bad I couldn't move my head – I would have liked a better look.

He looked so sad, so scared. I opened my mouth to say something smart-arse, but the only thing that came out was blood.

My gaze locked with his, and that was when I knew I was dying.

"Don't leave me," he whispered.

I heard voices around us, people running and shouting. I wanted to tell him I had no intention of going anywhere, that it was going to take more than a fucked-up hatters shifter-bitch to kill me, but I couldn't make a sound. When he took my hand, I couldn't even squeeze his fingers.

I gurgled. *I love you.*

Then, nothing.

CHAPTER 18

IF YOU ARE NOT AFRAID OF DYING, THERE IS NOTHING YOU CANNOT ACHIEVE

I woke up. That in itself was something of a surprise. Bit of a let-down, really. Dead would have meant I didn't have to worry about shit any more. Unfortunately, not-dead reminded me that it seemed the Prince of Wales was out to get me, and that I hurt like hell – everywhere.

I expected to find myself in hospital, but I wasn't. I was in Vex's bed, and it felt as though every inch of me was bandaged and wrapped like a bloody mummy.

A tall, skinny metal pole stood beside the bed. Attached to it were several bags of fluids – at least one of which appeared to be blood – that dripped through tubes and into needles that were taped to my arm where they pierced my veins.

I itched – healing wounds were always a bitch – but my hands were bandaged and I couldn't scratch. Could I just ignore it?

A soft growl turned my head. There, in a wingback chair pulled up close to the bed, slept Vex. His hair was a mess, there were violet smudges beneath his eyes and his jaw sported more than a day's worth of stubble. This wasn't the first time I'd woken up expecting to be dead only to find him near me.

How long had I been unconscious?

Long enough to really have to pee. Damnation.

"Vex?" It came out a strangled whisper. Had Ali severed my vocal cords? My face ached something horrible, and it was bandaged too. I cleared my throat – which, oddly enough, did not hurt. "Vex!"

He jerked upright. The startled expression on his face would have been comical if it hadn't immediately turned to such joyful relief that tears filled my eyes. I was not going to cry. If I started, I wouldn't stop for a good long time, and I wasn't going to go there.

My mind and soul would just have to be content with being alive, because all those might-have-beens hadn't happened and I had no time to entertain them.

"Xandra." Oh hell, his eyes were wet too. "Sweetheart . . . " Whatever else he planned to say never got said. Instead, he gently cupped my face with his hands and kissed me. Then we were still for a moment, his forehead resting against mine. That didn't hurt either, though the kiss had made my jaw twinge. I didn't care.

"I'll get William," he whispered, pulling back.

"I need to pee."

He stared at me for a moment, and then grinned. I guess having to pee was a good thing. "Can you move?" he asked.

I tried. "I can, but it's a bit dodgy with these bandages. Who the hell wrapped me like this?"

He arched a brow. "I did."

"Oh." I tried to smile. "Then I reckon you can get me out of them right quick, yeah?"

Turns out that was a great fat no. He did, however, pick me up and carry me to the loo. Those metal poles had to squeak along with us. I had to go so bad I didn't even care that he waited not far away, afraid to let me completely out of his sight.

When I was done, relieved and tidy, Vex carried me back to the bed and began unwrapping me. He also rang William, and sent a pack member off to fetch food and water for me.

Within moments William arrived – he must have been in the house, or just under it. Ophelia, Avery and Val showed up a few moments later, one by one. Val had a bouquet of bright, fragrant flowers.

"From Penny," he said, putting the vase on the night stand.

"She's so sweet," I murmured. "Be a love and scratch my nose, will you?" Vex hadn't taken the bandages off my hands yet. In fact, he'd only unwrapped one leg, and was inspecting it. He held the limb on his lap as he gently wiped away the dried blood with a warm wet cloth.

William then smeared the few remaining welts and cuts with a salve that smelled of blood and honey, and applied a light bandage over each area. I could wiggle my toes freely, and it felt lovely.

Watching the two of them fuss over me was comforting and touching. I knew they were responsible for me being alive. Maybe they had called a doctor, but I doubted it. They knew what I needed and had done everything in their combined power to make certain I got it.

"Thank you," I whispered. "All of you."

Ophelia didn't tear up, but Avery did. Of course Avery did. She felt so much and didn't care who saw. I would have hugged her if I hadn't had a werewolf and a goblin standing between us.

"Fill me in," I commanded of the visitors, so they wouldn't just stand about uncomfortably weepy as I was unwrapped like a bizarre Christmas package. "How long have I been asleep, and what has happened in the interim? What about Ali?"

My siblings exchanged glances. Vex and William continued unwrapping and inspecting.

"Right . . ." Ophelia stepped forward. "Guess I'll start, then. Rye is safe. He had a few deep cuts, and a broken collarbone, but he's all right. He's here, and wants to see you."

I was glad. To be honest, I expected Rye to be a little odd with me. I'd saved him from that lab, and now I'd saved him again – with Ophelia, of course. He already viewed me differently – his not wanting me to know about his drug addiction proved that he was afraid I'd see him as weak. I didn't want that deference, but I didn't want it to turn to resentment either.

"And Bedlam?" I asked.

Fee's expression tightened. "Most of the patients are fine, the dead have been buried and the survivors have scattered."

"Most?"

For a second I thought I saw the sheen of tears on her lashes, but then it was gone. "Livia is in quarantine at Prince Albert."

Livia. Was she the one that was raped by goblins? "Quarantine? What for?"

It was Vex who answered. "She was injected with a particularly virulent strain of the plague."

"No." God, I hoped this was just some sick joke.

Fee shook her head. "It's true. She's holding steady. They also injected Georgiana."

It took me a moment to place her as well. I'd only seen them once – the night Dede took me on a tour of Bedlam. "The little yellow-haired one with the metal in her head?"

My sister nodded. "She has great healing capabilities, and the plague seems to have ... changed her."

I arched a brow. "How?"

"Well, the metal in her head came out."

Fang me. "On its own? Through her skull?"

Another nod. "She's also become stronger."

My family and friends were all looking at each other as though they weren't certain what to tell me.

"Somebody bloody well explain what's going on!"

"She's mutated!" Fee blurted. "She's a full-blood."

I gaped at each of them. "How is that possible?"

"This new plague is particularly aggressive," Val told me. "So far it's killed two humans, but this halfie and another human case have resulted in a transformation. The former human is now a half-blood."

"What else aren't you telling me?" There was unease in all their features.

"Oh, for pity's sake!" Avery looked at all of them as though they were recalcitrant children. "The plague experts at Prince Albert seem to think the new strain was derived from your blood – at least part of it was. Or something."

I stared at her. "Or something?"

"Look, I don't understand all that science stuff! They made it from you, and used it along with your other bits – and Vex's son – to make Ali."

I whipped my gaze back to Vex. He watched me with an

expression I couldn't quite decipher. "Of course I knew," he said. "I had suspicions when she turned into him, but I saw bits of him in her later. The way she could shift." He shrugged.

"I wanted to be certain before I mentioned it," I whispered. It was a lame excuse, but honest.

Vex nodded. "I know."

I swallowed. I didn't think he was pissed off at me, but how could he not be? I just hadn't wanted him to get hurt. Why hadn't he confronted me with his suspicions?

Back to the bigger problem. "So, instead of trying to raise birth rates, these labs are trying to what? Make aristocrats?"

"It seems so," Val replied. "Killing two out of three humans is a brilliant way to level the playing field."

No shit.

"The League issued a statement demanding justice for the human victims," Fee interjected. "They've got some of the families of the victims involved as well. The fact that there were halfies killed during the Bedlam attack has made things even more tense."

So much for the Insurrectionists, but they weren't the real threat. It was the Human League who wanted blood. How much more would have to be spilled before they realised we were all being played like puppets? "What of Juliet?"

Fee glanced away. "She retired to the country. We thought it for the best given the situation. She doesn't have many friends in London right now."

Val filled in the rest. "What she does have is an alibi for the night Father was killed, and it was obvious she knew nothing about it. She was manipulated into trusting the wrong person, who then used her to get into Bedlam so he could recover two of his lost subjects."

I glanced at Fee, who was staring at the floor. I'd hug her if I was able. I reckoned Juliet's removal to the country meant she didn't want to see me, but that was fine. What would I say? "Sorry your fuck-buddy did you over, but what did you expect?"

"What of Ber— her friend?"

Vex looked up from unwrapping my right hand. "It's all right, love. Ophelia told us who's behind it all. Bertie's carrying on as usual and we're letting him, for now."

I nodded, not the least bit surprised. He'd fooled everyone for years; he wasn't going to slip up now. "No evidence?"

"Not a scrap." He glanced over his shoulder at Val. "Not yet."

"I managed to obtain a special warrant," my brother said. "Special Branch is poised to search all of his properties tomorrow evening while he's meeting with his mother."

"Victoria? Does she know?"

Val nodded. "I had to go to her for the warrant."

Good lord, my brother had bollocks the size of Big Ben. "How did she react?"

"My niece is leech queen." William spoke in that raspy voice of his as he tended my lingering wounds. "Arrogant. But stupid she is not. Suspected already. Feared it."

"It can't be fun to discover your child has betrayed you."

"We don't know the extent of Bertie's plan," Vex reminded me. "We need to move and gather actual evidence so that we can stop whatever he has in mind."

My brother agreed. "The horror shows, the laboratories and experiments. The abductions, deaths . . . we need to link him with those. Hard. Thanks to Ophelia's recognition of his voice, we're closer, though. Rye has given helpful evidence as well. We'll get him for the labs."

"And the attempt on his mother's life," I added.

"He probably killed Churchill too." Avery spoke up.

It was just for the span of a heartbeat, but I froze. Vex and William, however, continued.

"Likely, yes," my prince said with a sage nod. "Xandra, lady, most good it is to see you healing. Whole."

That one amber eye looked at me with more pride and love than my father ever had. I didn't care what sort of ointment he had on his furry hands; I wrapped my fingers – from the one unwrapped hand – around his and squeezed. "You and Vex are to thank for that."

"And you," Vex added, "for having the forethought to ring me first." He didn't look at me, but I didn't take it as an insult. I knew how seeing me like that had affected him, because I had felt the same way when Ali mauled him.

"I didn't want to be impulsive and reckless," I told him softly, with just a hint of a smile. And then, "Ali. Did she get away?"

William growled. "Yes."

Val cleared his throat – defensively, I thought. "She broke the neck of one copper and disembowelled another who didn't get out of her way fast enough."

"Have weapons, do you not?" William demanded, pausing to look over his shoulder. "Silver. Poison. Not used."

"I fired on her." My brother's face was dark. I had to hand it to him for not backing down from William. "How did she manage to escape *you*?"

A long, furry finger jabbed in my direction. "My queen needed blood."

"Ah, that's bloody convenient then, isn't it?"

"Enough!" Vex's snarl reverberated in the room. He looked from William to my brother. "I've had just about enough of the two of you. You both did what you thought was right, now shut the fuck up. Xandra is alive and that's what matters."

"The wolf is right." William bowed his head to me. "Your prince apologises."

Smiling, I patted his furry head. "I love you," I told him. I looked at my siblings. "I love you all." Then, to Vex, "And you . . . I don't ever want to open my eyes and not see you." That was as personal as I was going to get with an audience. The gold shimmer in his eyes made my chest tight.

Ophelia grinned at me. Avery burst into tears and turned to Val, who blinked profusely as he hugged her back.

A knock on the door interrupted the overwhelming emotion filling the room.

"What?" Vex demanded with an uncharacteristic scowl.

The door opened, and Argyle poked his head in. "Begging your pardon, Lord Alpha, but Her Majesty Queen Victoria is here." He sounded rather . . . shocked.

Vex and I stared at each other. This was unexpected.

"Send her up," Vex told him.

"Here, sir?" I swear Argyle's voice cracked a bit.

"Aye. I'm busy, so she can either come here or wait in my study, whichever she prefers." He went back to my bandages.

Argyle looked as though he might choke, but he disappeared and the door clicked shut.

"What do you suppose she wants?" I asked.

"Attention," William answered with a snort.

Vex slowly peeled away a piece of gauze that had become stuck to my skin by blood. "We'll find out soon enough, no doubt."

He was right. A few minutes later, the door opened, and Victoria walked in, no fanfare, no announcement.

Outside of the palace she seemed smaller. She really was

tiny as a sprite, but what she lacked in size she made up for in sheer presence; the room seemed to shrink around her. She wore black, complete with hat and veil, which she pushed back to reveal her face.

"Good evening," she said.

My siblings bowed and curtsied. Vex bowed his head. The only one who spoke was William. "Child," he said.

Victoria's cheeks flushed. Good lord, she actually curtsied to him. What the hell was that all about?

Oh, right. Her world was about to get all knobbed up too, wasn't it? Her son had tried to kill her, presumably so he could take that throne he had claimed to want no part of. And then what? He was going to unleash another plague?

I opened my mouth to say something, but ... I had nothing.

"Xandra, I am most happy to see you recovering from your terrible ordeal." Victoria sounded sincere. "I want you to know that every able body in service to the Crown is out searching for the creature who did this to you."

"Thanks." A little lame, but it would have to do. "And thank you for coming to call."

"Yes, well ... " She shrugged her shoulders. "I thought it for the best I come to you, given the circumstances. I received this earlier today." From her reticule she withdrew a small black box; she came forward to offer it to me.

"What is it?" I asked.

"A rather gruesome gift," she replied. "One that I believe means as much for you as for myself."

Intrigued, I opened the box. It was the hinged kind, used by high-end jewellery shops. It opened to reveal a bed of red velvet, in the middle of which was a severed finger wearing a signet ring.

It was my father's.

CHAPTER 19

BETRAYAL CAN ONLY HAPPEN IF YOU LOVE

To her credit, Avery did not scream or burst into tears. In fact, her face took on a hard set, as though the bones beneath had turned to stone.

"Why would someone send Vardan's finger to you?" she asked.

Victoria glanced at her, then back to me. "Because he wants me to know that he killed your father, and his own."

"Who?" I asked. Was it too cruel of me to make her say it?

The tiny queen drew herself up straight. How did a woman not even five feet tall manage to look so imposing? "The jeweller the box came from was one of Albert's – one of my favourites. Only a very few people know that."

"Is Bertie one of them?" I asked.

Victoria nodded, clasping her gloved hands in front of her. "Yes. I suspect he sent a similar trophy to your mother in the country." When I arched a brow, the hint of a smile curved her lips, but it wasn't one of pleasure. "Quite clever of her to hide her little uprising in a madhouse. You know, the previous goblin queen was much more forthcoming with information."

She'd played this card with me before – trying to rattle me with talk of a previous queen. "There have been other queens of England before too, ma'am. Do they have anything to do with the fact that your heir is a psychopath? You know, when they lock him up, the first thing they'll ask him about is his relationship with his mother."

Vex sighed. Or perhaps it was a growl – a long, low growl. "Am I surrounded by children?" he demanded, his brogue heavy with annoyance. "There are more important things afoot than pride and petty disagreements. With Juliet gone and the Bedlamites leaderless, the League is the only advocate the humans of England have, and they don't want equality, they want to *destroy* us. Our own kind conspire to unleash a plague that will kill countless humans and mutate others, not to mention the effect it will have on half-bloods."

He rose to his feet and looked around. "Half-bloods will not be safe if Bertie gets his way. Nor will wolves, or goblins. No one but those who follow him will be protected. Those who don't will be killed like Vardan, or Prince Albert." The look he shot Victoria was sympathetic, and I had to admit I loved him for it. It was exactly the sort of look one should give a woman whose son murdered her husband before plotting her downfall.

All these years Bertie had been plotting. Slowly and patiently. Had he planned to kill Albert, or had the opportunity fallen into his lap? He wanted to rule, and he wanted to crush the humans. He wouldn't be a king, he'd be a dictator.

Who else did he have in his pocket?

"Why?" It was Ophelia who asked the simple question, and

she directed it at Victoria. The tiny vampire didn't pretend not to understand.

"Years ago – before the uprising – Albert and I discussed the notion of trying to improve the relationship between aristocrats and humans. We knew we weren't so very different, especially when our kinds could interbreed. My son was vehemently opposed to the idea. He said we'd muddy the bloodline."

She shot me a droll look. "There's muddying, dear girl, and then there's breeding yourselves out of existence. We wanted to find a . . . balance. It was my Albert who thought of testing humans for the plague, and having teams of doctors and scientists work on how to better all the peoples of the empire, not just the entitled few. We tested ourselves; we even tried to test our children. Bertie refused. He said our line had already been polluted enough by my goblin uncle."

"Forgot our kind began as human," William said. He started removing the bandages from my face. Thankfully, I was wearing a robe so my bits weren't on display, but that meant having to keep my torso wrapped up for a bit longer until Vex and I were alone.

"Yes, well . . ." Victoria raised her chin. "I must take my share of responsibility for the boy. If it is determined that he is indeed behind all of these horrendous crimes, he must pay for them. Publicly so."

I raised a brow. "What are you going to do, behead him?" As far as I knew, that had been outlawed over a century ago.

Victoria stared at me. "If necessary."

I stared back. She would do that? To her own son? No. She wasn't that heartless. I could see how she clenched her jaw to keep her composure, how she blinked and looked away.

"I'm guessing if it was the prince who sent the finger, he won't be meeting you tomorrow evening?" Val asked.

"Oh no," Her Nibs replied. "He'll come. He's been working for this confrontation for a long time. Perhaps he'll have his little monster kill me and assume my appearance. I rather expect he'll try to lay all the blame on me and have me arrested for his crimes so he can enjoy seeing me brought low."

"He won't have to work too hard to sway opinion that way." Avery crossed her arms over her chest. "There was a rather nasty piece in *The Times* this morning that suggested you were behind the laboratories. They even insinuated that you should be investigated in several missing-person cases."

"Eating children now, am I?" Victoria didn't look too put out. I suppose almost two centuries on the throne would give you that sort of tough skin.

"A time there was when it was an honour to have the leech queen sup on your eldest."

I turned to William. "Really?"

He nodded, and cast a glance at his niece. "Were it Chesterfield or Marlborough?"

"Chesterfield," Victoria confirmed. "Chief Inspector Vardan, I would suggest you go ahead with your plans for tomorrow evening and leave my son to me."

"No," I said, even though it was the perfect and safest route for all of us.

No one looked more surprised by my announcement than Victoria. Vex glared at me as though he might tie me to the bedpost to keep me from inviting myself along.

"You're going to have backup," I informed her. "Bertie's going to bring friends with him. So are you. This affects all of us; it's not just about you any more." I gave her a hint of a smile as I threw what she had once said to me back at her.

The Queen of England gaped at me. Quite literally. "Are you *concerned* for my safety?"

"I know – it boggles the mind, right?" I squirmed under that piercing blue gaze. Fang me, it wasn't like I'd dropped to one knee and pledged my honour to her. "It's not safe, and you're not going to be alone. I'm going to be there with you."

"No you're fucking not." This came from Vex, the man who very rarely told me what to do. "I'm not letting you get back in the path of that thing. She almost killed you."

"She almost killed *you*," I reminded him. William had removed the rest of my visible bandages, and despite a layer of that salve, I felt unbelievably unburdened. "You plan on being there, don't you?"

A muscle in his cheek clenched.

I turned to Ophelia, who had been very quiet, probably because she was a known criminal. "You're coming too. Bring humans."

"What for?" she demanded. "Going to feed them to the freak, are you?"

I ignored that. "William, I want goblins there as well."

"Of course, lady."

"All the races together," I said, looking around at my friends, family and ... Victoria. "United against a common enemy. We'll keep the humans back to protect them. Val, you come armed to the teeth. If we drug Ali, we can bring her down."

I hated the idea of having to kill her, but there wasn't any other way. She'd been purposely made a monster, and Bertie had her under his control. I didn't see any way for her to walk away from this and be allowed to live.

I yawned and leaned back against the pillows. Vex shot me an assessing glance. "Look at you; you're not fit for fighting."

"I will be tomorrow," I promised, but it was all bravado. "We're going to train, remember?" That had gone by the wayside, hadn't it?

Ali had put me out for three days. Three fucking days. Who was I trying to fool? It was going to take every one of us to bring her down.

Wasn't it? I looked down at my hands. They looked as they always did, but when Ali and I had fought, I'd grown fur. Hadn't I? My mind was still a little cloudy. There had to be laudanum in the bags suspended above my head. I yawned again.

"We should let you sleep," Ophelia piped up. "The rest of us can hammer out the details." She began herding the others toward the door.

"Vex and William," I called out. "Could you stay, please? And Val?"

My brother turned. "Yeah, Xandy?"

I took the ring off our father's dead finger and tossed it to him. "This is yours now. Wear it tomorrow night and make certain everyone sees it."

Val looked at the ring for a moment before slipping it on his own finger. It was a good fit and the style suited him.

"Your Grace," I said, letting the gravity of that sink in. He clenched his hand into a fist, threw me a look bright with the promise of vengeance, and then left with Ophelia.

Avery put herself in the path of Victoria. "Beg your pardon, ma'am, but I'll accompany you back to the palace."

Victoria bestowed a rare smile upon her. "My dear girl, surely you do not believe I require *protection*, do you? I am a full-blood."

My sister pushed a strand of pink hair away from her face and met the Queen's gaze evenly. "Have you ever thrown a punch? Kicked someone in the face?"

The monarch's smile grew, with a hint of fang. "Not recently."

"Well you will have before this night is through. Come on, we've work to do. See ya later, Xandy."

And with that, they were gone, leaving me with the two most important men in my life.

"I don't want to fight about this," I told Vex.

"Nor do I," he replied.

"Good."

"But after this, we're getting married."

It was not the response I'd expected. "Married? We can't get married. You have to marry a were!"

"No I don't. I'm marrying you, and if you say no, I'll tie you to this fucking bed and you won't be going anywhere tomorrow night."

"You're coercing me into accepting your proposal?"

"You want to marry me as much as I want to marry you, and you know it, daft girl."

"I'm two and twenty years old! I'm not supposed to know what I want!" But a little voice in my head shouted at me to shut up.

He crouched beside the bed. I could see every line etched in his face. My favourites were the ones around his grey-blue eyes. He took my face in his hands. "I'm asking you to spend the rest of your life with me. Does that sound like something you'd like to do?"

"I think so."

He chuckled, and kissed me on the mouth. "That's a yes if I've ever heard one."

Sometimes it was frightening how well he knew me.

William bowed before us. "Congratulations, wolf, lady. Should your prince leave?"

"No," I said at the same time Vex said, "Yes." I made a face at him. "I need to talk to the both of you." I handed Vex the box with my father's finger in it. "Could you get rid of that, love?"

He put it in his pocket, then reclaimed his chair by the bed; William sat by my feet.

"Of all the people in my life, I trust the two of you most of all. When I fought with Ali the other night, something happened."

"She laid you open like a sandwich," Vex remarked.

I rolled my eyes. "Besides that. Look, the last few times I've gobbed out, it's been different."

"Gobbed out?" William's muzzle wrinkled like he'd bitten into something bad. "Is that what you call it?"

Deliver me from touchy, whiny men. "Had a visit from my inner goblin, or whatever. It was different. The first times my teeth were bigger and my face changed. I even got a bit of a muzzle."

Vex watched me, an odd expression on his face. He looked almost excited. "What happened last time?"

"I grew fur."

William barked. He actually barked. "The lady shifted."

"Started to," Vex amended. "She started to shift."

"You two look far too happy about this. Did you hear me say that I grew fucking fur? It was just like Ali's."

They looked at one another. "Just like hers?" Vex asked. "Are you certain?"

"As certain as I could be with my blood spraying all over the place, yeah. Why do you two look so ruddy smug?"

William turned to me. "If the lady can alter form, then perhaps future goblins might do the same – for longer times than now. No more looking like monsters."

It was like a punch to the solar plexus. This creature, who had terrified me so badly at one time, now inspired me to hug him. My heart broke for him.

"Shifting is primarily a were trait," Vex joined in. "I don't care what our children are, but they'll be shifters."

"We are not talking children yet," I informed him. "Not for a good long time."

He merely smiled. "I also suspect that Ali's ability to shift might be another trait she inherited from you."

"And others," I added. "Others that contributed to her gene pool were shifters." Such as his son.

"Yes, but your shifting ability was the dominant one."

Maybe it was all the drugs, but I still didn't get it. "I fail to see how fur colour and texture make any difference."

"Xandra, sweetheart – it means that maybe you have it in you to be like her. You're what she's copying when she gets all 'gobbed out', as you put it."

Right, it was definitely the drugs, because I felt like giggling. What he was suggesting was ludicrous, of course. Honestly, if I hadn't shifted to such an extent yet, what hope was there that I could?

But there was that little bit of me that held back whenever I felt the change come on – that part that flicked a switch before I lost complete control.

Maybe Ali did get it from me. Maybe all I needed to do was let myself go.

"It couldn't be that easy, could it?" That wasn't quite honest on my part, because there was nothing easy about it. Control wasn't something I liked to give up. That was why I was never particularly popular with boys, or had many girlfriends when I was younger. I was impulsive, but only on my own terms.

I was no fun.

Vex shrugged, but he looked the most hopeful I'd seen him look in a long time. "Nothing with you has ever been easy, sweetheart. But it may be worth a look."

I yawned again. "Right. What's the worst that could happen?"

CHAPTER 20

HEALING IS A MATTER OF TIME

After two hours of trying, I managed to fail spectacularly at this shifting business. I had one small success – the index finger on my right hand morphed into a claw just like one of Ali's – but it was a lone occurrence.

"It's the drugs," Vex allowed later. "You're still getting laudanum from the IVs."

"I'm not stoned," I replied, rather petulantly. Where was my big bad? My snarl? I was supposed to be the goblin queen, a nasty piece of work, a fighting machine.

Right then I was about as nasty as a mouldy old dishcloth. Nasty – but not in the right way.

"No, but you're not at one hundred per cent either. You've done enough for tonight."

"We're facing her tomorrow night, Vex."

"Aye, and you'll have several vampires, half-bloods, weres and goblins at your back. It doesn't all have to fall on you."

Was it completely twisted that I wanted it to fall on me? Ever since I'd jumped down this particular rabbit hole in my original search for Dede, I'd felt as though it had been all about me. Right. Now I knew it wasn't all about me – I was just a happy by-product. It was all about a boy and his mum, and that age-old chestnut about the heir itching to inherit. Victoria was obviously our longest-ruling monarch, and Bertie boy was the prince who'd waited almost two centuries to prove himself a man.

Still, he wasn't doing a very good job of it, was he? Making a monster. Killing my father. Poisoning his own father. Those all seemed to be the work of a coward, really. But then again, he'd hidden behind his mother's skirts for decades. Why show himself now if he didn't have to? Plus, if he was openly out there in his villainy, it would be that much more difficult to elicit sympathy and followers.

No, Bertie was setting himself up to be the saviour of his people, and he was going to make humans into a buffet and kill off as many as he could.

That realisation made me understand something else, something I'd thought before. "He's going to kill her."

Vex paused in unbuttoning his shirt. "Victoria? That's his plan, I wager."

I shook my head and enjoyed the view as he pulled the shirt off. He wasn't a heavily muscled man, but he wasn't lean and ropy either. He was sculpted without the bulk and sleek without being thin. Perfect, in a word.

"No, Ali. He's going to kill her when this is all done. I knew he'd have to do it, because he couldn't have her running about mucking things up. He can't risk losing control of her, so he's going to kill her to make himself seem the big hero. She shows up, kills his mum; he fights her off, kills her and gets a shiny new hat."

"And then he hangs all his crimes on his mother's tombstone and becomes a new hope for the aristocracy of Europe."

"He might even win a few human supporters with that."

"Until he rips their throats out. Or infects them with the plague." He unbuttoned his trousers. "You're staring."

"You're putting on a show, of course I'm staring." I smiled faintly. "Seems like it's been forever since I had the luxury of watching you undress."

Vex approached the bed, trousers tantalisingly low on his hips, just barely hanging on. "Let's get the rest of those bandages off you."

I was all too happy to oblige. Like the old gentleman that he was, he removed my robe and draped it over the footboard of his bed. Then he sat down beside me and went to work. When he was done, I was naked, my flesh marred by healing wounds, dried blood and the sticky salve William had used.

The salve had done wonders, as had food and blood directly digested. I had tender spots and bruised bits, but nothing open.

"Shower?" Vex asked.

"Yes please."

He offered me his hand and I took it, easing myself off the bed. My legs held surprisingly well. Maybe I'd be in better shape than I thought by tomorrow evening.

He called down to the servants' rooms and asked a maid to come up and change the bed. Then he carried me into the bathroom, and set me on a stool while he started the shower.

His tub was huge and the shower was no different. There was one attached to the tub, and then there was a separate shower off to the side that was easily big enough for four or five people. That was the one he ran for us.

"Expecting company?" I joked.

He grinned. "I like room to manoeuvre."

A little quiver twanged low in my belly. Oh dear. It felt like forever since we'd done that as well. I didn't know if he was serious about all that talk about marriage … No, who was I trying to fool? Of course I knew he was serious. He wouldn't have brought it up otherwise. There was no point questioning him or myself.

I wanted to be with Vex, and he wanted to be with me. End of discussion. The rest would happen as it happened.

"You've an odd expression on your face," he said, frowning. "Are you all right? Do you need a doctor?"

I lifted my chin. "Yes."

He started to leave the room. "I'll send Argyle."

"No! Vex, that's not what I meant." He stopped and turned towards me. I'd be damned if I wasn't stoned, maybe just a bit. The whole evening had a vaguely situation comedy feel to it. I pulled the IV needles from my arm. "I don't need a doctor. I meant that yes, I'll marry you."

He came back, knelt before me and wrapped his arms around me. I was naked and sticky and he didn't seem to care. I knew I didn't. "I love you," I told him. "So if you think you can put up with me for the next century or so, I'm all yours."

His lips came down on mine. Oh, it was better than the laudanum. Warmth spread through my limbs and swirled around in my stomach. That was how I knew I'd made the right decision the night I first went home with him. Neither one of us seemed to be able to help ourselves where the other was involved. Everything just happened so fast. Maybe that was how the right things were supposed to go, or maybe we'd break up in six months.

For once, I wasn't going to obsess over it. Coming that close to death made a girl take stock of things, and when I'd thought I was going to die, the last thing I'd thought of was Vex, and not because he was hovering over me, calling my name. It was because he was all that mattered.

That was the end of my romantic inner monologue. He carried me into the shower, and washed away all the blood and honey from my skin. He shampooed my hair, and massaged in conditioner that smelled like cloves. And then I washed him, and when he picked me up, I wrapped my legs around him, pressed my back against the warm stone wall and dug my fingers into his shoulders.

It wasn't the first time we'd had sex in the shower, or the first time we'd done it standing up, but it was the first time we'd done it after each of us had come so close to death. For all I knew, we were immortal, but that didn't mean that we couldn't be killed. Life meant so much more after you realised it could be easily taken away. And this wasn't the first time Vex had seen me teeter on the edge.

I clung to him, and let him and the water take everything else away. For a little while we were indeed immortal, and forever stretched out before us.

I'd think about dying tomorrow.

We were rudely awakened at eleven o'clock the following morning by a furious pounding on the door, followed by said door flying open.

It was Ophelia. I could see her perfectly despite the blackout curtains. Her blue hair was in a messy bun, and her eyes were wild. "They're saying the Human League bombed Clarence House!"

"What?" I sat up in bed, holding the sheets to my chest.

Vex made a noise that was half growl, half snort as he woke up. "Someone had better be dead."

"Most of the Prince of Wales's half-blood and human staff."

Fang me. That didn't sound like the HL. Usually they targeted places where they knew there would be few humans. "And the prince?"

"Was not at home."

"Convenient," I muttered.

Vex also sat up, blankets pooling around his waist. Fee didn't even look. Was she daft or respectful? "Bastard bombed his own house."

"You reckon?" My sister was calmer now. "Isn't that a wee bit extreme? He would have lost everything."

"Unless he cleared everything of value out first," I remarked. I'd seen it before. "It's an effective way of getting rid of evidence. The Yard probably won't find anything of any use in the rubble."

"Do you think he figured it out?" Fee leaned against the door frame. "Knew they were coming?" She didn't seem the least bit uncomfortable with the situation. Meanwhile, I wished she'd turn her back long enough for me to snag a robe.

"He's not stupid. It was ballsy of him to send Victoria my father's finger. He must know we're on to him." I couldn't get the image of Vardan's dead flesh out of my head. "Or at the very least realise we will be. And now he can pin this on the League and use it to incite animosity towards humans amongst the aristo population – and with the humans as well."

"His timing was impeccable," Fee agreed. "An hour later and Special Branch might have got in there. It's almost like he was watching for them."

"Or knew they were coming," Vex concluded, jaw tight. "Just like someone knew we were going to that lab where Ali attacked me. He's been one step ahead of us. I wonder if he knows his mother came here last night."

"You don't think we have a traitor, do you?" Really, that would just be the cherry on top of the last few months.

"Fee, be a love and go and rouse Argyle, if he's not up and around already. If anyone might have betrayed us, he'll find out who it was."

As soon as my sister left the room, I jumped out of bed, grabbed a robe and slipped it on. The thick velvet was so lovely on my skin. Vex also left the bed and pulled on his own dressing gown.

"How do you feel today?" he asked.

"Good. Almost one hundred per cent." I smiled and gave him a quick kiss. "You must have healed me."

He grinned in that lopsided manner I loved so much. "I have been told that my skills in the art of seduction are nothing short of therapeutic."

I laughed. "Because you want sex to be like a session with your head shrinker. No thank you."

Vex brushed a lock of hair away from my face. I'd slept with it down and no doubt looked a fright. "Now is probably a good time to tell you that you scared the hell out of me the other night. I thought I was going to lose you."

I wrapped my hand around his. "I thought you were too."

His other hand cupped the back of my neck and pulled me close so he could rest his forehead on mine. "I don't ever want to be that scared again."

"Neither do I, but I don't reckon that's the sort of promise either of us can make, is it?"

"No, I reckon not. Can you live with that?"

This was heavy conversation for having just woken up. I hadn't even had any coffee yet. I almost said that, but this wasn't the time for smart-arse remarks or pretending to be witty just to avoid the topic.

"I can." I didn't know if I could or not. Someday it might be too much, but for now it was a chance I was willing to take. Because maybe our lives would be quiet one day and we wouldn't have to worry about hidden dangers.

It was a good hope to cling to.

He lifted his head and kissed me on the top of mine. "Good."

Ophelia came back into the room. She looked worried – trepidatious.

"Vex . . ."

He turned away from me to face her. "Where's Argyle?"

My sister looked as though someone had kicked her in the chest. I immediately took a step towards her. "Fee? Are you all right?"

"No," she whispered. "It's just that . . . Stephen's gone."

"Gone where?" Vex demanded. He didn't understand yet, but I did. *Oh no.*

"I've no idea," Fee answered, "but his wardrobe has been cleaned out, and all his books are gone."

I could only watch helplessly as the full implication of that fell on Vex's shoulders. There was a second when his expression was one of complete and utter anguish – betrayal – and then it was gone, replaced by that steely look that meant he wanted to hit something.

"So, we had a traitor after all." He ran a hand over his stubbled jaw. "Ophelia, you're going to be my new secretary. Go tell MacGreggor about Argyle and see if his tracker is still online. Send word to every pack member that there is a price on Argyle's head. I want him alive."

She nodded. "Yes, sir. Oh, and thank you." Then she ducked out of the room.

"She won't be thanking me once the press get hold of this latest titbit and start calling for comments."

I wrapped my arms around his waist. "She'll be fine. How are you?"

He hugged me back. "Shocked, though I know I shouldn't be. Just because a person's family, it doesn't mean they can be trusted."

"That's true, but you did trust him, and he's betrayed you. That has to hurt."

"Of course it bloody hurts! It's like someone stuck an axe in my chest." Vex growled and ran a hand through his hair. "And I teased you for not trusting family. Fucking bastard. Christ only knows how long he's been feeding information about us to Bertie."

"He was here last night." I laughed even though this wasn't the least bit funny. "He announced Victoria himself. Bertie has to know she was here."

"No doubt that was why he chose to destroy his house. He knew Special Branch would strike soon." Vex shook his head. "He knows we plan to ambush him tonight. Fuck!"

He blamed himself; I knew it. I also knew there wasn't anything I could say to change that. Still ... "It's not your fault. Of course you trusted him. He's been with you for years." Even I had liked the back-stabbing bastard. "How did Bertie get to him?"

"The title," Vex replied without hesitation. "Stephen's my closest male relative in line for marquess."

The lengths people would go to just so they could ramble about in a huge house and stick a "lord" in front of their name. It was ridiculous, and not worth betraying family for.

"I'm surprised the little bastard hasn't already tried to kill you," I remarked bitterly.

Vex turned to me. The resignation in his gaze cut deeper than sorrow ever could have. "I think he did. He must have told Bertie about the raid on the laboratory. That's why it was easy to get in and not well staffed. They knew we were coming and had time to prepare. They counted on Ali killing me that night, I'm certain of it. Stephen was very . . . attentive. I wager the fact that Ophelia got me out of there and stayed with me drove him mad. Your sister – and you – probably saved me from being poisoned as well."

Oh, that was a kick. "He's the one who poisoned my father." It made sense. No one would think twice about Vex's trusted cousin skulking around. I was going to kill the little bastard. I'd rip him apart, piece by piece. Maybe suck the marrow from his traitorous little bones – and make him watch.

"Bertie won't make a move tonight. He's too smart for that. He's going to lie low. He may even leave the country. He can kill his mother just as easily from Paris, if he wants."

"He can set up new labs too." I shoved both hands into my hair and tugged at the roots to wake myself up. "With no evidence, he'll just walk. Think Argyle would turn on him?"

"At this point? No. Stephen's smart enough to know that what he's done is unforgivable. Plus, I'm fairly certain he'd realise that you'd kill him. He's afraid of goblins."

Then I'd make certain he got to spend a lot of up-close-and-personal time with a few of my favourites.

"We can't let them get away, Vex."

He went to the wardrobe and pulled out a pair of trousers. No going back to bed for us. "Special Branch doesn't have enough to arrest either of them without having to let them both go within a few hours. Stephen might have to spend time in a cell, but Bertie's solicitor will make certain he doesn't. We can kill them, but I doubt that will help our current situation other than giving us some satisfaction."

He was right. We could feed Bertie to the goblins, but the Human League would never know he was behind the labs. The vampires who worked for him would continue their work, or perhaps stop, but they would probably get clean away.

Vardan and Dede would have died for nothing. And Churchill would mock me in my dreams. I was not going to carry him around for the rest of my life.

I grabbed my rotary from my bag and began typing a message to Avery. She would still be at the palace. Then I reached for the handset of the telephone on the desk. "Do you have Victoria's number? I want to talk to her."

Vex glanced down at my hand. "Line's probably tapped."

I smiled. "I hope so."

CHAPTER 21

EVERYONE THINKS OF CHANGING THE WORLD

By evening, the VBC stations on the box were going to be positively wild with news leaked from Buckingham Palace. It might have happened sooner had Victoria not been such a stubborn cow.

She'd gone along with me on the telephone, as I had messaged Avery to tell her to, but the minute that connection broke, she rang me on a secure line and demanded to know if I had woken her up just to make sport of her, and that if I had, she'd wear my entrails to tea.

It took me two hours to convince her this was the right course. One hour on my rotary, and when the battery in that died, I hightailed myself to the palace and talked at her for another sixty minutes in person while the Human League picketed her gates. A young halfie – I'd heard from Ophelia – had been taken to hospital because of injuries inflicted by a gang of human ruffians. And then an HL-known gathering place had been trashed by a group of halfies in retaliation.

Our country was on the brink of something really terrible if we didn't act.

"Do you want another insurrection?" I asked Victoria. "Because you're going to get that and more if you don't do this."

She sniffed and looked down that imperious nose at me, even though I towered over her. "You do not know what it is you ask of me. No, I will not do it."

Fang me, but she was stubborn. Finally, I sighed and sank to my knees before her. Her eyes widened as I took both her hands. I think Avery might have even gasped.

"Don't get used to me being on my knees, Vic," I said. "Look, you need to listen. *Listen* to me. I am not asking anything of you that you and Albert did not discuss eighty years ago, before the Insurrection happened. If you won't do this for me, or your country, do it for him. Don't let his or my father's and my sister's death have been for nothing."

Her eyes filled with tears – they were pink. I'd never seen anyone cry blood tears before. "You are a terrible, manipulative, heartless girl to use him against me. Is it not enough that his own son was responsible for his death?"

"No," I told her. "It's not enough. You know it's not."

In the end, she relented, especially when I told her she was in charge of how far things went. Bit of a control freak, she was. I suppose I couldn't blame her for that, as it would be pot calling kettle, but she was old, and habits weren't so easily broken. She'd spent the last eighty years being afraid of and despising humans, and now, as they threw flaming bags of shit over her fence and called her names, I was asking her to show them fairness and extend an olive branch.

She would like to take said olive branch and roast one of the protesters on it. Honestly, I was desperate enough to take that as a step in the right direction.

I'd made arrangements with the morgue to be careful with today's delivery. Wouldn't do for a reporter or HL member to stumble upon the human corpse meant to feed my gobs, would it? But who would think to follow an unmarked van driven by a guy named Clive who smelled of ganja and Marmite?

The body was wrapped and in a wooden crate marked "Handle with Caution". It looked as though I was getting a delivery of china or crystal.

"Done this sort of thing before, have you, Clive?" I asked.

For a human he was very relaxed in my presence, a trait I attributed to the acrid smoke that clung to his person like an American starlet clinging to her youth.

"Nah. Just seemed like a good thing, right? Who's going to fret over a little box?"

It wasn't little – it stood almost as high as my waist. "How did you . . . get it in there?"

Clive smiled. "Come in fresh, right? Only been dead a couple of hours – rigor ain't set in. I folded her up just like origami. Course, she'll be stiffening up now, so you might have to break the crate to get her out. If not, just save it and I'll pick it up next time."

And with that – and a generous tip – he sauntered back to his van and drove away. I'd left his name at the Mayfair gates so he wouldn't have to go through all the security measures. I shouldn't have worried too much; he seemed morally content with our arrangement.

I took the crate down in the lift, and then down the stairs far below into the great hall of the plague den.

William met me, along with George and another male, who took the crate further into the hall to be opened and the meat shared. My prince was dressed in a new frock coat – black velvet with gold buttons. It fitted him perfectly. His fur smelled freshly washed, and had been brushed until it gleamed in the torchlight.

"Someone's all dolled up. What's the occasion?"

He smiled – even his teeth had been scrubbed. "Two things, lady. This night Elsbeth becomes my mate. Also, our lady becomes our lady."

"Congratulations. That last part lost me. How can I become what I already am?"

His smiled widened, canines glistening. "You understand."

Actually, no. I really didn't. I narrowed my eyes. "What's this about?"

He offered me his hand. "Come."

"William, I don't really have time for this . . . " I stopped in the centre of the hall. The torches had dimmed, bringing the altar to my notice. It was old and worn, and had blotches of candle wax that had to be older than Victoria herself dripped along its scarred surface. Beautiful white candles burned on it, flames flickering. And there on the dais was the body Clive had delivered. It was a woman of middle age, with full lips and a soft belly. She had laugh lines around her eyes and mouth, and even in death she appeared to wear a bit of a smile. She was lovely.

"The woman is perfect for what we ask," William said, stepping up to the altar and raising his right hand. I watched as the hand lengthened, fingers curving like talons as his nails grew and thickened, becoming wicked-looking claws. How much shifting power did it take to change just one body part? It was difficult for goblins to hold any form but their own for long because it required so much energy. But William made it look easy.

He brought his hand down, index finger neatly slicing through the woman's breastbone to make a standard Y incision. The air bloomed with the smell of blood, still relatively fresh, and the gathered goblins howled, their voices rising around me like a choir.

Something tugged at my trouser leg. I looked down to see little Alexandra there, grinning up at me. Today she looked like a cross between a puppy and a human toddler – huge eyes, long lashes and lots of teeth. She was the most adorable thing. When she held her arms up to me, I bent and picked her up, holding her so she sat on my forearm with her arms about my neck. She sniffed my hair and nuzzled her head against mine.

A cracking sound echoed around us – William had separated the ribs. He removed the heart and set it aside, then took out the other internal organs and divided those up amongst those who needed them most – the old, the sick and the young. Alexandra sucked up a piece of liver like it was pudding.

It didn't bother me so much any more. In fact, I dabbed away a little blood from her chin and licked my thumb.

William and Elsbeth shared a piece of meat, one feeding it to the other. That was the key element of the goblin wedding ceremony, the sharing of food. Then they shared a glass of blood and kissed. Voilà! They were goblin and wife.

It was time for me to go. I had to get to the palace. For that matter, so did William, or had he forgotten that he was going to accompany me to the meeting? How could he forget? It had to be on the news by now.

Queen Victoria and the faction leaders were going to sit down with the prime minister and human officials to broker a peace – the sort that should have happened a long time ago. The kind that involved Victoria giving up most of her power.

It was the only thing I could think of to remedy every issue. If Victoria made it so the monarch had limited power, or was abolished, Bertie had nothing. I was rather impressed with myself for thinking of it.

I was still holding Alexandra when William turned to me. "Xandra, lady, you will join me."

A command rather than a request. Hmm. I stepped up on to the worn platform. "What's going on, William?"

He drew a stiletto from an old leather sheath; the blade gleamed in the candlelight. Elsbeth held a golden goblet beneath his hands. He took the knife and made a small cut on his thumb, which he then squeezed over the goblet. A drop of crimson fell into the bowl. Then he handed the weapon to Elsbeth and held the goblet for her, and then for little Alexandra, who cried when he pricked her finger, but laughed when I stuck it in my mouth.

"William, what the hell?"

"Patience, lady," he said.

Once the goblet and blade had made their way to every goblin in the hall, William turned and took my crown, which sat on a pillow of red velvet, and placed it on my head. It was carved from bone – mostly a skull. It was morbid, grotesque, awesome and delicate, with perfectly sculpted points and smooth edges that had been lovingly fashioned.

That was when I noticed the other crown – the ancient one with Roman coins in its eyes, crystals glittering around it. Vines had grown through it at one time, and hand-hammered bronze formed its bone-spiked base. It was her crown – the first queen.

William held it out for all to see, then showed it to me. "Ancient was she whence we met," he began. "Saved your prince as a pup. Tossed out of the palace, denied my birthright. She took me in. Brought me here. Was a mother to me."

He didn't need to tell me this. "William . . . "

He held up one hand to silence me. The cut on his thumb had already healed. "Strong, she was. Wise. Kind. The first of us." Then he smiled. "Couldn't sing to save her life, but cared naught. She died protecting this den. Protecting her people on Insurrection Day. Humans killed her."

I knew where this was going. "I know how you feel about humans—"

"Please, cease flapping, lady."

My jaw snapped shut with a clack. William's smile returned. "We followed her, and we follow you – wherever you lead, you take us with you. Believe in you, does the plague. Trust in you. Honour you. Fight for you as you have fought for us." He turned the crown upside down. The lining had long since worn away, revealing the empty cavity of the skull. It was in that cavity that he placed the fresh heart.

The goblet came back half full of blood. William removed a small vial from inside his waistcoat. The stuff inside looked so red it was black.

"This is her blood – my mother, my queen." He popped the top and poured the blood into the cup. Then he poured the contents over the heart in the bottom of the skull.

It beat. Just once, but it beat. I gasped.

William reached down and pulled the bloody, dripping organ from the crown. "You ate of the Churchill for vengeance. You have taken meat for sustenance. Now you will take the meat given by your plague. The blood of your plague, the strength and hope of your plague. The heart of a mother. The blood of a mother. The blood of a warrior. Become what you are, lady. Know yourself as plague queen."

It all sounded very dramatic. I stared at that glistening lump of meat in his hand, smelled the blood of my goblins on it. Smelled the blood of that brave dead queen. I knew what he was demanding of me. I had accepted being their queen months ago, but in my heart I continued to feel removed. How could I ever truly be one of them when I was so different?

He was asking me to let go of everything I once held true. To embrace whatever lurked inside me, not as my monster, or my goblin, but as me.

Fuck, he had impeccable timing. And he knew me far better than he ought.

I took the heart in my hand. It was still warm, and the blood warmed it still. I turned to face the hall of goblins, baby Alexandra still in my arms.

"Eat," she said, prising my mouth open with her tiny dirty hands.

The goblins laughed. I laughed. And then I did what I was told – what I knew I had to do. What I wanted to do.

I ate the heart, and the cheers that echoed in the hall filled me as the blood and meat filled me, made my skin tingle and my veins pulse. After coming so close to death, I knew what this meant, what this moment was.

This was my rebirth.

CHAPTER 22

THE SUPREME ART OF WAR IS TO SUBDUE THE ENEMY WITHOUT FIGHTING

The palace was crawling with press when I arrived. I could see them pressed up against the gates like Newgate prisoners begging for bread. They were hungry for details. Word had leaked out that Victoria – a most reclusive queen – had requested a meeting with the PM and high-ranking humans. Was it true that she wanted peace? Or would she drain them all and throw their bodies to the goblins?

Of course there were protesters too, and the prerequisite hatters job with silver foil wrapped round his head who always showed up wherever there were cameras. A woman carrying a rotting turnip tried to claim it was her baby who had been eaten by goblins.

Please. There wasn't nearly enough meat on a baby.

My gaze scanned the surroundings – old habit from my Royal Guard days. Nothing seemed amiss, but then it rarely did until it was too late. Would Bertie show? Maybe. I wasn't worried about Bertie. He and I would meet again one day. To be honest, I was more interested in crossing paths with Stephen Argyle, but I doubted that would happen, and if it did I would have to get in line behind Vex for a piece of the little bastard. Still, I wouldn't forget that he poisoned my father. Vardan had never been much of a dad, but he had been my dad, and the only one I'd ever have.

Aside from William, that was.

Vex met me just inside the palace, where a security team of Royal Guards checked us and secured the area. It was odd, realising that I was now one of the people they were sworn to protect. At least while I was in this place. I watched them with their ear buds and stern expressions. Some of them couldn't be any more than twenty.

I was going to be three and twenty later this month. These halfies weren't much younger than me, but they seemed it.

"You look different," my wolf told me as we climbed the stairs together. The meeting was to be held in one of the public rooms at the palace. There hadn't been any public in it since the Insurrection, but such a space was still considered necessary for some reason.

"Do I? I actually put some make-up on." I usually loved preening and getting dressed up, but lately I'd been a minimalist with both. I think it was high time I got some ruffles back – and maybe a new lipstick.

Perhaps I'd dye my hair. Candy red was fun and all that, but I'd had it my entire life.

"No, that's not it." He stepped in front of me in the upstairs corridor to prevent me from walking ahead. He was dressed in a formal coat, white shirt and his dress kilt, along with black boots. He looked terribly sexy in his kilt, but tonight he was extra so. Must be all that goblin blood and fresh meat sizzling in my veins. I felt . . . free.

I gazed up at him adoringly. "I feel good."

His lips curved on one side, deepening the lines around his eyes. He always seemed to find me amusing. Maybe I made him happy. He leaned closer – almost close enough to kiss – and sniffed. "You've fed."

I grinned. "William. By the way, he and Elsbeth are married now. Do I have anything in my teeth?"

"Lovely. Xandra, sweetheart, what did you eat?"

"A heart – it was dead when I got it. And some ancient goblin blood."

Vex's eyes narrowed. "Ancient indeed. What else?"

That was it. Oh, wait. "More blood. I think from the whole plague."

"That explains it." He shook his head. "That bastard William is a wily one."

"Why do you say that?"

He took my hand as we began walking again. Thankfully there was no one around. "Bleedings like that have been used for years amongst wolves and goblins – it's to give strength in battle, like the whole pack is fighting with you."

"It's certainly a pick-me-up."

He laughed. "Woman, you are madder than a hatter."

"That's so nineteenth-century of you. The term is hatters."

"The term is ridiculous. Now, do you think you can sit quietly for a bit?"

I took a deep breath. I might feel a little anxious, but this was important. I could totally do this. "I'm good."

We were greeted at the door by a footman, and announced

to the room. William had already arrived, as had Lord Ainsley, who had been chosen to represent the vampires in my father's stead. Technically, Bertie was the leader of the vampires, but my father had always done most of the work, despite how little he'd been trusted. The PM was there as well – a striking black woman who was almost as tall as Vex. I noticed that she and the other human invitees sat as far away from the aristos as they could. Not good, but understandable.

Avery was there, dressed in head-to-toe black. Victoria was a stickler for the old ways, so my sister wore a gown rather than her usual modern attire. I'd bet the skirt had concealed slits in it, however – in case things got dicey. Probably had a handgun under her bustle, too.

After all this build-up, I had to admit I was hoping for dicey.

A few moments later the doors were closed, and Victoria entered the room from another point. We all stood as she approached. We sat when she sat.

"Thank you for coming here on such short notice this evening," she said. "I know many of you have families you would rather be with, so I will attempt to make this process as abbreviated as possible." That was a nice touch – a nod to the humans and their rampant breeding.

"I realise that these are difficult times for all of us in our country." When one of the humans snorted, Victoria fixed her gaze on him and arched a brow. "Queen Alexandra has lost both a sister and her father due to the recent violence. Lord MacLaughlin has lost a son and friends. I have lost people I have known for more than a century. Whom have you lost, sir?"

The man flushed dark red – clashing with his ginger hair. "Uh ... ahem. No one."

Victoria's chin lifted. "Indeed."

I wanted to clap. Maybe even cheer when the little ponce averted his gaze, but I kept still, cheering on the inside. I was not going to knob this up by behaving like I'd eaten a handful of hallucinogenic mushrooms.

The tiny queen turned her attention to the PM. "Madam Prime Minister, I would like to propose that a formal agreement be made between the Crown and the human people of the empire. Between the Crown and *all* people of the empire." She glanced at William when she said that last part. "Eighty years ago, His Royal Highness, my husband Albert, drafted a proposal that would limit the control of the monarchy and increase the participation of the human race. In honour of his memory and his fairness to all races, I would like to go forth with that proposal."

The PM blinked. One of the humans whispered excitedly to her, but she might as well have voiced her speculation out loud, because we all heard her doubt our sincerity.

"No one's going to eat you," I said to her. She flushed too. You'd think that humans would take pains to prevent all that yummy blood from rushing to their faces. It made them look like ripe cherries on an ice cream dessert. "She's proposing a new regime that will give a portion of lawmaking and government to humans as well as aristos and half-bloods. Equality through a slow process of removal of the monarchy."

Every head turned to Victoria to validate my claim. "That is it in a nutshell, yes. In fact, I will have it made law that upon my death the monarchy is to be formally abolished."

Now *that* would raise a ruckus. I thought Ainsley was going to have a fit of some kind, and the humans looked as though they'd been set in the middle of a Chinese opera and were expected to perform.

Victoria banged her hand on the table. The blow sent a shudder down the entire length of the polished surface. I'd be surprised if she hadn't left a handprint.

Everyone fell quiet and looked to her. "What I want is for the people of this country to find a way to exist with one another. What we were doing eighty years ago didn't work, and what we're doing now isn't working either. We're afraid of you and you are afraid of us when we all came from the same place. We were once a great nation whose age and historical importance drew visitors to our museums and theatres. Now, we have busloads of Americans taking photographs of us like we're sideshow freaks or visiting clubs where they can have a sexual encounter with an aristocrat or half-blood. We have come to a place where we find sport in watching each other die, where you are thought of as food and we are thought of as monsters. We are *not* monsters. And we would very much like to find a way for all of us to live together. Do not you think it time?"

Amazing. She was really into it – really inspired. I could imagine her eighty years ago, she and Albert both passionate about reform. Before the Insurrection made her afraid to leave her home for fear of attack.

She spoke some more, but I wasn't paying attention. A familiar scent drifted to my nose, tickling and taunting.

Ali. Bertie had sent his monster. He might have other friends here as well, but Ali was the only one I was worried about. She'd make short work of the humans and halfies. She only needed to take out Victoria for Bertie's plan to work. If she killed the Queen before she signed the new constitution, he would be in charge.

Under the table, I nudged Vex's knee with my own. I felt his fingers squeeze my leg in return. He smelled her too.

Where was she? Was she one of the humans? One of the aristos? I couldn't turn around without looking suspicious.

And what was that other smell? I sniffed again. There was something else, and it was new. It smelled faint and sickly sweet. I couldn't quite place it. Bloody annoying. I couldn't determine if it was a harbinger of bad things or not.

My gaze fell on Avery, and that was when I knew Ali had shown herself. My sister stood near to Victoria, but her face was pale and her eyes were wide as she stared at someone behind where I sat. I didn't have to turn to know whose face Ali would be wearing. There was only one that I would hesitate to hit, and it was my fault she knew that. Dede. She was wearing Dede as her disguise.

When I saw Avery's hand reaching for her bustle, I knew things were about to heat up. "Avery," I said, cutting off Victoria mid-sentence. "Get Her Majesty out of here, now."

The humans were uneasy – I could see it. I could smell their delicious fear.

Victoria glared at me. "I'll have you know that I am just as ready to fight as any of you."

"Lady, if she kills you before those new laws get made, your mad-as-fuck son takes over and everything Albert wanted will die with you."

She nodded. "Miss Vardan, you may escort me to the panic room."

Panic room? Why did that surprise me?

I pushed back my chair. "Vex?"

He didn't fight me. "I'll take the humans." There was no way those people would go with William. It was either Vex or Ainsley, and I didn't know if we could trust him. Although when he looked up, I watched the blood drain from his face. He'd seen Ali too.

And that *smell* . . . Oh, fuck.

"Vex, it's the plague. He's pumping the plague into the place through the air ducts. I can smell it."

Vex swore, and hurried towards the humans. How much exposure did they need before the new strain kicked in? And could he get them to safety in time? Christ, two of them were already coughing.

I turned as I stood, braced for her attack as the others scattered. My job wasn't to worry about humans. My job was to keep Ali from going after Victoria. William's job would be to keep any friends she had with her from going after anyone else.

And she did have friends. Three of them. They looked like halfies, but then so did I.

"Be careful," I said to William. "But take them out quickly."

He flashed fang. "As you wish."

I was prepared to see Dede come at me, but that didn't stop my heart from lurching when she did. Even though the smell was wrong, and the expression too severe, it was still my little sister's face.

My hesitation got me a punch in the face that sent me flying backwards over the table. I hit the carpet on my back. Fuck. How could I have been so easily caught off my guard?

I pushed against the floor with my shoulders, bucked and came up on my feet fast. Just fast enough to kick her in the face. Now she was the one on the other side of the table.

When Ali rose, she wasn't wearing Dede any more. She was just herself, except there was a mad gleam in her eyes and an odd twist to her mouth. She looked . . . well, vacant. She was driven by the madness Bertie had put upon her. There was nothing of that naïve, scared creature who wanted me to help her, who claimed me as her mother.

I was glad that girl was gone. I wouldn't want to kill her. This thing, though? I could kill it without remorse.

But Ali didn't keep her own face for long. She cried out as a change overtook her. Her body contorted and spasmed as her limbs thickened and lengthened. Fur grew longer, providing added protection. Claws came out, and fangs glistened. She was an impressive sight. When she came at me, I barely dodged a swipe that would have taken the head off a bull.

This was not how I had planned it. Had I really thought it would be so simple to take her down? Of course I knew better. I reckoned it was a bit more choreographed in my head.

The next time she came at me, I jobbed her between the eyes with a hard right. It knocked her back a pace or two. She grinned.

"He wants me to kill you," she taunted. "It's going to feel so good to kill you and the old bitch."

"Awww," I whined mockingly. "Why can't I be the bitch?"

She punched me hard in the solar plexus and I went down, gasping for breath. That was when she kicked me in the head and sent me sprawling.

I blinked. Lights danced before my eyes. Change hadn't come yet. I hadn't shifted. Not even my usual bit.

Maybe it had to be invited.

As I rolled out of the way of another kick and scrambled to my feet, I tried to let go of my control – just toss it away. It clung to me like a spiderweb. When she backhanded me and sent me into the wall, I looked up and saw William attending to the last of the three opponents he'd taken on. Good, he could help me with Ali.

But Ali had no intention of waiting that long. When she came tearing at me, snarling and snapping, I knew there was only one way I could win this.

I invited change. I thought of all my loved ones, both alive and dead. I thought about goblin babies and a goblin matriarch whose blood was inside of me. I took the anger and despair – the sorrow – packed it up and tucked it aside. Those emotions sometimes triggered a shift, but this time I wanted to choose it.

I felt my bones move. My God, I could see them moving under my skin – skin that had started to grow that fine velvety fur once more.

Ali paused. Thank fuck for curiosity. "What are you doing?" Her voice was a low growl.

"What does it look like?" The words came out slurred as my jaw lengthened. Ali charged me, but I managed to dodge once again, giving me time for my claws to appear.

It was amazing, this rush of transformation. It wasn't easy, but once it started, it came quickly and painfully. Bones separated and repositioned themselves, muscles lengthened. Everything became more – more claw, more fang. It was bloody amazing.

Ali stared at me. "How did you do that?"

I grinned. "Where do you think you got it?" Oh, why had I fought this for so long? I could feel the blood of my pack racing through me, giving me strength and speed. I felt strong. Powerful. *Whole*.

This time I was the one on the offensive. I leapt at her, claws out, swiping her cheek and laying open the skin to a torrent of blood. She screamed, and for a moment I saw that formerly scared creature in her eyes – the one that had jumped on me in joy and wanted me to be her mother. But then it was gone as she snarled and started swinging her own terrible claws.

She tore open my arm, but I twisted out of the way before she could dig in. As I did so, I whipped my leg up and gave her a boot to the frontal lobe. She staggered and came back with a kick of her own that should have knocked my jaw loose but didn't. This new form – this *true* form – was stronger than my usual self.

Fighting is a bit like dancing – it's all about following your partner's lead. Ali and I could probably do this all night if we both weren't in such a hurry to end it.

"I really don't want to kill you," she lied. How easily it rolled off her tongue. She learned fast. "Why don't you just step aside and let me go after the old woman?"

I punched her in the mouth. "Because five minutes ago you told me just how much you were going to enjoy killing me, and because I've become rather partial to that old woman."

Another shot aimed at my solar plexus. I blocked and sliced the inside of her wrist. Cheap shot? Yes. I was not, however, going to feel badly for it when she'd be healed in a short time.

"Why won't you just die?" she screamed swinging wildly and missing. "You were so easy to tear apart four days ago!"

I grinned. "I wasn't myself then." My elbow slammed into her face. I felt her nose break before I danced just out of her reach.

The noises she made had more to do with rage than pain. I knew this because they were the same grunts I made when I felt that way. We were both sticky with each other's blood – gory little dancing dolls.

I saw her glance over my shoulder and smile. I didn't have to look to understand her. Vex had returned – I felt his presence. He was fighting her friends alongside William. She was going to go for him.

And she did. She jumped right over my head and ran for him. I gave chase. I was faster in this form as well, but she still managed to give him a good swipe before I reached her. Nothing serious, just enough to piss me off. I grabbed her by the hair and pulled her head back so that her neck was exposed.

"You know I can't let you live," I said to her.

"I know," she whispered. For a moment I thought for certain that she wanted me to kill her. Then she jobbed me in the face – just missing my eye.

"Fucking cow!" I still had her hair, and I pulled hard on it now. I didn't think; I simply acted. Fangs grew even longer in my mouth, and saliva started to flow.

I latched on to her hard, pulling on the surge of her blood until I felt her weaken in my arms. Only then did I lift my head. Our gazes met. Hers was dim and narrow.

"Do it," she whispered. "Please?"

How could I deny her? I stared at her a moment, seeing myself and Dede, and everyone else whose face she'd worn.

I grabbed her neck with my teeth and ripped. Blood flooded my mouth, ran down my chin and front. I ignored it as I gently guided her to the floor. Glassy eyes looked up at me as her fingers stroked my cheek, the strong line of my jaw and the velvety fur that was so like her own.

"Found you," she whispered, a bloody smile curving her lips.

And then she died.

CHAPTER 23

LOVE WILL FIND A WAY THROUGH PATHS WHERE WOLVES FEAR TO PREY

It was Avery and Val who caught Bertie when he came to finish his mother. Too bad she'd already signed the papers changing the future of England and had them witnessed by the PM.

Bruised and winded, with dried blood on my face and in my hair, I let Vex and William escort me to the parlour where Victoria, her son and my siblings waited. The Prince of Wales was bound to a very sturdy chair.

Bertie stared at me when I walked in. I was still in my new form, holding it without the rage. He must have thought I was Ali. I willed myself to change back to my normal appearance, if for no other reason than to see the look on his face.

His disappointment was delicious.

"She's dead," I told him. "She asked me to kill her so she didn't have to be your puppet any more."

The prince shrugged. "She filled her purpose."

"You cunt," I sneered. "Everyone was put on this earth to be your plaything."

He met my gaze without a hint of expression. "That's one of the perks of being royalty. Surely you know that, Alexandra."

"No," I answered. "I really don't."

"Where's Argyle?" Vex demanded.

Bertie laughed at him, bright blue eyes twinkling. I wanted to dig my thumbs into them and pop them like bubble-wrap. "Your little traitor? He was so very easy to seduce, Lord Alpha. A promise of a little power and he did whatever I asked of him. He's in my apartments." He looked past Vex to me. "So sorry about your father, Alexandra. Did you get the package I sent?"

Vex left the room. I wanted to go with him, but it wasn't my place. Instead, I kept my face blank and tucked my fists behind my back so I couldn't use them. I took a calming breath. "You're being awfully conversational, Bertie. I almost feel like a priest in a confessional. Aren't you worried about incriminating yourself?" Oh, it would be lovely to pound that smug smile off his face.

With Vex gone, Bertie reverted to his obnoxious self. "I don't know what you're all upset about. I'm bringing about a new dusk for this country – a world where the British Empire will be great and glorious once more. Mother, you know I'm right. Release me."

Victoria walked around the desk to stand in front of her son. She drew back her arm and slapped him so hard the chair tipped over backwards and fell to the floor.

"You do not speak to me," she told him. "And you most certainly do *not* call me mother."

We let him squirm like an overturned beetle for a moment, and then Val pushed the chair and prince upright once more. "We need to take him into custody, Your Majesty."

Victoria nodded. "Of course. Do what you must."

As Val placed special aristo-strong shackles on Bertie's ankles, I asked what no one else had. "What about a cure?"

Everyone looked at me, but I kept my attention on Bertie. "Every human and half-blood in this palace has been exposed to the new plague. The majority of them will die if they don't mutate. There must be a treatment, right? Just in case it didn't go as planned?"

Bertie grinned as Val applied shackles to his wrists as well. "I'll tell you what won't work – tetracycline. You'll find my lovely creation terribly resistant to all forms of antibiotics. It's a persistent little beauty."

I couldn't believe it. "There's no cure?"

The grin widened. "Now you understand. No, my dear freak, there is no cure. There's no treatment. No hope." This last word came out almost like a kiss. "There's absolutely nothing you can do now that I've set my lovely free."

Cold spiked through my core, down into my feet. "What have you done?" And what was taking Vex so long? It felt like he'd been gone for hours.

Bertie glanced towards the clock on the mantle. "One hour ago the airborne plague I've named *Pestis albia* was released in underground stations in London, Hong Kong and Paris. It was also released in hospitals across Europe and Asia, in schools, universities and prisons. I believe that at this moment it's being discharged into the air at a celebrity gathering in Los Angeles in America, as well as the New York subway and a hockey game in Toronto."

Victoria staggered backwards. I admit I almost did the same. Oh my God.

"How could you do such a thing?" his mother asked.

He shrugged, fixing her with a gaze of pure hate. Freed from the chair, he stood, silver-treated restraints jangling discordantly. "I did what you and my father could not. In a few days' time, much of the world's human population will begin to die very painful deaths, or they will transcend. A few will survive, as they always do, and they will go on to feed the rest of us. But we will be the dominant species. Why so shocked, Mother? Haven't you always talked of uniting humans and the aristocracy? Well, they're united now, or they soon will be."

The rest of us shared astonished and horrified glances as Bertie laughed at us.

"Not quite," came Vex's voice from the door.

My shoulders sagged when I looked and saw him standing there with Argyle. I had a little business to finish with the traitorous halfie when this was over, but for now, seeing him was a good thing.

Bertie turned, and regarded the arrivals with that smug smile. "Ah, Argyle. No hard feelings, dear boy, but I think you know that a man who would betray his own so easily is also very easy to betray."

"Well said," Vex replied. "So it won't surprise you to know that a little over an hour ago, one of your little cabals was prevented from carrying through your plans by their local aristo law enforcement, thanks to Stephen's realisation that it was easier to betray you than face me."

Bertie's smile melted away, like blood down a drain. "What?"

I walked up behind him and clapped him on the shoulder.

"All halfies have trackers in them, Bertie. The pack found Stephen not long after he left us." I didn't add how tense the last few hours had been, not knowing if all the agencies would comply, if Argyle had given us the right information. Vex had kept me practically in the dark about the whole thing so that all I needed to worry about was Ali.

"All that work," I whispered in the prince's ear. "All that planning. For nothing. You failed, Bertie."

I stepped back with a smile, enjoying his stunned silence. Then he lifted his chin defiantly, a little of the old arrogance returning. "You haven't stopped me. Lock me up and I'll start again. I have contacts all over the continent. You will not sto—"

His words died abruptly, turning into a terrible gurgle as Queen V ripped out her son's throat.

We all watched his blood drain out in satisfied silence.

"Is it done?" Avery finally asked. "Is it over?"

"Yes," Vex answered, shoving Argyle at Val to be taken into custody. "Some of the gas did escape into the palace, but so far none of the humans are exhibiting any symptoms."

My knees trembled. I wanted to sit down, but I didn't know if I'd ever get back up. And I was terribly concerned about getting blood on Victoria's furniture. I stared at Bertie's corpse, then lifted my gaze to meet Victoria's. For a second, I saw a mother's sorrow in her eyes, and while I hadn't been a mother long, I knew a little about having no choice but to destroy your own child.

"We'd better call a press conference," she announced, all emotion vanishing as she slipped back into monarch mode. I had to admit, I admired her for it. "Xandra, Vex, Uncle William – you will join me. As will Madame Prime Minister."

My eyebrows lifted of their own accord. "Now?" I was covered in blood – and she was still holding on to part of her son's trachea.

"Now." She tossed the lump of meat at William, who caught it and practically swallowed it whole. "We do this now. No more hiding. No more fighting. My son was right about one thing – this empire was great once upon a time. And it will be great again, with all of its peoples united. I will see this happen if it is the last thing I do."

Oh, she was good. I felt a little thrill at her words. Inspired.

There was a knock on the door. It opened to reveal the prime minister. Poor woman looked nervous. I didn't blame her. Here we were, all bloody messes. She must have felt like a mouse entering a hawk house.

"You wanted to see me, Your Majesty?" Her voice cracked slightly.

"Yes," Victoria said. "Join us, please."

The woman did, putting herself closer to Avery and Val – the safest-looking of the lot.

Victoria held out her hand to me – the bloody one, of course – and I took it without hesitation. Her other reached for William, while I reached for Vex. He gestured for Avery and Val to join – but not Argyle, who was trussed up behind us – and offered his other hand to the PM. She hesitated only a second before taking it.

"No more hiding in the dark," Victoria said, her gaze meeting each of ours. "No more lording it from behind armed guards and fortified walls. As of tonight, we reclaim our own place in this city – in the world." She glanced at William and gave him a small smile. "Tonight is a new beginning for the British Empire, with all of us going forward as equals. What say you?"

Starting with William, she looked to each person in the circle. Every one of them said "aye", even the PM, who still looked a little confused. However, she was a smart, strong woman who had no problem ignoring the corpse of the Prince of Wales at her feet.

Vex gave his agreement next, and then all eyes were on me. Vex gave my fingers a little squeeze. I smiled at him before turning to Victoria, the woman I had thought was my enemy, who was now turning into something more, though I didn't imagine we'd be going for pedicures any time soon.

The little woman looked at me expectantly. "Xandra? What do you say?"

I gazed around at all my friends and family. I would do anything for any of them.

"I say . . ." I lifted the small, bloody hand that stuck to mine, "long live the Queen."

GLOSSARY

aether – slang for airwaves, usually applied to telephone, telegraph and video communications not broadcast over private channels.

aethernet – international network of logic engines that share government, educational, personal and commercial information using the same protocols.

Albert's fangs – curse seen as taking the late Prince Consort's name in vein ... er, vain.

aristocrat – collective term for vampires and werewolves, particularly those of noble birth.

box – television.

Britme – electronic service provided by Britannia Telephone and Telegraph where people can leave a voice recording for the person they're trying to reach via stationary line or rotary.

bubonic betty – human who injects aristocrat hormones to gain enhanced senses, strength and speed.

cobbleside – above ground.

courtesan – human woman employed by the aristocracy to breed half-bloods. These women are plague carriers, their blood rich with the Prometheus protein necessary for full-term, healthy pregnancies.

digigram – electronic text-based message sent between wireless devices and logic engines.

fang me – being fanged means being used for food by an aristocrat – a practice beneath most halfies.

job – to hit or get violent with. Comes with the violence often attached to halfie occupations: "He really did a job on that human"; "She jobbed the betty hard in the kidneys."

halfie – a half-blood. Half vampire/were and half human.

hatters – derived from "mad as a hatter". Slang for crazy, insane.

horror show – illegal spectacle at which vampires or weres consume a human or halfie victim for the audience's titillation.

logic engine – electronic device that stores and processes information, and allows for many kinds of digital communication over the aethernet.

meat – goblin term for anything warm-blooded, and therefore edible.

Met, the – Metropolitan Underground Railway.

motor carriage – transportation. Modern carriage propelled by an engine rather than horses.

Motorrad – what Americans refer to as a "motorcycle".

plague, the – responsible for the Prometheus mutation that made vamps and weres, and goblins. Also the term the goblins use to describe a group of themselves. The London plague is used to refer to all the goblins in London.

radiarange – counter-top oven that cooks food using non-ionising microwave radiation.

rotary – portable wireless telephone. Has a rotary dial.

rutting – vulgar, but slightly more polite than "fucking".

tango – halfie slang for a fight.

TrackNav – a system of tracking people and vehicles via satel-
lite and uniquely trackable devices.

underside – underground.

VC – video cylinder. A cylinder used to record and play back
video, such as films.

ACKNOWLEDGEMENTS

I want to take a minute to thank the fans of this series. You are all so unbelievably cool! Thank you for letting me know you've enjoyed the books.

Thank you to Miriam Kriss for hand-holding, lunching, butt-kicking and just being the best agent ever.

Thank you to Devi Pillai for knowing exactly how to deal with me, and for being understanding when disaster strikes! Oh, and for being the most evil editor I've ever worked with. ☺

Thank you to Lauren Panepinto for the best covers ever, and to Jeximé for bringing Xandra to life. And thank you to the entire Orbit/Hachette crew on this side of the pond and the other. I don't want to try listing you all for fear I'll forget one of you, but all of you ROCK. I have been so extremely lucky to work with you. Special thanks to Joanna Kramer for a certain signed book that will be treasured for ever.

Thanks to my family for just being their crazy selves. I'm so lucky to have you all! And thanks to my friends for understanding why sometimes I'm not fit for company.

And thank you to Emilie Autumn, for releasing *Fight Like a Girl* as I was writing this book, providing much musical inspiration.

extras

orbit

www.orbitbooks.net

about the author

Kate Locke is a shameless Anglophile who wrote her first book at age twelve. Fortunately, that book about a British pop band is lost for ever. When not experimenting with new hair colours, Kate likes to hang out with her husband who, while not from England, can do a pretty convincing accent. She spends her days being bossed about by five fur kids and making stuff up – often while wearing a "uniform" that looks suspiciously like pyjamas. During "off" hours Kate often screeches along to *Rock Band* (being a rock star was her second career choice if the writing thing didn't work out), watches BBC America, or plays with make-up. She loves history, the paranormal, horror and sparkly things. The author's website can be found at www.katelocke.com.

Find out more about Kate Locke and other Orbit authors by registering for the free monthly newsletter at www.orbitbooks.net.

if you enjoyed
LONG LIVE THE QUEEN

look out for

THE SHAMBLING GUIDE
TO NEW YORK CITY

by

Mur Lafferty

Chapter One

The bookstore was sandwiched between a dry cleaner's and a shifty-looking accounting office. Mannegishi's Tricks wasn't in the guidebook, but Zoë Norris knew enough about guidebooks to know they often missed the best places.

This clearly was not one of those places.

The store was, to put it bluntly, filthy. It reminded Zoë of an abandoned mechanic's garage, with grime and grease coating the walls and bookshelves. She pulled her arms in to avoid brushing against anything. Long strips of paint dotted with mold peeled away from the walls as if they could no longer stand to adhere to such filth. Zoë couldn't blame them. She felt a bizarre desire to wave to them as they bobbed lazily to herald her passing. Her shoes stuck slightly to the floor, making her trek through the store louder than she would have liked.

She always enjoyed looking at cities—even her hometown—through the eyes of a tourist. She owned guidebooks of every city she had visited and used them extensively. It made her usual urban exploration feel more thorough.

It also allowed her to look at the competition, or it had when she'd worked in travel book publishing.

The store didn't win her over with its stock, either. She'd never heard of most of the books; they had titles like *How to Make Love, Marry, Devour, and Inherit in Eight Weeks* in the Romance section and *When Your Hound from Hell Outgrows His House—and Yours* in the Pets section.

She picked the one about hounds and opened it to Chapter Four: "The Augean Stables: How to Pooper-Scoop Dung That Could Drown a Terrier." She frowned. *So, they're really assuming your dog gets bigger than a house? It's not tongue in cheek? If this is humor, it's failing.* Despite the humorous title, the front cover had a frightening drawing of a hulking white beast with red eyes. The cover was growing uncomfortably warm, and the leather had a sticky, alien feeling, not like cow or even snake leather. She switched the book to her left hand and wiped her right on her beige sweater. She immediately regretted it.

"One sweater ruined," she muttered, looking at the grainy black smear. "What *is* this stuff?"

The cashier's desk faced the door from the back of the store, and was staffed by an unsmiling teen girl in a dirty gray sundress. She had olive skin and big round eyes, and her head had the fuzz of the somewhat-recently shaved. Piercings dotted her face at her nose, eyebrow, lip, and cheek, and all the way up her ears. Despite her slouchy body language, she watched Zoë with a bright, sharp gaze that looked almost hungry.

Beside the desk was a bulletin board, blocked by a pudgy man hanging a flyer. He wore a T-shirt and jeans and looked to be in his mid-thirties. He looked completely out of place in this store; that is, he was clean.

"Can I help you?" the girl asked as Zoë approached the counter.

"Uh, you have a very interesting shop here," Zoë said, smiling. She put the hound book on the counter and tried not to grimace as it stuck to her hand briefly. "How much is this one?"

The clerk didn't return her smile. "We cater to a specific clientele."

"OK . . . but how much is the book?" Zoë asked again.

"It's not for sale. It's a collectible."

Zoë became aware of the man at the bulletin board turning and watching her. She began to sweat a little bit.

Jesus, calm down. Not everyone is out to get you.

"So it's not for sale, or it's a collectible. Which one?"

The girl reached over and took the book. "It's not for sale to you, only to collectors."

"How do you know I don't collect dog books?" Zoë asked, bristling. "And what does it matter? All I wanted to know was how much it costs. Do you care where it goes as long as it's paid for?"

"Are you a collector of rare books catering to the owners of . . . exotic pets?" the man interrupted, smiling. His voice was pleasant and mild, and she relaxed a little, despite his patronizing words. "Excuse me for butting in, but I know the owner of this shop and she considers these books her treasure. She is very particular about where they go when they leave her care."

"Why should she . . . " Zoë trailed off when she got a closer look at the bulletin board to the man's left. Several flyers stood out, many with phone numbers ripped from the bottom. One, advertising an exorcism service specializing in elemental demons, looked burned in a couple of places. The flyer that had caught her eye was pink, and the one the man had just secured with a thumbtack.

Underground Publishing
LOOKING FOR WRITERS

Underground Publishing is a new company writing travel guides for people like you. Since we're writing for people like you, we need people like you to write for us.

Pluses: Experience in writing, publishing, or editing (in this life or any other), and knowledge of New York City.

Minuses: A life span shorter than an editorial cycle (in this case, nine months).

Call 212.555.1666 for more information
or email rand@undergroundpub.com for
more information.

"Oh, hell yes," said Zoë, and with the weird, dirty hound book forgotten, she pulled a battered notebook from her satchel. She needed a job. She was refusing to adhere to the stereotype of running home to New York, admitting failure at her attempts to leave her hometown. Her goal was a simple office job. She wasn't waiting for her big break on Broadway and looking to wait tables or take on a leaflet-passing, taco-suit-wearing street-nuisance job in the meantime.

Office job. Simple. Uncomplicated.

As she scribbled down the information, the man looked her up and down and said, "Ah, I'm not sure if that's a good idea for you to pursue."

Zoë looked up sharply. "What are you talking about? First I can't buy the book, now I can't apply for a job? I know you guys have some sort of weird vibe going on, 'We're so goth and special, let's freak out the normals.' But for a business that caters to, you know, *customers*, you're certainly not welcoming."

"I just think that particular business may be looking for someone with experience you may not have," he said, his voice level and diplomatic. He held his hands out, placating her.

"But you don't even know me. You don't know my qualifications. I just left Misconceptions Publishing in Raleigh. You heard of them?" She hated name-dropping her old employer—she would have preferred to forget it entirely—

but the second-biggest travel book publisher in the USA was her strongest credential in the job hunt.

The man shifted his weight and touched his chin. "Really. What did you do for them?"

Zoë stood a little taller. "Head researcher and writer. I wrote most of *Raleigh Misconceptions*, and was picked to head the project *Tallahassee Misconceptions*."

He smiled a bit. "Impressive. But you do know Tallahassee is south of North Carolina, right? You went in the wrong direction entirely."

Zoë clenched her jaw. "I was laid off. It wasn't due to job performance. I took my severance and came back home to the city."

The man rubbed his smooth, pudgy cheek. "What happened to cause the layoff? I thought Misconceptions was doing well."

Zoë felt her cheeks get hot. Her boss, Godfrey, had happened. Then Godfrey's wife—whom he had failed to mention until Zoë was well and truly in "other woman" territory—had happened. She swallowed. "Economy. You know how it goes."

He stepped back and leaned against the wall, clearly not minding the cracked and peeling paint that broke off and stuck to his shirt. "Those are good credentials. However, you're still probably not what they're looking for."

Zoë looked at her notebook and continued writing. "Luckily it's not your decision, is it?"

"Actually, it is."

She groaned and looked back up at him. "All right. Who are you?"

He extended his hand. "Phillip Rand. Owner, president, and CEO of Underground Publishing."

She looked at his hand for a moment and shook it, her small fingers briefly engulfed in his grip. It was a cool handshake, but strong.

"Zoë Norris. And why, Mr. Phillip Rand, will you not let me even apply?"

"Well, Miss Zoë Norris, I don't think you'd fit in with the staff. And fitting in with the staff is key to this company's success."

A vision of future months dressed as a dancing cell phone on the wintry streets pummeled Zoë's psyche. She leaned forward in desperation. She was short, and used to looking up at people, but he was over six feet, and she was forced to crane her neck to look up at him. "Mr. Rand. How many other people experienced in researching and writing travel guides do you have with you?"

He considered for a moment. "With that specific qualification? I actually have none."

"So if you have a full staff of people who fit into some kind of mystery mold, but don't actually have experience writing travel books, how good do you think your books are going to be? You sound like you're a kid trying to fill a club, not a working publishing company. You need a managing editor with experience to supervise your writers and researchers. I'm smart, hardworking, creative, and a hell of a lot of fun in the times I'm not blatantly begging for a job—obviously you'll have to just take my word on that. I haven't found a work environment I don't fit in with. I don't care if Underground Publishing is catering to eastern Europeans, or transsexuals, or Eskimos, or even Republicans. Just because I don't fit in doesn't mean I can't be accepting as long as they accept me. Just give me a chance."

Phillip Rand was unmoved. "Trust me. You would not fit in. You're not our type."

She finally deflated and sighed. "Isn't this illegal?"

He actually had the audacity to laugh at that. "I'm not discriminating based on your gender or race or religion."

"Then what are you basing it on?"

He licked his lips and looked at her again, studying her. "Call it a gut reaction."

She deflated. "Oh well. It was worth a try. Have a good day."

On her way out, she ran through her options: there were the few publishing companies she hadn't yet applied to, the jobs that she had recently thought beneath her that she'd gladly take at this point. She paused a moment in the Self-Help section to see if anything there could help her better herself. She glanced at the covers for *Reborn and Loving It*, *Second Life: Not Just on the Internet*, and *Get the Salary You Deserve! Negotiating Hell Notes in a Time of Economic Downturn*. Nothing she could relate to, so she trudged out the door, contemplating a long bath when she got back to her apartment. Better than unpacking more boxes.

After the grimy door shut behind her, Zoë decided she had earned a tall caloric caffeine bomb to soothe her ego. She wasn't sure what she'd done to deserve this, but it didn't take much to make her leap for the comfort treats these days—which reminded her, she needed to recycle some wine bottles.